Dedication

For Anne Madeline Masson (Jackson)
who had stoot hert for a stey brae.

'There are many kinds of faith. It is not law but conscience that determines when they crack.'

Shirley McKay

Chapter 1

Lesmahagow village in the County of Lanark. Monday, 3rd April 1679

In another time Lucas Brotherstone might have been an actor. Pretence came easily, especially when he allowed his Sunday sermon to become a theatrical performance. Sometimes he even convinced himself.

Today he was pretending to be practical, clearing weeds in his vegetable garden. He knelt down and his knees sank into the soft soil. Not that it bothered him. He'd always kneel when seeking guidance from his God. And it seemed to work. How else had he become such a confident preacher?

"Mornin sir."

Lucas recognised the voice. He stood up, dusted his grimy knees, then turned towards a burly figure standing on the path beside him. "Morning John. Whit can I dae for ye?"

"Sir. If ye can spare a meenit ah'd like a word aboot yer sermon yesterday?"

"The prodigal?" Lucas smiled to himself.

"Ay." A pair of brown eyes issued a challenge. "An aw yon forgiveness."

"Which we must try to practice oorsels."

The brown eyes hardened. "That's the problem."

"Indeed? Ye surprise me."

"Lucas." His wife appeared at the kitchen door. "There's a man here, saying he's frae the sheriff. Ye best come. He's brocht a paper for ye tae sign."

Lucas frowned.

"On ye go sir," John said. "Forgiveness can wait."

"Not at aw. It'll be naething important." Lucas turned towards his wife. "Send the man oot here." He wiped his hands on his breeches and headed for an old metal bench at the end of the garden. John shrugged and followed him, and they both sat down to wait.

A small, stout man, his face screwed up like a wizened plum, marched down the long path towards them. "Whae's the meenister? Ah've a paper here needin signed."

"I am." Lucas held up his hand. "Whit's this aboot?"

"Official business. Ah'd prefer tae speak indoors. Mair private like."

"Oot here is fine. Please, sit doon." Lucas indicated a space on the bench beside him.

"Ah'd raither staund."

"As ye wish."

The little man shuffled his feet. "Name's Thrum. Clerk tae the sheriff an the court at Lanark." He took a rolled up parchment from a large, leather satchel strung across his chest, undid a red ribbon tied round it, then held out the document. "Ye've tae sign this."

Lucas made no move.

Thrum thrust the parchment into his hands.

"Haud on a meenit," Lucas protested. "I need tae read it afore ony signing."

"Please yersel." Thrum sniffed. "But ye also need tae be law abidin. That's whit this paper's aboot."

Lucas spread the parchment on the bench and began to read lines of tight scripted words. A moment later he paused, muttered something, glared at Thrum, then continued reading. Finally he rolled up the paper and handed it back. "I canna sign this nonsense."

"Hoo no?" Thrum snapped. "It comes frae the king himsel."

"It maks nae difference. I canna sign." Lucas turned to John as if expecting support.

John said nothing.

Undeterred Lucas went on. "This paper talks aboot bishops in my Kirk, even accepting the king as oor spiritual leader. It's madness sir, sheer madness tae even suggest sic a thing."

"Tak care." Thrum's face darkened. The lines round his

4

mouth grew tight. "Unless ye agree tae sign ye're oot o here. As for preachin, forget it. Ye best chew that ower afore ye utter ony mair treasonous words."

Lucas was speechless.

Thrum shrugged. "The sheriff thocht ye wudna be keen on signin, an bein a generous man he's prepared tae gie ye some mair time. Ye've seven days tae think aboot it, an come tae yer senses afore ah come back wi a mounted platoon. If yer answer is still no ye're oot on yer lug, an dinna expect the military tae be gentle wi ye." He stuffed the parchment into his bag. "On yer ain heid be it. Guid day."

Lucas stared after the clerk as he strode back up the garden path. He was still staring after the man had gone.

"Sir."

Lucas neither moved nor spoke.

"Did ye unnerstaund aw that?" John asked gently.

Lucas nodded. His face was chalk white, his grey eyes clouded with fear.

John stood up. "In that case sir, ye've plenty tae think aboot, so ah'll leave ye tae it. But if ah wis ye ah'd be wary aboot ma future. I've heard aboot the sheriff at Lanark. His reputation gangs afore him. He'll no tak kindly, if ye get my meanin."

Lucas nodded.

Six days later Lucas Brotherstone climbed the twelve steps to his pulpit. Below him rows of upturned faces waited as they did each Sunday.

He gripped the polished brass rail and closed his eyes before lifting his arms wide in an enclosing gesture. The sleeves of his black robe swung out like some great crow spreading its wings before flight. There was a gasp from below. Lucas didn't notice. He was wrestling with the temptation to deliver his normal sermon and pretend that nothing was amiss. But it was. He took a deep breath, forced himself. "My friends. I'm about tae break the law."

Every back straightened. His voice steadied. "Six days ago the sheriff at Lanark sent his clerk tae demand my name on a miserable paper agreeing tae bishops in oor Kirk. Even worse, I'd tae accept the King's superiority ower aw things spiritual and temporal. I read each word twice tae mak sure afore I refused tae put my name tae sic blasphemy." His voice grew louder. His arms reached out, palms open, every finger stretched wide to pull his audience in. "Bishops wi their fancy claes and ways hae nae place in oor Kirk. Nor dae we believe their mealy moothed words aboot respect for oor betters. And hoo they're in the richt position tae intervene afore the Almighty. The route tae oor Lord is direct and can never be disowned. We ken that. The Bible tells us braw plain. Hoo can we respect a monarch misguided enough tae believe he has divine power ower us aw?"

Words bounced off the white painted walls while every ear strained forward, desperate to miss nothing.

"Tomorrow that same clerk will return wi his accursed paper. He has already warned what will happen if I still refuse tae sign. This time he'll bring armed support tae drive me frae this parish. In spite o this threat I must haud firm tae the truth. If my action is considered treasonable, so be it. Changed times are being thrust upon us, telling us aw tae look within and grasp the truth."

Lucas was carried away with his own eloquence, almost imagining himself a prophet chastising the children of Israel. Lost in his own performance, he didn't notice that one dissenting face, or how John Steel leant forward to watch his neighbours. He missed the warning in John's stare, and ranted on with every last, angry, spiteful word.

At last he announced the 15th psalm, and the congregation stood as one to sing:

> *"The man that walketh uprightly,*
> *And worketh righteousness*
> *And as he thinketh in his heart,*
> *So doth he truth express."*

The words rang out while Lucas climbed down from his pulpit to stand on the stone floor. It sounded grand. A justification of his defiance. But did he really believe his own words? He swallowed this moment of weakness, straightened his shoulders and lifted his face to say the benediction before his faithful beadle could open the heavy outer door.

A widening patch of bright light beckoned. He longed to be

there, anywhere, other than in this kirk. For a moment he was wrapped in a still silence, no shuffle of feet, no cough as everyone waited. Eyes fixed beyond the opening door he pulled his black robe tight across his chest, and managed to take the first step, then a second, a third. Blurred faces loomed out of the pews on either side as Lucas Brotherstone walked slowly out of his church for the last time.

He hesitated on the broad step but did not look back. Behind him he could hear the scrape of feet and muted whispers.

"Can we no wait tae a meenit or twa?" Marion Steel tried to resist as John steered her across the church square.

John kept walking.

"But the Reverend did himsel proud."

"Mibbe so. But these days the law has the last word. If the meenister thinks itherwise he's a bigger fool than ah thocht."

They stopped by their tethered horse and trap, and John lifted her into the front seat. She glared at him. He dared a smile then turned to lift up their two small sons. Neither boy smiled nor said a word.

The warm sunshine usually had them laughing and joking as the trap rattled along between the high beech hedges. Today was different with every turn of the wheel grinding out *Brotherstone, Brotherstone*. No one spoke during the two-mile drive back to Logan Waterhead.

At dinner the two boys slid into their places and barely moved while they ate their meal. At either end of the table Marion and John maintained their silence, the only sound the repeating scrape of a knife on a pewter plate.

When the meal was finished the boys made no move; faces white, they didn't ask permission to leave. Marion forced a smile and held out the egg-collecting basket. They grabbed it and raced off with the basket between them.

Meanwhile John was scraping back his chair, muttering about feeding the calves. Before she could speak he slipped round the kitchen door and was gone.

She stared at the closed door then bustled through to the wash-house and banged the plates down on the stone shelf.

Standing there in the tiny space she noted bowls stacked, mugs in a tidy row, two buckets of clean water waiting in readiness with no need to go out to the well. This had her whirling round to stomp back into the kitchen and push each chair into place around the table.

There was a rap at the door. "This is aw ah need." She smoothed her apron as the outer latch lifted.

The door opened and her brother stepped into the kitchen.

"Guid aifternoon, sister dear." He winked at her and skimmed his felt hat across the room to land on the dog curled up by the fire.

In spite of her mood Marion gave a half smile. "Och Gavin, ye've that beast as daft as yersel."

"She enjoys it."

The dog thumped her tail and peered out below the hat brim.

"Aye, weel, ah'm no in the mood for nonsense."

"Whit's up? Is it this mornin? Ah noticed John had·ye awa richt aifter the service."

"He wasna keen tae bide."

The two boys burst in, dumped the egg basket, and flung themselves at their uncle. They rolled over on the floor, the dog joining in, and the kitchen rang with fun.

John appeared in the doorway. He grinned at the wrestling figures then stepped forward to pull both boys from the young man's back. "C'mon. Twa against ane isna fair. Noo mak yersel useful an fetch some ale frae the larder. Ah cud dae wi a drink. Yer Uncle Gavin certainly deserves yin."

Gavin scrambled up. "That pair's turnin intae a richt handful."

"An whae encourages them?" John said.

"Ay. It's guid fun. But no why ah'm here. Faither sent me tae ask if ye'll come by the manse in the mornin. He thinks the meenister micht need support when the sheriff's clerk arrives wi the military."

"Tae arrest the eedjit or worse."

Marion stared at John. "So that's whit ye meant."

He nodded. "Ah didna like tae say but the man's daft. Is that plain enough for ye? Whit he's daein tae himsel is bad enough. Noo he's tryin tae involve ithers in somethin they micht live tae regret."

"Whit's wrang wi the meenister speakin oot aboot richt an wrang? Ah didna hear a voice raised against him."

"No in the kirk, ah'll grant ye."

"There ye are then."

"Whit aboot them in power? Maister Brotherstone's words hud a ring o rebellion. They canna ignore it. The law is there tae be obeyed, no tae be liked. The man's aither a complete fool or doesna realise the danger he's in."

Marion's voice rose. "A man lik that kens whit he's dain."

"Is that so? Weel, whit aboot nae job, nae hame, an mibbe endin up in prison or worse? Whit aboot his pair wife? Has he asked her hoo she feels?"

"Why wud he no?"

"Why indeed? An whit aboot us?" John's voice sharpened. "We were in the kirk listenin. Next thing the sheriff will hae spies oot here checkin on us. God kens whit stories they'll tak back."

"But – " Marion began to argue.

"But nuthin." John stopped her. "Why is it ye nivver see beyond the end o yer nose?"

"Whit's that supposed tae mean?"

John shrugged.

She glared at him. Her face and neck reddened. Her fist clenched.

Everyone in the room watched. They too said nothing. The room grew still, so still the only movement was the tick, tock of the big wall clock. It didn't last. With a sudden whistle Marion summoned the dog, and was out and away. She didn't even bang the door shut behind her.

William stared at his father. "Ma's awfy angry." He turned to his uncle. "Is she angry wi ye tae?"

"Maist likely." Picking his hat off the floor Gavin glanced awkwardly at John and headed for the door. "In the mornin then?"

"Mibbe." John turned to his sons and tried to appear calmer than he felt. "Ye ken hoo Ma aye goes for a walk when she's angry. Weel, hoo aboot ye twa feedin the hens while ah brush up in here, an then we micht get a smile when she comes back?"

The boys ran into the scullery for the feed-bag and were gone.

John took the birch besom from behind the kitchen dresser and began to sweep the flagstone floor with even strokes. He was half way across the floor before he noticed the trail of tiny, broken twigs behind him. He stopped, turned back to start again. This time no twig or crumb escaped. Marion couldn't have done any better.

Besom stowed away again he fetched four potatoes from the pantry and placed them in the little brick oven beside the fire. After so long in the fresh air her anger would be mixed with hunger. Maybe a wiff of baked potato would foster a little forgiveness. This made him think of Lucas's sermon only a week ago. How things had changed.

Everything in the kitchen was tidy, and something tempting was in the oven. Nothing else to do but be patient. He added two logs to the fire then settled down to watch the flames flicker and dance. Within the changing shapes it was easy to imagine Marion striding through the heather. Wrapped up in her own anger there was every chance she might catch her foot on fern or heather root, or even stumble into a hidden pool of peaty mud. This would be the last thing on her mind. As for the words being mouthed into the wind he could feel his ears burning with her resentment. In spite of this he knew she'd be fine. She always was.

He leant back and allowed the heat from the fire to flood over him. After that it was easy to close his eyes and listen to the sound of the wall clock with its pendulum measuring every minute as everything was gently gathered in.

When Marion marched into the yard her two boys were sitting on the doorstep. They stared up at her tense face and said, "Da's sleepin."

"Is he then?"

"Ay. But he brushed up first an we fed the hens. He said ye'd be pleased."

"Did he?" She lifted the latch and pushed the door open.

There was a tidy kitchen, and four clean platters on the table beside hunks of bread piled high in her favourite woven basket that she'd won last year at Lanark Fair. There was even the welcoming smell of potatoes baking in the oven.

She smiled at the still figure by the fire and tiptoed into the kitchen.

It had been a long, anxious night and dawn would bring the seventh day since the sheriff's clerk had come to frighten the wits out of Elizabeth Brotherstone. The more she thought about that day the more she blamed Lucas, and she'd been angry enough to tell him. He'd listened when she raged about his precious conscience. He hadn't liked that. And the look on his face when she said he must sign the sheriff's paper before it was too late. Not that he'd argued or even answered. He'd left her to wonder, then stepped up to his pulpit and did what she dreaded. She could almost see herself sitting there, blinking back tears.

The lines of daylight began to filter through gaps in the wooden shutters yet the figure by her side didn't stir. She listened to the quiet, regular breathing and the pretence of it all made her teeth grit. The past few days had brought a terrible change in Lucas till she barely recognised him. Silence had been his only defence after she'd spoken out. And all that pacing up and down the big room as if rehearsing his sermon when it was obvious he was terrified. But he'd dredged up enough fine words to fool his congregation. He'd even convinced them of his respect for the truth.

Respect. Elizabeth sat up and pulled the sheet tight. To her surprise Lucas reached out to touch her bare arm. She started and pulled away.

"Bett. Please."

She clung to the sheet.

"I had tae. Tell me ye understand."

She turned and glared at him. "Why should I? It's aw aboot yersel, wi never a thocht for me, nor whit I micht want."

He blinked at her but said nothing.

"Ye still intend saying no when the military arrive. Is that it? We tak oor chances?"

He dared to nod.

"So be it. But when it aw goes wrang jist mind whae's tae

11

blame." She jumped out of bed, and her bare feet thumped on the floorboards as she crossed to the dressing table. Back turned against Lucas she lifted the jug to pour icy water into the big, earthenware bowl then picked up the tiny bar of soap and square of soft, clean muslin neatly placed beside the big crock. She slipped off her shift and stood within the crumpled circle of fine cotton. The glow of smooth skin was tempting as always but the taut curve of her body defied him to step up close, to circle his arms, to kiss the back of her neck as he usually did.

He closed his eyes but could still feel the resentment. Not that he blamed her.

When he dared look again Elizabeth was dressed, standing beside him holding a small pile of neatly folded clothes. "It's nearly six. Time tae get dressed." How normal she sounded.

"Thank ye," he whispered.

"Whit for?" She hissed the words. "For seeing whit ye're really like?"

"I'm sorry."

"It's too late for that. Get up. Get dressed. At least try tae look the part." She lifted his best linen shirt from the top of the pile and held it out.

He slid out of bed, took the shirt, and stood there like a guilty child while she opened the big press door to pull out his best Sunday suit of dark serge cloth, the fine weave, the even colour, the symbol of his calling, that cost more than the first month of his first stipend. He knew she'd been proud of him then, but there was no sign of it as she laid the suit on a chair and slipped from the room without another word. Only her hard little shoes clipping down the bare wood stairs told him what she thought.

He crossed to the dressing table and stared at the delicate pink roses painted round the edge of the pale blue washing bowl. It had been a wedding present, on a happy day when they'd stood within a circle of well-wishers and felt the strength of their support. He blinked and noticed it had been filled with fresh water. Elizabeth had seen to it. He touched the water. His reflection rippled across the icy surface. He watched it move and reform, then widen before the surface stilled. His finger trailed across the surface and the little waves created the same effect again. Feeling better he looked up and peered into the tiny looking glass on the table to find a pair of grey eyes, full of uncertainty and questions he knew he couldn't answer.

He took the leather strop from its hook on the back of the door then opened the long razor to slide the edge up and down till it gleamed. With careful wrist movements he began to guide the sharp blade across his stubble, back and forward till his skin glowed and stung. Finally he ran his fingers over his face, checking for any nick or cut. It was smooth. He grabbed a towel to pat his burning face. Now for his dark, wiry hair. A few heavy strokes with his hair-brush forced it to lie flat against his scalp, ready to be scraped back and neatly tied with a short length of black silk braid. What an effort it was. This looking the part. With a wry smile he pulled on his fine linen shirt and caught the merest whiff of sweet lavender. And when he slipped on his formal coat and breeches the heavy black cloth only added to his mood. Maybe a lace ruff would help, the one he kept for marriage ceremonies. But his hand sought the plain, white length of cloth he usually wore as a cravat. White stockings and buckled shoes completed the picture and he stood before the long wardrobe mirror to inspect the result. It was a fine reflection, yet he barely recognised himself.

Elizabeth was in the kitchen. Outside the door he stopped to adjust his jacket, check his hair. And so they met in the empty kitchen, either side of the wide table like two strangers sharing a small jug of goat's milk and two thick bannocks.

Neither spoke, nor looked at the other in the quiet room. Both stiffened when the outdoor bell clanged. At the second ring their eyes met and held. Elizabeth nodded. "It's early. Bide here. I'll see whit it's aboot."

In the hall she paused to straighten her dress. It was the first time she'd worn such fine brown cotton so nicely finished off with the tiny pearl buttons she'd saved up for, and sewn on with such care; the dress she'd been keeping for a special occasion.

She sighed and went on down the long hall towards the big front door with its coloured glass panel. The sun was shining through the glass and the scrubbed wooden floor danced with a mosaic of reflected hues. She stepped inside this bright circle and allowed the shades of light to slide across the discreet brown of her dress and give it an almost gaudy look. She'd stood here many times, usually smiling. Today tears welled up.

The bell clanged again and she stared at the glass panel, with the shadow of someone waiting on the other side of the door. Every part of her wanted to ignore this summons. But she stepped forward and used both hands to turn the big key. After the loud click she waited a moment then grasped the big round handle and pulled the door open to find a group of familiar faces.

"Mornin, maam." John Steel stepped forward and removed his cap.

"Morning Maister Steel."

"We were wonderin if the meenister's still o a mind?"

"Indeed." Lucas appeared beside Elizabeth wearing his formal kirk face.

"In that case ye'll be needin a hand tae load the cart afore the sheriff's man arrives wi the troopers." John turned to his companions. "Ah'll awa an hitch up the horse an cart. The rest o ye, intae the hoose an start bringin oot whitever the mistress means tae tak wi her."

Chapter 2

The church clock chimed eight. Metal hooves clanged on the dewy cobbles like angry hammers as a fast moving military troop turned off Lesmahagow main street, heading up the lane to the manse. At the sound of the approaching thunder John fastened the tail-gate of the cart then signalled the others to group round the minister. So there they were in a tight little circle facing the snorting horses when they plunged into the tiny courtyard.

The leading horseman reined in. Faultlessly turned out from top to toe in a fine uniform, sword and pistol by his side, well polished buttons and breastplate gleaming in the morning sun this platoon lieutenant tried to present the picture of the grand commander he probably imagined himself to be. Only the glint in his deep-set eyes gave any hint of an unpredictable nature.

Lucas stepped forward with a polite nod.

The lieutenant's hard eyes flicked across the slight figure. "Are ye the meenister here?"

"I am. Lucas Brotherstone, ordained minister tae this parish."

"No muckle longer." Turning in his saddle the lieutenant indicated a flustered looking man flopped across a small, dappled mare. "Here's Maister Thrum, the sheriff's clerk, back tae see ye."

Thrum nodded and pulled a rolled up parchment from his saddlebag. He waved it at Lucas. "Ah've brocht yon paper ye were supposed tae sign last week. Ah tak it ye're willin tae oblige noo?"

"My answer remains the same."

Thrum took off his wide brimmed hat to fan his red face. "An here ah wis hopin a few days tae think aboot it micht bring ye tae yer senses."

"I've never been mair sure o my senses."

"Is that so? Weel, ye need tae unnerstaund sic antics are no jist offensive, thur unlawful. That's no a personal opinion, nor frae the sheriff, it comes aw the way frae the King himsel."

"In that case I regret giving any offence." Lucas's voice remained steady. "And I dinna want tae break the law. But I canna sign a paper that denies everything I believe in."

"That's aw very weel, but dinna forget thur's a price for sic disobedience. Are ye prepared for it?" Thrum's experienced eyes watched for any sign of weakening. None came. He sucked in his cheeks and turned to the lieutenant. "Weel, Crichton, ye heard whit the man said. By his ain admission Maister Brotherstone is noo a renegade agin the crown. As such he has nae richt tae live an preach in this parish. Yer duty is tae escort him beyond the parish limit by noon an warn him tae bide there."

"Dinna fash yersel. We'll see tae the meenister. He'll be awa in nae time."

"That's guid news for my maister is no a man tae thole failure."

The lieutenant flushed but said nothing.

Thrum turned to Lucas. "Aince across the parish boundary thur's nae comin back."

Lucas looked as if he'd been struck but he didn't react nor break his silence.

Thrum stared at Elizabeth. "Ye as weel, maam." With a curt nod he stuffed the unsigned parchment into his saddle-bag, edged his mare past the row of soldiers and left the newly declared outlaw and his wife to the lieutenant's mercy.

Crichton wasted no time in signalling his men to surround the minister's cart. As they obeyed he edged his own horse forward till he towered over Lucas and the little group of villagers. He glared down at the wary faces. No one spoke or moved. This seemed to please him. He waited a moment then pointed towards a tall beech tree which overhung the manse garden. "See they guid, thick branches? Wi a hemp rope flung across they should be strong enough tae swing a man's heels aff the ground." He stared at Lucas. "And we aw ken which man it micht be."

"Please sir." Elizabeth stumbled forward. "My husband means nae harm. His concern is only the truth as he sees it."

Crichton glared down. "Yer stutterin words mean naethin maam. Ma concern is his defiance agin the law. Ane wrang word an he swings. Ma orders are tae run yer man oot this parish. If he has ony fancy ideas aboot arguin ah'm within ma rights tae deal wi him in ony way ah see fit." He pointed towards the loaded cart. "No anither word. An climb up there afore we find oot if they branches are strong enough for twa."

John stepped up behind Elizabeth. "Dae as he says."

"But he doesna understand." She was staring at the lieutenant.

"It's too late for that." He took her arm.

She tried to pull away.

He tightened his grip. "Richt noo understaunin disna come intae it. Ye need tae dae as the soldier says."

Eyes blinded with tears, her lips trembled as she stood in silent appeal.

"C'mon maam," John whispered. Gently but firmly he led her towards the cart.

Crichton watched Elizabeth being lifted into her seat then signalled John to approach. John stepped closer and looked up. The soldier leant over. "Whae gied ye permission tae interfere?" He lunged forward and smashed his clenched fist against the upturned face.

John reeled back, almost fell. His heels dug into the dirt. He swung his arms to steady himself then leapt to grab the lieutenant's sleeve. He pulled hard. His weight and strength rocked the soldier, forcing him sidewards, almost enough to slip from the saddle, but someone had the tail of John's jacket and was pulling equally hard.

"Dae that again an it's yer last." Crichton drew his pistol and aimed it at John's brow.

John held up his hands in submission and stepped back.

"That's mair like it." Crichton pointed towards the cart. "Noo, get ower there. An bide there afore ah dae somethin ye'll regret." He replaced his pistol in his belt and waited till John obeyed.

With a satisfied smirk Crichton turned his attention to the villagers standing by the loaded cart. Lucas was in the driving seat with Elizabeth sitting beside him, two helpless figures awaiting his pleasure. It was too good a chance to miss. Easing his horse closer to the cart he leant forward and cracked his whip in front of the minister's horse as it patiently stood between the shafts of the cart.

The brown head jerked up. There was a loud whinny. The

beast danced within the shafts and the harness strained as Lucas grabbed hold of the reins and struggled to gain control. Crichton grinned, raising the whip again. This time it came down to cut the soft, fleshy muzzle. The animal squealed and jumped with fright. The leather hit again. With another squeal the beast reared back as far as the cart shafts would allow then plunged forward with such force that Lucas could do nothing to stop it. The cart shot forward, out through the narrow close mouth and into the cobbled lane. Those who'd gathered to watch pressed back against the wall as the horse galloped past, foam streaming between its champing teeth. The speed, the rocking, the uneven cobbles were too much for the stacked furniture and baskets. A chair fell, then a basket, to be followed by another which burst open leaving a pathetic trail of creased and filthied clothes. Two heavy iron pots bounced on the ground and rolled into the gutter, and a long length of thick blue satin ribbon trailed beside two bone hair-clasps and a little heart-shaped dish, which shattered leaving shards of glass to sink into the mud.

The horse raced along the narrow lane. Straight ahead loomed the gable end of a house. There was nowhere to go but sharp right into the main street. Elizabeth screamed and clung to the metal hand-rail while Lucas tugged on the reins and roared at the beast to stop.

It made no difference. Nothing would stop the horse lunging to the side in an attempt to avoid the wall. The cart followed. It was too wide. The corner clipped the lime washed wall and Lucas ducked back, holding his breath. White paint scuffed past his nose and sparks flew from the metal edge of the cart as it scrieved a long, deep groove on the smooth surface before the unstable load tipped the cart on its side to bump a few more yards along the cobbles then embed itself in a deep drainage runnel at the edge of the lane. Forced to stop the horse strained to escape from the shafts, hooves champing, wild eyes defying anyone to come near.

Lucas's elbows crunched against the edge of the wooden seat and a sharp pain shot down his arm, into his fingers. He let go of the reins then tried to grab them again before they disappeared.

As the cart slid further, the reins swung upwards again,

looped round his arms, then his waist, and tightened as he lost his balance. The strong leather straps held firm, and he was left dangling like an ungainly parcel, his nose almost touching the rough cobbles.

Nothing broke Elizabeth's fall except a glancing blow from the metal rim of a spinning wheel before she hit the ground. Small stones skittered across the narrow lane and a dust cloud rose to hide her fallen body before those who'd followed the runaway cart caught up with it. Willing hands released the minister and pulled him upright, held him steady while he stared about, dazed. Others ran to help his wife who lay in the dirt beside the half upended cart. There was a cruel twist to her body; her bonnet was torn off, yet the ribbons remained tight round her slim neck. Everything about her was still, and the absolute white of her brow was marked by a long purple weal.

Confused by the shouts around him, and dizzy from his fall it took a few moments before Lucas became aware enough to see the group by the cart. He stared at them bending over, whispering, looking back at him. He couldn't hear the words but their expressions spoke clearly enough. He guessed, then tried to deny it, but the look on those faces was telling him otherwise. His mouth opened and shut. He tore himself free, ran forward, and pushed into the centre of a growing crowd. And there she was.

Dropping to his knees he scooped up her head while the nearest villagers stepped back to form a protective circle. He stroked some of the grime from her tangled hair and leant closer to press his ear against her upturned face. They watched as he listened. No sound. No movement. No sign of breath. He tried again. Nothing. He kissed her fingers, and stared into the soft hazel eyes, willing a reaction. Nothing. No accusation. Only blankness.

He looked up at the watchers and nodded. They lowered their eyes, moving back to give him a private space to cradle his wife's head, whisper her name over and over.

No one spoke. They stood and watched until the innkeeper pushed forward from the crowd and tapped John's shoulder. "Here." He held out a clean, folded sheet. "Ye'll need this for the mistress."

Lucas saw John take the sheet, the sight of it so final he closed his eyes rather than accept the message of the neat, white folds. When he looked again the innkeeper was gone among the crowd and a dark shadow loomed over him. He blinked at the lieutenant's horse then saw the soldier's moonlike face peering down, its expression goading him, expecting him to drop to his knees and plead for his own safety.

Only a surge of shame kept him upright before he turned away from the horse towards John, who was leaning forward offering him the sheet. Lucas drew back as if afraid to even touch the sheet, and the two men froze, the length of cloth between them, while one willed the other to do what was needed.

The lieutenant leant forward and tapped Lucas's shoulder with the end of his whip. "Yer cart's been righted so get movin. We canna wait only longer."

Lucas didn't answer.

"Dae ye hear me?"

Lucas seemed to come back from somewhere far away and stared up at the impatient face. "My wife's deid."

"An ah hae my orders," the soldier snapped back. "Deid or alive ye've a boundary tae pass afore noon. So wrap her up. Put the body in the back o yon cart."

Elizabeth's prediction had come true. Lucas's only option was to obey. He opened the sheet and John helped him gently wrap it round the still little body till it was hidden from the watching eyes.

The lieutenant pointed towards the cart and slowly the light bundle was eased over the tailgate, in beside the remaining baskets and chairs.

Crichton pointed at the driving seat.

Lucas clambered into the cart. The platoon lined up on either side and the trembling horse was coaxed forward, Lucas staring ahead as if unaware of the silent people lining the main street. Breastplates flashed in the sun, the metal links in the reins jingled, and two lines of fine horses trotted along in close escort as Lesmahagow's minister was forced out of his parish like a common felon.

When the cavalcade reached the boundary signpost Crichton ordered Lucas to stop. "See that sign? Bide on the ither side o it frae noo on. Nae comin back or ye'll find the law waitin wi a hemp rope."

Lucas turned towards the soldier and treated him to an unblinking stare. "Rest assured, sir, I intend to follow my conscience." The cart then passed the line of mounted soldiers, crossed the parish boundary and crawled away down the road.

John stood outside the manse, on the same spot he'd stood that morning. The same blank windows of the house stared out as if they'd seen nothing. He stepped back and admired the building. It was a fine sight with a golden sandstone frontage. A building to envy. Five broad steps led to the shiny black door with its coloured glass panel and polished brass bell hanging alongside, bordered by thick metal railings as proof of how grand it was. Yet Lucas Brotherstone had left without protest, as if none of it mattered.

He thought about his own farm. He'd built it up carefully. He was proud of it and the other two farms he rented to tenants. Losing them was unthinkable. He shook his head then turned his face up to the warm sunshine. It felt good, the only good thing he'd felt since morning. As for attacking an armed soldier, and in full view, he cursed his stupidity and silently thanked whoever had hung on to his coat-tail. And Mistress Brotherstone. What a fate her beloved husband had brought on her, and yet he'd stuck to his conscience. John could understand none of it.

Juno snorted. He patted her neck and loosened the tether. "C'mon, lass." He walked the full length of the main street with Juno clip-clopping alongside. The reassurance of the slow, steady rhythm, the fitting of his steps to those of the horse helped contain his rage and frustration.

Once beyond the village he turned onto the old droving road which skirted the edge of the moor with its mile after mile of heather and fern and swirling air. Here man meant nothing. Just what he needed. No questions, no answers, only empty space. He stopped and stared into the distance. After that it was easy to step away from the hard shale and lead the willing horse across rough grass towards the banks of heather.

Marion listened wide-eyed to John's story of what had happened at the manse. When he mentioned Crichton she rounded on him. "For God's sake John, whit wur ye thinkin aboot tryin sic a thing against a man lik that? An armed tae."

Instead of answering he leant back and closed his eyes. This was a mistake. It allowed a pretty oval face to flood his mind, every detail as clear as it had been three hours ago. He jerked upright and opened his eyes. "She doesna deserve that. No yon fine, wee lass."

"Stop." Marion shook him. "It's me."

He stared at her and shook his head. "Ah canna stop thinkin aboot her."

"It's by wi. It happened. Ye need tae accept whit's done." She grasped his outstretched hand and squeezed it.

"Whit aboot Maister Brotherstone drivin aboot the countryside wi her body in the back o his cairt? Yon lieutenant ordered meenister an wife oot the parish. Deid or alive, it made nae difference. Aifter whit's happened ah doubt he kens whit he's daein, or even whaur tae go. He's no the maist sensible man. Folk lik that need help. An ken whit? We aw stood an watched him drive awa, an did naethin."

"Ye cudna."

"That disna mak it richt. That lassie needs buryin. An in her richtfu place."

"But the meenister's been driven oot. He'll need tae tak her somewhaur else."

"No if ah can persuade him tae come back."

"He micht no want tae come back."

"He has tae."

Marion's hand flew to her mouth. "Please John, leave it be."

"Ye werena there or ye'd unnerstaund."

They stood there several moments with fingers entwined. Neither spoke. Finally she sighed. "If ye must."

With a quick kiss on her cheek he was away through the house and out to the stable. Minutes later Juno's metal shoes rang across the cobbled yard as John set out to find Lucas Brotherstone.

Chapter 3

Late at night, just outside Lesmahagow, a cart lurched over the ruts and hollows of a little used track. The axle groaned and creaked in the still air and the noise woke an old tinker who'd been asleep in a bed of ferns. Sam Galbraith, Gaby as he was known, sat up and rubbed his eyes. "Whit's happenin?"

His voice carried in the air but was drowned by the noise of the cart and two heavily plodding horses. Neither the driver nor his passenger noticed the grimy face now peering through the tangled hawthorn hedge.

Gaby sucked in his breath. "Weel ah nivver. That's yon farmer John Steel. An whae's that alang wi him at this time o nicht? My oh my if it's no the meenister. Him as wis flung oot his kirk a few hoors ago. This ah must see." The bent little figure grabbed his pack and left his ferny bed to follow in the shadows.

After another mile John steered the cart towards a narrower track where it lurched down a steep, gravelly slope overhung with elderberry bushes and yellow gorse. At the bottom John stopped then edged the cart onto a little stone bridge over the Logan Water Burn.

Gaby peered into the gloom while the horses and cart continued towards the shadowy outline of farm buildings on the edge of the next hillock. Takin the meenister hame wi him when he kens the man's a declared felon. The raggedy figure smiled. "Noo jist supposin the sheriff got tae ken. An if ah wis the yin tellin him ther micht be a bawbee or twa in it. He micht even want tae hear a wheen mair snippits." His fingers itched at the thought of a few coins. "God kens whaur else this micht lead. Mibbe ah shud bide here a wee while." He stared over at the farm then down to the little bridge and smiled again. "Onybody comin or goin crosses there. An if ah'm unnerneath ah'll miss nuthin. Better still ah'll hae a bit a shelter an a wee sit doon." He hurried down the steep path. Just before the bridge he pushed through the overhanging birch and rowan, then slid down between the rushes on the steep bank to reach the stony edge of the burn.

Pleased with his hidey-hole he took off his packman's bag and slumped down among the stones piled against the supporting wall of the bridge. With a bit of twisting and shuffling he managed to make himself reasonably comfortable. "Ay, this'll dae fine." He leant his head against the soft moss covering the wall and closed his eyes. The water of the burn rippled past his feet, the sound repetitive, gentle, persuasive. Soon the old rascal was drifting into sleep.

When the cart-wheels rang through the cobbled close Marion ran into the yard with the storm lantern to meet John and their visitor. "Whaur did ye find him?"

"Jist afore the Glesca road. He'd stopped the cairt an wis sittin there starin intae space. He wisna keen aboot comin wi me." John nodded towards the back of the cart and whispered, "The mistress is in there." Louder he said, "Doon ye get sir. Awa intae the hoose wi Marion here while ah stable the horse an put this cairt awa somewhaur safe."

Lucas obeyed and allowed Marion to steer him indoors where she settled him on the best chair, in the warmest corner of the kitchen. "Sit doon, sir. Warm yersel."

There was neither a word nor a nod of recognition.

She let him be and busied herself with adding a few logs to the dozing fire and encouraging the golden fingers to crackle round the dry wood. Within minutes there was enough rising heat to swing the soup pot over and leave it to simmer while she cut some hunks of bread and cheese. She laid the table, walking back and forward in an awkward silence while Lucas sat there as if unaware of her presence

When John came into the kitchen she whispered, "Not a word. An jist luk at him, sittin there, starin at the fire lik a bairn."

"Dinna worry. Ah'll see tae him." John bent over the still figure and almost lifted Lucas from his seat by the fire to lead him towards the table while Marion ladled out the soup.

Politely she offered her minister the first bowl and a piece of bread.

He made no move.

John pushed the bowl closer and held out a spoon.

Lucas took the spoon and stared at the steaming liquid.

"C'mon sir. When did ye last eat? Some broth will mak ye feel better."

Lucas hesitated then took a first mouthful. The taste seemed to persuade him to keep going and he managed to finish the bowl but the bread was untouched.

Marion and John ate their own supper. Talk seemed pointless. The only sound was the crackling of the fire, its sharpness like a warning against blundering into something that would best be left alone. But it was too late. Lucas was here in the farm. And what about the next step? John's mother had often said, "Look afore ye leap." How many times had he ignored these words? And here he was doing it again. He thought about the tight-rolled bundle he'd left in the stable. Another day. That's all it would take. All the same, he didn't dare look at Marion.

As soon as supper was over John leant forward and said, "Time fur bed."

Lucas pushed his chair back and stood up.

John lit a fresh candle then grasped the limp arm to lead his strange guest through the dark hall to the front room. He stopped within the flickering circle of light and pointed into the shadows, towards the outline of the big square bed. "Bed sir. Ye must be tired."

No answer.

John almost pushed Lucas forward and sat him down on the edge of the bed where he stayed like some wooden puppet, lifeless, relying on someone to pull the strings.

"Alloo me." John eased off the fine serge jacket now covered with dust and mud. No argument, no resistance as he tipped his guest over and laid him across the bed. After that it was easy to pull off the heavy, buckled shoes and roll the man on his side before covering the rigid figure with a thick, grey blanket.

His eyes were already closed.

John stared down at the white face as young and helpless as the pretty oval face he'd stared at that morning. The memory reminded him this wasn't about Lucas Brotherstone but a kind, gentle young woman, who'd soon lie beneath the grass of the village graveyard. Lucas and his precious conscience had triggered off a terrible sequence of events. As for thinking about travelling to the city with his dead wife in the back of his cart, John shuddered at the thought of such madness. Whatever else it was it wasn't right. Uncertainty and tiredness washed over him, telling him to leave things be till morning. He blew out the candle and crept from the room.

It was a relief to click the door shut and stand a moment in the velvet dark of the hall. Ahead he could see light flickering below the gap in the kitchen door. It was tempting to stay where he was, lean against the wall and close his eyes. But that solved nothing, and an anxious Marion was waiting in the kitchen. She'd need reassuring before anything else happened. Reluctantly he walked the few steps back to the warm kitchen.

"Weel?" Marion demanded as soon as she saw him. "Oot wi it."

John looked uncomfortable. "When ah caught up wi him he wisna for listenin, an kept mutterin aboot goin tae Glesca, tae his brither in law. An much guid that wud dae. Ah tried tellin him, but it wis nae use. Finally ah jist said he had tae come back an dae whit's richt. Ah even reminded him they were his ain words frae the pulpit. He didna like it. But he gied in an haunded me the reins, an allooed me tae turn his cart roond. No that he said a word aw the way back so ah'm nane the wiser if he's on wi buryin the mistress. But richt noo ah dinna care. Ah jist want tae shut ma een and let it aw go. C'mon lass, bed."

Hooves. Gaby struggled out from under the bridge in time to see John Steel urging his horse along the beech avenue towards the village. Here was a chance. Gaby grinned and muttered. "Mistress Steel an the meenister are left on their ain. Perfect. The guid lady has her guest tae luk aifter an mak his breakfast. Whae's tae notice the likes o me takin a wee luk aboot the place?" He crossed the bridge and cut across the nearest field to the farm buildings.

Life on the open road often depended on the tinker's ability to hide. The farm collie gave no warning bark. It seemed to ignore the little figure creeping from one shadow to another, heading for the byre door. Once there Gaby stopped to look round and listen. No sound. No movement other than the remnants of dawn mist rising from the cobbles. All he had to do was lift the wooden bar and push the door open just enough to slip through. Once inside his fingers gripped one of the upright planks and pulled the heavy door shut again.

Now he laid his cadger's bag among the nearest pile of straw and peered into the half-light where the cows were still dozing. Sweet drifts of steam rose from their broad flanks and the air felt pleasantly warm to the tinker's old bones as he slipped past ten contented creatures to the stable at the back where a horse and an old donkey occupied the first two stalls. Beyond them he could see the shape of the minister's cart.

Both animals opened their eyes and stared at him without a blink. The horse's ears pricked. Wary of its next move he stepped up close to whisper gently and stroke the smooth brown neck till he felt the big body relax again. Careful as ever he then spent a few moments fussing over the donkey, rubbing its brow, encouraging it to get used to his smell and snuggle in against his old coat. Once the beast seemed happy he carried over a big armful of fresh straw. Both heads went down and the animals began to eat. No problem now. All he had to do was reach up over the tailboard of the cart and pull himself aboard.

He rolled across the top tarpaulin then lifted the edge of the waxed cloth to look underneath. There it was, wedged among the boxes and baskets, what looked like a roll of best white linen. He began picking at the folds. Almost immediately his probing fingers touched cold skin. Just to make sure he pulled the fine cloth back and met Elizabeth Brotherstone's still face with its frame of dark brown curls. Such marble smoothness startled him. He drew away. But something about its stillness held him, pulled him back. Heart thumping he leant over to study the perfect arch of the eyebrows, the shadowy lashes. The closed eyelids, and what might lie below, pulled him even closer till he was almost touching the tiny upturned nose and small sweet mouth. There was much to admire. His lips began to skim across that perfect skin. Cold as it was he longed to linger but his own held breath was rising in his throat, pushing to escape. With a gasp he jerked upright as a surge of long forgotten feelings reminded him of a time when he'd relished a loving touch, or even a kiss.

Another breath and a quick shake of the head put a stop to that. He brushed aside the frame of dark curls, leant close again to lift the lobe of each perfect little ear, and quickly remove two delicate pearl earrings. He smiled to himself. The vera thing. Ah've a guid story tae sell an a wee bonus forbye. He replaced the folded cloth exactly as before and jumped down from the cart.

His hand was about to push the byre door open when light footsteps pattered on the yard cobbles. He peered through the gaps in the wooden planks and saw Marion coming towards him. She was carrying a bucket. He hoped she was heading for the well in the middle of the yard.

She was.

She laid the bucket on the stone rim then reached up for the rope and hook. Another moment and she'd be back across the yard and into the house.

The old donkey shook his head and snuffled, the sound seeming to fill the quiet space. Marion stopped, squinting towards the stable as the donkey snuffled again.

She let go of the hook. Gaby half turned, ready to grab his bag and hide.

The kitchen clock chimed six. Marion turned, looking towards the house, then drew up the water and hurried indoors.

Gaby stayed where he was and waited till the farmhouse door clanged shut.

The kitchen fire was glowing. Time to cook the porridge. Marion hurried through to the scullery where she kept the big pot. Fine oatmeal had been added and left to soak in water overnight. All she had to do was fetch the pot and hang it over the fire. With a little more water and a spoonful of salt an occasional stir would do the rest.

She turned towards the big dresser in the corner, lifted down her best bowls from the top shelf and opened the centre drawer to pull out the horn spoons her father had carved as a wedding present. She was admiring them when the kitchen door opened and Lucas Brotherstone stood there. Washed and dressed he looked more presentable than the night before. His eyes were no longer blank, but his face was tense and white.

"Mornin, sir. Breakfast in a meenit."

Lucas opened his mouth to reply when there was a light tap on the outer door.

They both froze. Marion put a warning finger to her lips and pointed towards the inner hall.

Lucas nodded and retreated.

The tap came again but she didn't move.

It came again. A little louder this time.

Marion straightened her apron and walked slowly over to open the outer door a few inches.

"Guid mornin Mistress Steel." There was a familiar brown face grinning at her.

"Oh, it's yersel, Gaby. Ye're early on the go."

"As ever maam, an bringin somethin nice in ma bag."

"Dinna be daft." She looked at him suspiciously. "Whit are ye aifter?"

"Ah'm a pair auld man whae's been sleepin in the dew till ma bones are fair frozen."

Marion saw his bright little eyes slide over her shoulder into the empty kitchen and almost closed the door again.

He reached out a hand as if to stop her. "When ah saw smoke curlin up frae yer chimney ah had tae come an ask Mistress Steel if she'd a wee corner in her heart for a cauld, hungry traveller."

She hesitated.

"Ah wis hopin." Gaby pulled a miserable face. "My, that's a grand smell."

Marion relented. "One bowl of porridge an on yer way."

"Ay, mistress. Jist whit ah'm needin."

"In ye come then." She opened the door wide.

He hurried over to the table and sat down while Marion fetched an old bowl and ladled out a portion along with a small mug of milk.

He took out his own horn spoon from one of his many jacket pockets and slurped up the hot porridge. She noticed his eyes scour the kitchen, but this was nothing unusual. He was always nosing about. No matter, there was no sign of any jacket or bag, or anything that might belong to the minister. And then she saw the line of fine bowls with a beautifully carved spoon carefully laid beside each one. These didn't see daily use and the old rascal was sure to notice. Still, he knew nothing about the minister.

Gaby was licking his spoon clean when the children burst into the kitchen.

Marion stiffened but he didn't seem to notice and simply turned to welcome the boys. "Mornin young gentlemen. Hoo are ye?"

Both boys grinned. Here was a chance to look through his pack of trinkets and maybe hear a new story. They ran forward. "Hae ye brocht yer bag?"

"It's here. But yer Ma's no fur lukin at it this mornin. She's jist giein me a bite tae eat then ah'm awa."

"No even a story?"

"No indeed." She pushed the boys towards the door. "C'mon ye twa. First things first. Oot tae the water trough an wash yer faces. Whit'll Maister Galbraith be thinkin?"

Gaby stood up and wiped his mouth with the back of his sleeve. "Ah'm thinkin ye're a kind lass."

"Awa wi ye."

"As ye wish." Gaby bowed. "An since ah canna tempt ye wi ma trinkets ah'll leave a wee somethin. Yer porridge has set me up for the day an ah'm gratefu." A length of blue ribbon appeared beside his empty bowl. "The very colour for yer bonny hair."

"There's nae need."

"Every need." He bowed again.

Marion walked behind Gaby to the outer door and stood there while he hopped down the four steps to the cobbled yard, nodded to the boys by the water trough and began to cross the yard. At the close mouth he turned, waved to her, and was away through the arch. A cheery whistle drifted back into the empty space but Marion stood where she was till the sound died away.

Back inside she found Lucas in the darkest corner of the front room and tried to reassure him. "It wis only an old tinker. He often comes tae the door. Ah gied him a bowl of porridge an he's awa." Just then she became aware of a tiny movement outside. No more than a flicker or a shadow, or maybe it was a bird's wing passing the window.

Crossing the room she peered out.

Nothing.

She turned and hurried back to the kitchen. The first thing she saw was Gaby's present lying on the table. She scooped up the blue ribbon and pressed the soft silk in her fingers. When she opened her hand again the strip of delicate material curled round and round, like a tiny blue snake resting in her palm. She blinked then dropped it into the fire.

Lucas had followed her into the kitchen and stopped short when he met the two boys coming in from the water trough. They stared at this second unexpected visitor and Marion quickly signalled a warning to ask no questions. She signalled again and they mumbled, "Guid mornin."

Lucas returned their greeting and they all stood there while Marion turned towards the porridge pot and ladled out four full bowls.

Maybe she was imagining too much. Nothing had gone wrong while Gaby was in the house. Everything was just as it should be. She carried the bowls to the table. "Sit yersels doon." She nodded to Lucas. "Sir. If ye'd be guid enough tae say grace afore we eat."

When John returned from the village he led the minister through to the front room and told him Elizabeth's burial was arranged for after midnight. "Nae offence sir, but it needs tae be kept secret," he explained.

"Secret?" Lucas shook his head. "In this village?"

"We tak that risk," John admitted. "But we go aheid onyway."

Lucas opened his mouth as if to argue when Marion came into the room.

"Whit's up?"

"Ye shud ken, Gaby cam tae the door this mornin jist aifter ye left for the village. Ye ken hoo he aye gets roond me when he's aifter somethin tae eat. Ah let him in an gied him some porridge. Only thing wis ah had ma best china bowls oot on the table an he'd ken that meant a visitor. No that he said onythin. An he didna clap een on Maister Brotherstone."

"That settles it," Lucas cut in. "I must leave at once."

A moment later heavy cart-wheels rattled into the cobbled

yard. John peered out the window. "That's the joiner arrivin tae dae whit's needed afore the nicht."

"But - " Lucas began.

John rounded on him. "Nae but. Get that intae yer heid. Richt noo yer wife comes first. In ma book it's time ye gied a thocht for somebody ither than yersel."

Lucas flushed but said nothing as John hurried outside to greet the new arrival.

After a few words the two men lifted down fresh cut planks from the cart and carried them into the nearest shed. The joiner stayed inside. John pulled the door shut then fetched the big yard brush to begin sweeping round as he usually did of a morning. After a while the joiner opened the door again and signalled to John who backed the cart up close to the shed then lowered the tailboard. Both men gently slid a long, simply made box among bundles of straw then covered everything with a thick tarpaulin. The joiner climbed into the driving seat, gave John a final nod then the cart clattered out of the yard and away.

John came back into the kitchen.

Determined to have his say Lucas confronted him. "I ken ye mean weel, and yer concern is touching. But yer plan is ower risky."

"Maks nae difference," John stopped him. "A few mair hoors and yer wife is laid tae rest. Surely ye can dae that much for her?"

Lucas hung his head.

"Richt. That's settled." John glared at him. "Ah'll awa an get on wi some work. An while ah dae, ah'd raither ye bide in here sir, weel oot o sicht." With that he went out and banged the outside door behind him.

Lucas retreated to the silence of the front room. At first he sat on the edge of the bed and stared at the wall. But soon the pacing began, back and forward, same distance covered each time, each step measured and regular. He counted them as he tried to blank out the last few hours as a reluctant guest in this house, obliged to obey the wishes of a man set on thinking for him. Everything had changed. Bett was gone. He doubted he'd ever have a normal day again.

Not so long ago Bett had been proud of him. They'd been

happy. And then his conscience had spoilt it all.

Why did ye dae it? a small accusing voice whispered inside his head.

Unable to answer he turned away to look out the tiny window and saw John working in the yard, every inch a useful man.

Look at him, the voice taunted. He kens whit he's aboot.

Lucas blinked back tears and looked past John's busy figure to the jumble of farm buildings, then along the long slope towards the first field, and on to the top of the next field where sunset gold was flooding across a broad strip of rough grazing. Bordering this was a drystane dyke like a barrier against the mounds of tangled heather and waving fern that climbed and dipped among mile after mile of changing moorland where nothing was enclosed. Down below the gentle pastures and tended crops belonged to an organised, more complicated world, a world he no longer wanted.

Doing anything seemed impossible, doing nothing no option. A sense of reason, even purpose had to be found. Some ousted ministers had travelled the roads, traversed the hills and made the open air their kirk. Lucas was different. He knew that. But all the same.

He went on peering through the tiny window panes until moor and sky merged in gathering dusk and velvet black took over. He was still there when Marion appeared in the doorway holding a candle. "Supper's ready, sir. Will ye join us?"

He shook his head. "The quiet."

She stepped forward to touch his arm. "There's baked trout, an ah jist happen tae ken it's yer favourite. Can the quiet no wait till ye eat?"

Politeness won. He followed her guttering candle through to the warm kitchen where John and the two boys were seated at the table. They smiled awkwardly and no one spoke. Marion bent down to lift the large ashet from the oven by the fire. Everyone watched as she carried the heavy dish to the table and laid it in the centre. There were the promised trout, baked to perfection on a bed of fresh cut leeks. Lucas sniffed the salty-sweet aromatic steam and was suddenly as hungry as he could ever remember. He looked up at Marion's anxious face and said, "Thank ye."

She smiled.

"Shall I say grace?"

She nodded.

A subtle change crept into the room. Some of the tension slipped away as everyone closed their eyes for the brief prayer.

Marion served the meal and began to speak about Elizabeth. At first Lucas resisted but gradually he responded to her gentle persuasion. His dull eyes flickered then lightened and his Bett came into the kitchen as he spoke of her likes and dislikes, and how she often teased his seriousness. Once or twice he almost smiled. Every scrap of fish and bread was eaten and he didn't notice how much he'd eaten. He forgot about returning to the heavy silence of the front room, and after their meal was content to sit by the fire reading aloud to the two boys from the big, family Bible.

Just before midnight John went out to the stable and saddled up Juno. Marion and Lucas waited by the farmhouse door as he led the big horse across the yard and stopped beside them.

Marion shivered. "It's startin tae rain."

"Less chance o meetin onybody." John patted Juno's flank and leant over to grab the minister's wrist. "Hop up, sir. She's steady as a rock an weel able tae cairry us baith." His strong arm pulled the slight figure astride the great beast's back. Lucas gripped his jacket and John could feel his fear, and imagine the poor man's expression. He smiled in the dark. "Ye're safe enough, sir. Nae need tae worry." He leant down towards Marion and whispered, "Keep the door locked till we come back."

Marion stood on the doorstep listening to the metal hooves fading down the long track from the farm before she turned indoors and locked the door. She looked round her shadowy kitchen. Here was the centre of her world. Everything familiar, everything in its place. Tonight this was far from reassuring when she thought of a fresh dug trench just waiting for the moment.

A basket in the corner by the fire always had some stocking or vest in it needing repair. She lifted a sock with no heel then poked about in the bottom of the basket for a length of matching wool. "Keep busy," she told herself. Lighting an extra candle she carried it to the little shelf by the fire. Safe in her favourite corner she sat down to begin her task. Once the wool was squeezed through the big eye of the needle she began to move the strand back and forward, darning a new patch to cover the gaping hole. It was difficult to pay attention, to weave over and under when her head buzzed with questions and fears.

Eventually she gave up the struggle and put down the needle to stare into the quiet gleam of the log embers. Blue merged with gold then red, and all in a shimmering haze. Often at night, when all was quiet, she'd sit by the fire, enjoying the flames dancing, images coming and going, triggering memories or fanciful thoughts as strange and wonderful as her imagination would allow. Tonight it was an uneasy picture of John's horse hurrying through the rain and dark to meet with shadowy figures waiting in the graveyard. And then there was that poor woman, beautiful, kind, young, yet not allowed to live another day. And what if word got out about the burial, would John be in trouble, maybe arrested? As for the minister, he should be miles away, not here defying the law. What if the troopers came back to the village? Would they come to the farm?

Rain pattered from one overhanging leaf to another and grew into a steady drumming which almost hid Juno's clip-clop across the loose stones of the farm track. Not that it mattered. Gaby saw them come. He'd been waiting a long time and had seen the joiner's cart pass hours ago. Now he was sure where they were going.

At the end of the track John turned Juno onto the beech avenue beside the Lesmahagow road. She began to canter and the old man cursed his legs as he splashed through the rain, determined not to be left too far behind.

At the top end of the village Juno was reined back. Behind him John heard Lucas breathe a sigh of relief at the slower pace. No lights to be seen. Every house seemed asleep. Still cautious, John edged her towards the mud at the side of the road and made sure her hooves didn't ring on the cobbles. As they passed he studied each dark window for any sign of movement. Half way down the hill he stopped the horse outside the joiner's yard and waited for the agreed sign. A candle flared in the workshop window then snuffed out.

On they went along the main street, past a long row of double-storey houses which led to the church square in the centre of the village. The horse plodded through the deepest shadows, her hooves sliding on the soft mud as John strove to remain invisible.

In the near side of the square was an ornate metal gate, the main entrance to the graveyard. John ignored this and kept going to the end of the square where a tiny cobbled lane led directly to the manse. "Slip aff here, sir," he whispered. "Keep tae the dark side of the lane. When ye reach the manse cut across the garden tae the wee side gate. Wait there till ah catch up wi ye. Ah'm takin Juno alang by the Glebe field tae tether her in the birch wood."

Alone in the dark of the lane Lucas's heart thudded and his face burned as he inched forward trying not to slip in the thick mud. The slightest sound terrified him, made him feel even more of a fool. Worse was to come when he reached his own garden gate and touched the familiar cold metal to discover he felt like an intruder.

As instructed he waited. Minutes passed. It felt longer, much longer as he stood there shivering while the pattering rain soaked further into his best serge jacket. Still no sign of John. More minutes passed before the big man was beside him. Lucas started at such stealth and wished he had half this ability.

"C'mon sir. Ye ken the way." John's strong hand steered him across the wet grass towards the furthest corner of the graveyard.

Ahead faint shadows flitted between the solid lines of stones towards a lantern glow on the ground. The shadows became men. They stood in a line behind a freshly dug trench with the outline of a long, narrow box sitting alongside. He stared at the eerie scene and could scarce believe those strange figures belonged to his own parishioners.

Realising they were waiting for him Lucas took his place opposite them. For a moment he was lost for words and stood half expecting one of them to take over and do the needful.

John gave him a gentle push. "Jist a prayer, sir, then yer wife can be left in peace. It's no as respectful as we'd like, but we need tae be quick."

This was Elizabeth's moment. He must do his best and speak to the Lord on her behalf. With a gulp of cold air he began the familiar words of internment while the rough coffin was lowered into the trench. Even as it touched the bottom shovels of earth spattered over the clean lid to cover it before a pile of turf was unrolled and patted back in place. Finally a large, round stone was placed to mark the spot.

"Ah brocht it frae the Nethan." Wull Gemmell turned towards Lucas. "Ah thocht she'd like that."

Tears stung Lucas's eyes.

"Ah often met her walkin by the river."

"Wheesht," John urged. "We havena time."

The lantern dimmed. The strange group dispersed through a fine curtain of rain while the rest of the village slept on.

John grasped Lucas's arm again and hurried him out of the graveyard. They headed for the small birch wood where Juno was tethered. As they drew near the horse's ears pricked up. She gave a soft snort. John stopped to listen. Juno rattled her bridle. John stiffened. "Ah think we hae a visitor."

"Surely no," Lucas said.

"Juno thinks ay. And ah need tae ken whae's oot there."

"So, somebody did ken aboot this nicht's business aifter aw."

John untethered the horse. He held out the leather straps. "Jist walk her furrit as if ye're on yer ain. Keep goin thru the village an we'll see whit happens."

"Masel? Wi this big horse?"

"Jist dae as ye're tellt." John thrust the reins into Lucas's hands. "On ye go an ah'll see aboot oor visitor."

"And then whit?"

"Never mind, sir. Jist dae it."

Horse and man walked forward, the man reluctantly and a little unsteadily, in contrast to the steady beast by his side.

John waited among the birch trees and watched them walk down the lane. He was alert for any other sign of movement.

Juno was right, he knew that, and whoever was out there would probably be tempted to follow the slow moving horse and man. Gradually they became faint shadows, almost merging into nothing. And that's when a third, equally faint shape, appeared and began to creep across the grass. The very care of the movement, low and close to the ground, stealthy as a stalking fox, told him who it was. Old Gaby. First at the farm. Now here.

John ran forward. But quick as he was some sixth sense seemed to warn the old tinker of approaching danger. He dived sidewards into the ditch and rolled out of reach as John skidded past on the wet grass. By the time the big man slithered to a stop his would-be captive was over the stone boundary wall, crawling under a low tabletop gravestone.

John opened the gate and stood a moment. All he could hear was pattering rain and loud drips of water bouncing from the leaves of the spreading beech tree in the centre. The dark was relentless, no benefit of moon or stars on a night like this. The rain grew heavier, a dancing curtain, which made it difficult to see at all let alone make out the outline of someone like Gaby.

John walked from one side of the graveyard to the other. He stopped, listened again, then turned to cross in the opposite direction. Nothing. He checked each row of headstones. Still no sign of the old tinker, who only needed to stay put and stay safe. John continued his methodical search but saw nothing, heard nothing other than his own fast breathing. Gaby's ability to hide and remain hidden had scored again.

Eventually the hunter was forced to give up. He walked back to the gate, turned and spoke into the dark space behind him. "Ah ken ye're there, Sam Galbraith." His words rang in the silence. "Ah've a guid idea whit ye're up tae. So be warned: if onybody gets tae hear aboot this nicht, ye're for it."

The old tinker shivered. He well understood that John would have no hesitation in dealing with him. He began to wish he'd never left that bundle of ferns when the cart rumbled past. And then he thought about all this dodging here and there to survive. Soon it would be beyond him, so why give up this chance of earning a few sly bawbees? Even a little rest and comfort cost money. He'd take his chance with John Steel's threat. Happy again he snuggled into the pile of dry leaves that had gathered under the thick stone table. His bones began to thaw, and the constant pit-pat of rain on the stone shelf above his head was almost hypnotic. Safe and warm, and not in the least bothered about lying only inches above some long dead corpse, he closed his eyes. His excitement gave way to exhaustion, and he slept.

A few hours later he was up and away through the breaking dawn, heading for the sheriff at Lanark.

John jerked awake. He sat up in bed and listened. It was barely daylight. Somebody was moving about in the kitchen.

"Whit's up?" Marion turned towards him with a start.

"A noise in the kitchen."

"It's likely the meenister. He wis awfy restless aifter ye came back frae the village."

"Ah'll go an see." John dressed quickly and went through to the kitchen. No one. Hurrying down the hall to the front room he knocked politely on the door. No answer. He stuck his head round the door. There was an empty bed, and the minister's clothes were gone. Back in the kitchen he found the outer door off the latch and peered out to see if the man was washing himself at the water trough. The yard was deserted. Surprised that Lucas was up so early John grabbed his jacket and went to investigate.

On the opposite side of the yard he saw the bar was off the stable door and it was slightly ajar. He crossed over and pushed it further open. There was his visitor packing a few possessions from his cart into a leather satchel. "Here, here," he snapped, "whit's up?"

Lucas turned and looked guilty. "I'm sorry. I didna mean tae disturb ye."

"So ah see."

"It's jist - " Lucas sounded apologetic. "Aifter aw ye've done, and aifter last nicht, weel it's time I wis awa afore I bring real trouble on ye."

"Withoot a word?"

Lucas straightened. "Of course I'm beholden. But it canna go on like this."

"So?"

"Look John, I'm supposed tae be beyond the parish. As long as I bide here I'm a danger tae ye and yer family That's the last thing I want. Onyway, I need tae be aboot my Faither's business."

"Business?"

"With or withoot a kirk I must continue God's work as my conscience dictates."

"Has that no been yer problem so far?"

Lucas flushed. "Indeed. And aw the mair reason tae mak it mean something."

"So whit's yer plan?"

"I'll head for Ayrshire, travel by foot and cross the moors where I'm less likely tae be seen. I'll try tae find Alexander Peden, the preacher who lost his ain charge a while back. I ken he travels the country, speaking the truth for ony willing tae listen. I mean tae try and follow his lead. If I can find him he'll help me on my way."

"That's as maybe but Reverend Peden's an experienced hill man. Nae disrespect sir, ye've never set foot on a moor let alane tried tae find yer way across these open spaces."

"But I must."

John took a deep breath. "In that case far be it for me tae try and stop ye. The best place tae start is Priesthill Farm. Reverend Peden passes that way an bides there wi my freend John Brown. But ye need tae unnerstaund it's a guid lang walk tae the farm. It's on the ither side o this moor an ye cud easy git lost."

"God will guide me."

"That's as maybe but whit aboot yer horse an cairt? Hae ye thocht aboot that?"

"I hae nae need o either."

"Ah cud git a guid price for them at the market. Send the money on tae ye."

"Keep them John. Ye'll mak better use o them than I ever could."

"If ye say so."

Neither spoke for a few minutes then John took up where they'd left off. "Jist mind the moor seems pleasant enough when the sun's shinin but dinna be fooled. The going's rough, an when the weather chainges it can turn a mite unfriendly. Maybe ah shud see ye on yer way."

"Thank ye."

"No afore yer breakfast." Marion appeared at the stable door. "Ye need fed first, an then ah can pack a bit extra for Maister Brotherstone."

An hour later two figures climbed the long slope behind the farm, crossed the last patch of rough grazing, and headed for the moor. At first Lucas stumbled over loose stones and tripped over heather roots, but he kept going. His persistence paid off. He began to sense the shape and feel of the ground and place his feet with more care. Gradually both men settled into a steady pace through the grass and heather hummocks, some tall, some steep, some a gentle rise, some topped with thick clumps of dark, spiky rushes, but all similar enough to confuse the unwary.

Uneasy silence walked with them. Eventually Lucas stopped. "Ye're a busy man John. Too busy for this. If ye point oot the way I'll go on by masel."

John hesitated.

Lucas held out his hand. "Thank ye. Ye've done mair than I deserve. Noo I must mak my ain start."

John grasped the offered hand then pointed towards a pair of distant hillocks. "Pass atween these twa. Dinna veer aff if ye want tae come oot on the top edge o Priesthill valley. From there ye'll see the smoke frae the farm chimney. Mind an tell John Brown ah sent ye. He'll dae whit he can tae help wi the next stage o yer journey. He micht even ken the whereaboots o Sandy Peden."

Lucas nodded his thanks and walked away.

John watched till the slight figure had disappeared. Only an idiot would set out with no idea where he was going, or what might happen. In that moment John felt akin to that idiot. Each was as bad as the other in his own way.

The truth of it shocked him and brought a bitter laugh.

The harsh sound hit the air and was whisked away by the wind, leaving only the swish of grass around him. He stood there listening, and soon could make out the wheep of curlews rising and calling, then the scratch and rustle of tiny moorhen claws scuttling among the heather roots. In the distance came the bleat of a lamb and then the answering baa of the mother.

A bee buzzed past his ear. He watched its progress across the heather bells towards the sound of rabbit paws digging and scraping, and flinging the earth behind them. Each and every creature knew its own purpose and accepted it.

With a lighter step he turned towards home.

Chapter 4

Lucas strode through the heather. Clouds raced towards him from the horizon then passed overhead in an instant. Their speed and singular direction seemed like an omen, a sign of a fresh start, and swollen with pride he walked along, his head buzzing with Bible quotations.

Wrapped up in himself, or busy cloud watching, his toe would catch on a root, or slip into a runnel in the soft soil, or dislodge a loose stone. Once or twice he almost fell over but even this didn't jerk him back to reality. He forgot John's warning to mind where he walked, keep track of the weather, and to stay between the two main hillocks on his way to Priesthill farm.

An hour later his legs ached. He stopped for a rest and took out two bannocks from the pack Marion had given him. They smelt good. Mistress Steel was kind to take such trouble. And this walk was doing him good, clearing his mind, affirming his determination. He looked round the vast, treeless space and his sense of well-being faltered as a white mass of cloud rose above the nearest grassy slope. On either side of it the moorland was clear, the sky blue, but within that pillar everything had disappeared. As he watched it swirled towards him, swallowing the ground as it came.

Even as he grabbed his bag, made to run, a wet blanket dropped over him, and cold fingers spiralled up from his toes to wash his face. He could see nothing other than water droplets, each one beautiful and perfect, but terrifying in their ability to link and become such a dense curtain. He huddled against this wet cold and felt it suck out every vestige of his earlier high spirits. He'd forgotten the warning of how the moor could turn unfriendly and now he was stuck in this awful nowhere with no idea how to escape.

The sun was out there beyond this watery wall. He could just make out its faint gleam. But how to get there, to feel its warmth? All he could do was close his eyes and pray for strength against these clawing tendrils that left him with barely a sense of himself.

When he opened his eyes God had heard. The mist was sliding away. Nearby heather and fern re-appeared, glistening in the brighter light, fresh washed to greet a shaft of sunlight which cut through the curtain of blindness. Normality returned as if nothing untoward had happened. A bird began to sing. Maybe it was safe to rise and walk on.

He stood up to lift his bag when a figure emerged from the tail of the departing mist. Tall and ungainly it strode out of the pale slivers and came towards him. A dark cloak flapped around the long, thin body and made it easy to imagine the arrival of some harbinger of doom or mythical bird. A leather mask covered the face, and atop it all danced a wild black wig.

Lucas made to turn and run, but a deep voice called out, "Bide whaur ye are ma freend an ah'll join ye." A moment later a large hand reached out to shake his own and the same voice asked, "Whaur are ye headin?"

"Priesthill." Lucas tried not to stare at the dark sockets of the leather mask. "I'm on my way tae see John Brown."

The mouth below the mask smiled. "Noo there's a thing. So am ah. We can go thegither."

Lucas's eyes flicked from mask to wig and back again.

This seemed to amuse the stranger who laughed. "Ah'm a strange lookin beast am ah no?"

Lost for words Lucas didn't even nod.

"That bad eh? This pair wanderin thing wi its face hidden frae ony it meets."

"But why sir? Whit hae ye done?"

"Tellt the truth as ah see it. An preach the Lord's word in a way the law neither likes nor approves."

"Whit aboot the mask?"

"Ah've a thoosand merks on my heid an the threat o prison for ony man or woman found harbourin me. As yet ah'm as free as a bird, an guid folk still gie me a bed an a meal. But jist in case, ah wear this disguise. That way ony strangers ah meet can honestly say they havena seen me."

"Ye sound like a wandering meenister."

"Ay." The figure bowed. "Put oot ma charge for denyin the king's misguided whims aboot the Kirk. Ah'm no a man seekin confrontation but the truth wis in sic mortal danger ah'd nae option but speak oot and warn folk whit wis happenin. Aifter that the law taen hard agin me, an noo ah'm worth a bit siller if caught."

"I'm a meenister tae, newly ousted," Lucas announced. "Frae Lesmahagow."

"An ye paid a heavy price my man. Did ye no?" The voice softened.

Lucas blinked. "Hoo dae ye ken?"

"Ah ken ye're mournin the loss o a fine lass an takin much o the blame on yersel."

"Whae tellt ye?" Lucas's skin prickled.

"Ah jist ken." The great head nodded and the black wig waved in the wind.

"Sometimes ma inner mind sees things. Whiles they're guid, whiles no sae guid, whiles best no seen at aw. Folk say it's the second sicht which is a guid enough name ah suppose."

Lucas flinched. Words like these scared him.

The black wig nodded again. "Ah saw yer trouble, an yer pair wife. Ah felt for ye, an wept as ah said a prayer. An noo ye're here. Mibbe ah can help ye."

"I doubt it." Lucas had heard enough. "I'm seeking a Reverend Peden, tae follow in his footsteps, tae spread the true word as he does."

"Weel, whae'd believe it?" The mouth smiled. "Oot here in this wild place ye've jist happened on auld Sandy. Is that no a strange coincidence, or wis it meant tae be?"

Lucas gaped at the tall figure wrapped in a well-patched cloak, face part hidden by the leather mask and ridiculous black wig bobbing above. Could this apparition really be Alexander Peden, the man whose name was whispered with reverence as one of the great men of the Kirk, who carved his own reputation wherever he went? The more he stared the more Lucas was prepared to accept that out here there was no such thing as normal, and anything was possible. He began to mumble, "Sir. I had nae idea. It wisna my intention tae seem rude."

"An neither ye were, for Sandy Peden weel kens hoo odd he looks. So nae mair aboot it an we'll walk on thegither tae Priesthill."

"I'm no sure o the way," Lucas admitted. "I wisna paying attention and then this mist came doon."

"Ay. It can be scary. But it has a guid side tae. Aince or twice ah've been gled o it when the troopers wur aifter me. Ah'd jist sit within its tendrils an they'd nae idea whaur ah wis as they passed by as close as ye like. But enough. On we go. Anither hawf hoor will see us safe in Priesthill."

Lucas trailed behind the gaunt figure as his new companion ploughed through the ferns and heather. By the time he saw smoke rising from the farm chimney he was several yards behind, and well out of breath.

The door of the house opened on their approach. A tall, well built man came out. His wary expression vanished and he smiled. "Sandy. It's yersel. Guid tae see ye. An whae's this ye've brocht?"

"I'm Lucas Brotherstone, meenister frae Lesmahagow. John Steel sent me."

The big man nodded. "Come awa in then. Ye're welcome"

Sandy Peden made to remove his mask and wig then stopped and turned towards Lucas. "John here kens me weel enough an I've naethin tae hide frae him. But mibbe ye'd prefer if ah didna?"

"Go aheid, sir. Mak yersel comfortable."

Sandy Peden pulled off his wig and mask and Lucas was able to see the brown, weather-beaten face, sharp and lined, not unlike an elderly eagle.

A bright pair of eyes twinkled with amusement. "Ah hope ye'll no regret seein ma face. In the richt circumstances it micht cost ye dear."

Before Lucas could answer John Brown ushered them indoors.

Here was an ordinary farm kitchen, a familiar place Lucas could relate to. The fire crackled and heat filled the room suggesting comfort could be had within those thick walls. And he needed it after the terror of that mist and the weirdest figure he'd ever met.

John Brown ladled out two small bowls of broth from the

pot by the fire. "Here, sit doon, warm yersels, an hae some soup. An then gie me yer news."

Sandy described his long walk across country from Galloway, spoke about the outdoor services he'd conducted, the people who'd come to hear him, and the kindness they offered. Lucas realised this strange man was brave. If the law caught up with him the gallows would follow, yet here he was roaming the country, defying the law as if it was the most natural thing in the world.

Lucas's story brought nods of sympathy. Sandy said, "Dae ye still want tae follow in ma footsteps?"

Lucas flushed but didn't answer.

"Wise man," Sandy nodded. "Ye're no cut oot for the open air an a rough moor. But dinna despair, there's ither ways tae cairry the truth an dae richt by oor Kirk. Letters need tae be passed, an them in the touns need tae hear the word. Ye cud dae that. It wud be dangerous but still possible. Whit dae ye think?"

Lucas slowly nodded.

"Guid man." Sandy seemed pleased. "But first things first. Yer wife's brither deserves tae ken whit happened. Ye need tae visit him an no jist leave it be."

This time Lucas accepted that Sandy just knew and didn't query it.

"Aifter that ah'd be gratefu if ye'd deliver a letter ah hae for a Maister Middleton. He's a weel kent merchant on the Broomielaw. He has twa ships that ply atween here an Holland. He's a guid freend tae the Kirk an has seen a few meenisters across the water tae safety."

"I'll be happy tae pass on yer letter."

"Here ye are then." Sandy pulled the letter from one of his many pockets and handed it to Lucas. "Mind an gie it tae Maister Middleton. Nae ither een are tae read it. Och, whit am ah sayin? Ah ken ye'll dae yer best."

Lucas nodded and slid the letter inside his jacket.

That evening John Brown's wife gave them a good dinner of thick barley broth and the best of fresh vegetables along with a tough but tasty old hen. They ate well and the kitchen rang with talk and laughter. Later they settled into a long debate about the king and the law, their voices echoing the worry over the unfairness of it all. Lucas listened to Sandy's words which were mostly about the merits of peace, so different to the Kirk's fire brand aggression. He began to wonder if maybe this old man had the truth of it.

When the candles were finally snuffed out the two travellers shared the warm flagstones before the dying fire. For Lucas they felt hard and uncomfortable, so unlike his normal soft bed. But Sandy seemed quite at home, wrapped up in his old cloak and asleep in minutes.

Lying there alongside this revered minister of such odd appearance Lucas felt comforted by his presence. For the first time since Bett's death he was calm enough to almost think logically, to admit his failings and strengths, and try to put them into some semblance of order. It took a long time there in the dark but sleep, when it came, was deep and undisturbed.

Lucas woke at dawn to find himself alone in the kitchen. Alarmed he jumped up and hurried outside and found Sandy talking to John Brown, who already had his cart loaded, ready for the off.

"Ah'm aye up early," John Brown explained. "Best pairt o the day for thinkin. Richt noo ah'm thinkin aboot takin ye doon tae the end o this track tae meet up wi Gus MacPhail."

"Whit for?" Lucas asked.

John Brown pointed to the painted letters on the back of his cart. "That says carrier. Gus an me share work. Ah dae Ayrshire, he gangs roond the toun. If ye're still on wi Sandy's suggestion an headin for Glesca, wud a ride on a cart no be better than a lang walk?"

"If that's the best way I can be o service." Lucas turned to Sandy. "But whit aboot yersel, sir?"

"Dinna worry aboot me. Ah'm awa tae Muirkirk an Cumnock. Aifter that ah'll double back by Lanark, an mibbe as far as Biggar afore the end o the month."

"That's a wheen miles tae walk by yersel."

"Ah'm used tae it. The Lord shows me my path, ah jist follow."

There was no answer to that.

"A bite tae eat afore ye go," John Brown suggested.

"Naw, naw. Ye fed me ower weel last nicht. Ah need tae walk it aff. As ever, ah'm obliged tae ye." Sandy lifted his staff from the long grass and crossed the yard towards the moor.

"Sir." Lucas ran after him and grasped the back of the old man's cloak. "I jist want tae thank ye."

Sandy's dark eyes twinkled at Lucas's serious face. "Smile man. That'll dae me."

"It's jist, weel, I'm glad we met up. I'd never hae got here withoot ye. And yer talk."

Sandy stopped him. "Last nicht ye were a guid listener. An ye need tae hear mair afore ah go. My inner ee has shown me yer road is lang, an hard, an shud tak ye across the water for a while. If yer wise ye'll neither fight it nor think yersel a coward for leavin this land. The Lord wants it. Jist trust him an dae as he asks." With a wide grin Sandy walked away, whistling as if he hadn't a care in the world.

"He's a mite unpredictable," John Brown said as they watched the ungainly figure fade in the distance. "An nane the worse for it."

Sandy's parting words repeated in Lucas's ears. He shook his head in disbelief. This could never happen.

"Trust him. It'll aw mak sense in time." John Brown nodded as if he'd seen this reaction before. "But richt noo sir, we need a bite tae eat afore we meet Gus MacPhail. He'll see ye richt an deliver ye safe an soond."

Late that night Lucas found himself outside his brother in law's door, at the bottom of the High Street in Glasgow. This was an important address. Andrew Spreul was an important merchant, a wealthy man.

Here in this strange place he felt anxious about the shadowy figures that seemed to flit past in the deepening dark. In Lesmahagow folk would be indoors, in bed, not like this city of the night, pulsing with uncertainty, and its mix of human smells and stale cooking, even the occasional cough or bray from an animal stabled nearby. Being alone on this chilly street seemed unwise and he rattled the brass door-knocker several times.

"Whae's there?" A woman's trembling voice called out

behind the big, black door. "Whit is it?"

"Lucas Brotherstone. Brother in law of Andrew Spreul. I wish tae speak wi him."

"At this hoor?" There was silence for several minutes then a familiar deep voice demanded, "Is that yersel Lucas?"

"Ay. I'm sorry aboot arriving sae late. Can I come in?"

Before he could say any more bolts were drawn back, a big key grated round, and the door swung inwards a few inches. A heavily whiskered face peered out, and a small circle of light appeared.

Lucas leant towards it. "Ay, it's me."

"God sakes man." A strong arm grabbed hold of his jacket and yanked him forward, the door opened wider, and he was inside. Nothing was said while Andrew Spreul slammed the door shut and slid all the bolts back in place. He turned the big key again then held the guttering candle up to examine Lucas's face. "Ye luk terrible. Whit's wrang?"

Lucas said nothing.

"Richt. Follow me intae the kitchen. At this time o nicht it's the warmest room in the hoose. We can talk there." Andrew turned to a shadowy figure hovering behind him. "Richt Mearn, we need a bit supper for oor guest, and fling a wheen logs on the fire. Aifter that awa back tae yer bed."

Minutes later Lucas was sitting by the familiar fireside drinking his first cup of strong, hot tea. He drank without asking what the strange liquid was. He didn't much like the taste, but thought it uncivil to say so.

"Weel?" Andrew could wait no longer. "Whit's aw this aboot?"

"It's Bett."

"Bett?"

"She's deid." It sounded raw and unfeeling. Not the way he meant to begin.

Desperate to make things right everything else burst out, every last moment of that final encounter with Lieutenant Crichton.

Andrew pursed his lips, seemed on the verge of saying something, then continued to stare at Lucas. After a long silence he stood up and began to pace the shadowy room. Finally he asked, "Whit noo?"

"Ane way or anither I must mak aw this mean something. I must continue my defiance by preaching the word tae those as will listen. Here in the toun I can gather sma groups."

"No ye'll no," Andrew snapped. "Indeed ye will not. Whit ye did tae my Bett is unforgivable. Wis she no worth mair than yer so cawed conscience? God sakes she'd still be alive if ye'd been man enough tae swallow yer pride."

"I had nae choice."

"Nae choice? Of course ye had a choice. No that I'm surprised. It's aye been yer ain way or nae way. And noo my pair sister has paid the price for yer damned selfishness. Whit ye did is beyond endurance and I'll no hae it. Frae noo on ye're neither freend nor relation o mine, so bide oot ma sicht. We're feenished."

"Ye dinna understand." Lucas drew back from the angry face.

"Oh but I dae. Only too weel. In my book ye're despicable." Andrew's hand reached out and grabbed Lucas's wrist, pulling him closer.

"Leave aff sir." Lucas looked down and hated each one of those grasping, podgy fingers. "Leave aff." His voice rang with meaning. "Or God help me."

"Ye wudna dare - " Andrew jumped back. "No in ma ain hoose."

"Try me."

"And whit will yer God say then? Man, ye're laughable. They say pride comes afore a fall. If there's ony justice ye'll fall aw the way and burn in hell."

"And ye'll relish it nae doubt."

The two men glared at each other then Andrew said. "Ay weel, I'm Christian enough no tae turn ye oot lik I shud. Ye can bide here in the kitchen but come mornin ye're oot. And if I ivver see yer face again it'll be ower soon." With that he marched out the room and slammed the heavy door behind him.

Lucas listened to the footsteps clump down the hall then up the long curved stair and fade to nothing on the floor above. He stared into the darkest corner of the room and heard every one of Andrew's words again. Not that he accepted their sincerity.

He knew his brother-in-law well enough to know his reaction had more to do with steering a careful business course than love of his only sister. Right now the Kirk was seen to be a problem. The great and the good were far from happy with it. There were even mutterings of treason. Best not show sympathy. In fact best not lean either way. For this clever merchant it was all a balancing act and had nothing to do with right or wrong.

At least Andrew knew why he behaved as he did. And it brought its own rewards for his ever expanding purse, and ever more important position among the other merchants. *If only*, Lucas thought resentfully.

As for the memory of Bett's blank eyes staring up at him while he cradled her head, he'd known then whose fault it was, and yet he still couldn't admit why he'd taken such a stand against the law, other than that it was expected. The Kirk expected and the faithful servant delivered. Now his pretence was wearing thin. Worst of all, he'd had to hear it from the likes of Andrew Spreul.

It made him want to escape, anywhere, so long as it was away from this house. But that was another pretence, especially in the middle of the night, in a strange city with whatever lurked out there in the dark streets, waiting to do him harm.

He stood up and stretched, sniffing the food laid out on the kitchen table. Turning towards it he reached for a slice of dark rye bread, fresh, thick cut, moist, liberally spread with good butter. He bit into it and savoured the taste, best he'd ever had, and only to be expected for Andrew Spreul was one of the wealthiest merchants in the city. A man like that could afford the best. Several excellent slices of boiled ham came next, and upset as he was, hunger kept him eating till the plates were cleared. Afterwards he slumped down by the dying embers of the fire to sit out the rest of the night then slip away with first light.

He tried not to think, especially about Bett. It was difficult, here in her family home where she seemed almost alive, emerging from the shadows to torment and tease his imagination. He sat up straight, tried to resist but she kept appearing, her perfect oval face pale and faint, but as tempting as ever. He had to get closer.

He stood up and crept into the hall, feeling his way in the dark till he reached the door of the room she'd had throughout her childhood. Once inside he clicked the door shut and stumbled over to pull back the heavy shutters. Moonlight flooded in and lit up Bett's collection of knick-knacks, the things she'd touched, played with, even the doll's house specially made by her father. Lucas stared at each piece then shuddered. Moonlight indeed. He turned to close the shutters again and stop this madness; weary, alone, confused, grieving, he flopped back on the bed and cried himself to sleep.

It was well into the morning when he woke and heard the noise of household servants busy about their daily chores. He heard Andrew receiving his visitors, the deep voice talking business, steering the conversation to suit himself. No one seemed aware that Lucas was still in the house. He thought about opening the window, jumping into the yard and creeping away unseen, but couldn't bring himself to do it. Out by the front door was the only way.

He stood up, straightened his dusty clothes, re-tied his hair, and hoped he looked better than he felt. He opened the door and saw Andrew conducting an elderly customer down the hall, no doubt whispering whatever it took to keep a smile on the old man's face.

The door creaked and Andrew whirled round. Lucas nodded to the two men.

"Chris sake," Andrew gaped at him. "I thocht ye were awa hoors ago." His eyes strayed to the open door of the room. His face darkened. "Whit were ye up tae in there?"

"I wis - " Lucas stopped. Andrew wouldn't understand.

"Ay richt." Andrew pulled the front door open and pointed towards the street beyond. "Oot ye go. And mind it's for the last time. There's nae welcome here onymair."

Lucas stalked past, half expecting a shove to help him on his way. Nothing came although his toes barely touched the bottom step before the door clanged shut behind him.

Glasgow was about its daily business, and none of it seemed to relate to the stranger in its midst. Lucas stood, looking up and down the busy street, wondering what next when he remembered Sandy's letter still inside his jacket, and his promise to deliver it to the merchant Middleton. At least he could do that.

He set out for the Broomielaw, determined to find the man. Much later, and after many questions, he ended up at the corner of the Trongate, outside the city's first coffee house, opened only a few months ago. It was a grand building, already the place for those and such as those to be seen meeting and doing business, and anyone he asked about Middleton had directed him there.

Once past the tall fluted pillars and massive double doors complete with carved panels of full rigged ships, Lucas plunged into a huge, smoke laden hall, full of noise and the smell of cooked food.

Lucas had no idea who Middleton might be but when he mentioned the name to a serving girl he was directed to a corner table where a group of well-dressed merchants seemed to be having a business meeting while eating from huge platters heaped with a selection of meats and fried fish. Talking and eating at the same time seemed no problem to these men. He approached the group and politely said, "Maister Middleton?"

A round faced, stout man looked up. "Ay. Whit is it?" His soft, brown eyes were wary.

Sensing this Lucas said, "I hae a letter for ye sir." He didn't mention Sandy's name.

The merchant rose from his seat, took the letter then stood under the steady glow of an oil lamp to read it. When finished he waved Lucas forward. "Come awa in sir. Join oor group. We've mair than enough tae satisfy oor needs and happy tae share."

Lucas took a seat at the end of the table. He was offered a selection from the nearest plate. He tried to be polite and ate a little but business talk was beyond him, and he could only sit and listen to the lively debate without understanding much of what was said. An hour passed. One by one the merchants rose from the table and went about their business. He and Middleton were left alone.

Middleton turned to Lucas and nodded. "I cudna ask afore

but is he weel?" Even now he didn't mention the name.

"Indeed."

"Busy as ivver if this letter's onything tae go by."

Lucas nodded.

Middleton studied Lucas as if making up his mind about speaking more freely. After a moment he said "Move yer chair in a bit, sir. Ye canna be too careful aboot here."

Lucas shuffled closer.

Middleton did the same then leant forward and spoke softly. "The man mentioned in this letter canna undertake the task in mind."

Lucas blinked. He'd no idea where this conversation was going.

Middleton shook his head. "It's a sad business but the pair soul wis lifted yesterday and charged wi secret preaching. He's been flung in the Tolbooth, and they say he'll be shipped oot tae the Bass Rock when he should be heading for Utrecht."

"Utrecht?"

"Ay. Utrecht, Holland. And God kens hoo I'll find somebody tae tak his place."

"Ye've lost me," Lucas admitted. "Oor freend didna tell me the contents o that letter."

"Ay weel, sir. Let me fill ye in. My sympathy is wi the Kirk and as a merchant I'm in a position tae help when needed. Last month I had twa meenisters keen on a quick way oot raither than face a hanging."

"It's as bad as that?"

"Ay. And getting worse. But aince across the water they're safe enough. And it's no as if they let things lie. There's a school ower there, wi mony a scholar ready and willing tae wrestle wi scripture and learn hoo tae present the word as it shud be heard. When the time comes weel versed men will return and tak the Kirk furrit in the richt way."

"I'm an ousted meenister tae."

"Are ye noo?" Middleton's bushy eyebrows rose. "Whaur frae?"

"Lesmahagow."

"In the country I tak it?"

"Ay."

"Nae maitter. Hoo's yer theology and scripture? Are ye guid at arguing? Can ye haud yer ain and get yer point across?"

"I've completed several essays on the disciples and had them printed. And there's naething I like better than a lively debate."

"Is that so? And whit aboot yer family? Ony ties tae keep ye here?"

"Nane."

Middleton leant closer. "Hoo wud ye feel aboot a wee sail doon the Clyde and then oot tae sea, aw the way tae Holland, and Utrecht in parteeclar? It's a fine toun wi guid folk, and sympathetic tae the cause. Ye'd hae keen students and plenty debate, even arguing. Jist think whit an influence ye cud be on the Kirk's future."

"And if I did consider yer suggestion when wud this be likely tae happen?"

"It's supposed tae tak place the nicht, at the turn o the tide. My sailing rig, the *Elizabeth*, is anchored aff the tail o the bank by Greenock. She's loaded, ready tae go. If William Service hadna been arrested and flung in the Tolbooth he'd be setting oot on her. But noo ye're here."

The *Elizabeth*. Suddenly Lucas saw the sense of it all. He smiled. "Ay sir, I'll go."

Late that night Lucas Brotherstone was punted down the Clyde, out to Middleton's fine rigged ship then hoisted aboard. The anchor was lifted, the sails unfurled, and he was off for Holland with Sandy Peden's prophecy ringing in his ears.

Chapter 5

The shoemaker, Sandy Gillon, hurried down Lanark High Street towards the garrison. The captain there always expected special attention so it was no surprise when his boots were handed in at the shop that morning with a note to have them back at the garrison by twelve noon. The worn out soles had been replaced and the scuffed leather carefully oiled. The boots were looking good but that would be forgotten if Sandy was late with their return.

He didn't like delivering to the old stone fort with its tiny barred windows high above the street. There was something unpleasant about this peering out with no chance to look in. And the main gate was shut most of the time. Visitors gained entry by a small side gate where they were interrogated and sometimes flung back into the street. Most Lanark citizens rarely ventured within those walls. Nor did they want to, for Sheriff Meiklejon had his own special approach to the law.

The town clock was about to chime the hour and the road was blocked by a crowd milling around the main gate. "Whit's goin on?" Sandy tried to push past.

"A notice," someone called out. "Luk for yersel. It's pinned tae the gate."

Sandy peered over the heads in front of him and read:

> *Post of curate in Lesmahagow Parish*
> *Apply in writing to Sheriff Meiklejon at Lanark Garrison*

He was reading the notice again when the captain shouted to him from the rampart above. Sandy waved and rushed along to the side gate and rattled the heavy knocker. A small panel slid back. A pair of suspicious eyes peered out.

Sandy held up the boots.

A gruff voice said, "Fur the captain?"

"Ay."

The gate opened a fraction. A strong arm pulled him in. "Ye're cuttin it fine. The platoon's aboot tae go."

Outside the garrison might look like a fortress but inside it resembled a badly constructed maze with much of it used for storage and stabling horses.

A whole section of the building was given over to the sheriff, who lived and dictated in grand style while his soldiers made the best of two rows of wooden shacks more or less bolted to the walls.

The main garrison store and kitchen were directly below the men's quarters and whatever time Sandy called servants and soldiers came and went with constant noise. And he'd heard about the cells. Sited down a steep, narrow stair, below the big store, they'd be damp and dark. And further down there was supposed to be a specially built corner with extra thick walls, where interrogations, or worse, could go on with no fear of interruption.

The exercise yard was the only open space. The other half was covered by a thatched canopy that cast shadows into every corner. During the day roosting pigeons were a nuisance and at night tiny bats flew back and forward above the flickering sconces that lined the inner walls.

Sandy's only thought was delivering those boots. Soldiers and horses almost filled the yard but he squeezed past then ran up the wooden steps to meet his client on the way down.

"Ah thocht ye'd lost track o the time." The captain grabbed his boots and sat down on a step to pull them on. "But nivver mind. Ye've done a guid job."

"The crowd millin aboot held me back."

"Ay. It's a bit steery wi folk tryin tae read that notice."

"Ah had a luk," Sandy admitted. "But ah didna unnerstaund whit it wis aboot."

"Nae wunner. It's a queer business. Aw aboot the king bein at loggerheids wi the Kirk."

"Hoo come? He's miles awa in London."

"That doesna stop him wantin his subjects tae dae as thur tellt. Richt noo he's richt annoyed. As far as ah can mak oot the king says he's heid o the Kirk wi a direct line tae the Almichty. The meenisters say he's no. Noo he's tellt them tae gie way or git flung oot on their lug, wi nae job an nae hoose if they dinna sign a paper declarin their loyalty tae the crown. There's a wheen haudin oot agin it, an we've a government platoon hoisted on us tae dae the needfu. The sheriff's ragin aboot sae mony extra mooths tae feed. Noo he's been tellt tae find curates tae replace the meenisters. An it's no as if he kens whit a curate is let alane whaur tae luk. He's no the maist even tempered man so richt noo he's findin fault wi everythin."

"Whit is a curate onyway?"

"Ah think it's kind a lik a meenister. But the sheriff's no fussed aboot them havin the richt papers for the job."

"Does that mean onybody can apply?"

"So it seems."

"Whit aboot me?" Sandy asked.

"Ye must be jokin. Ah hudna ye marked doon as a preacher or a prayin man."

"Suit me fine." Sandy didn't admit it was the idea of becoming a somebody instead of a mere tradesman, at anybody's beck and call.

"Ye're no the man ah thocht ye wur." The captain shook his head. "Still, each tae his ain madness ah suppose. Mind ye, it's weel paid, an thur's a free hoose wi a Glebe field. The sheriff's even offerin a horse an trap tae the richt applicant."

Sandy's eyebrows rose. "Micht be worth thinkin aboot."

"Jist be carefu," the captain warned. "It's Sheriff Meiklejon makin the offer."

A bugle sounded.

"Time tae mount up." The captain dropped three half groats into Sandy's hand then rattled down the stairs two at a time. At the bottom he turned and grinned up at him. "Jist mind whit ah said."

Sandy smiled back as expected, then looked at the three silver coins in the centre of his palm. All that effort for next to nothing. Didn't seem fair somehow. He was capable of much more than repairing boots and shoes.

He waited till the horses cleared the yard then slipped out the main gate behind them. The gate clanged shut and its sound reminded him of the notice. He turned to read it again. With a job like that he'd have a steady income. And he'd be Maister

Gillon, not just common Sandy. As for living in a free house with a Glebe field, and driving about the countryside like a gentleman, there was nothing there to dislike.

Lost in thought he walked away from the garrison and began to make his way back up the main street. Half way up he stopped outside the provost's house and looked at its fine, stone frontage. Here lived a respected man who'd come from a background no better than his own. Sandy knew which narrow vennel had originally been the provost's home, and not so many years ago either. Maybe a step up like this was possible. Before he could change his mind he grasped the bell pull and rang it several times.

The provost appeared in a fluster. "Whit is it man? Ye're ringin that bell as if yer tail's on fire."

"Sorry sir. It's important. Can ye spare me a few meenits?" Sandy smiled his best please-will-you-help-me smile and was relieved to see the frown begin to soften. For good measure he added, "Ah'd appreciate yer advice."

The provost turned and led him down the long hall, into the big front room where they stood facing each other.

"Weel. Whit is it?" the provost demanded.

"There's a notice on the garrison gate aboot a curate for Lesmahagow. They seem tae be needin yin an ah'd like tae apply."

The provost's lips pursed. He frowned and sighed. "A curate. Is somethin lik that no a wee bit ootside yer usual line o work? Lesmahagow ye say?"

"Ay sir. But onybody can apply, as long as it's in writin." Sandy began to explain, delivering the facts in a way that implied he could be part of it all. He ended with, "Ah had it frae the garrison captain himsel."

"But ye're a shoemaker. Ye've nae religious trainin." The older man shook his head. "An whit aboot the Bible? Hoo weel are ye acquaint wi that? Can ye quote plenty scripture?"

"Nae problem. My faither had me at the catechism frae an early age an ah read my Bible every day."

"Ay, weel. Ye'd certainly need tae be familiar wi the word."

Sandy said nothing. This was not the moment to push. He could almost see the older mind ticking over. At least the frown had gone, and the silence in the room didn't seem heavy.

Eventually the provost said, "Ye've a guid hand at the writin. As guid as ony. An ye understaund the wordin on official papers as weel as helpin me wi mony a letter for the toun an nivver giein a word awa aboot the business. Kennin when tae keep yer mooth shut wud be important tae. An ye're reliable. Aye willin when ah ask ye. An ye've guid manners. An ye speak weel. God's sake Sandy, it's mibbe no sic a daft notion aifter aw. Ye micht jist manage tae haud yer ain an mak a decent fist o it."

Sandy kept his voice measured and calm. "Thank ye. Ah'd like tae gie it a try."

"Guid luck then."

They shook hands then Sandy dared to push a little further. "Ah wis wonderin sir. Cud ye see yer way tae gien me a reference? Yer opinion maitters aboot here an ah'm sure yer approval wud carry weight wi the sheriff."

"The sheriff?"

"Ay sir. He's the man wi the final say. Wi yersel ahint me, weel, it micht mak aw the difference."

The provost gave him a hard stare then shrugged. "Och, why no? Ane guid turn deserves anither. An ye've aye done weel by me."

There was an amused glint in the provost's eye which might just be hinting that he was less than convinced, or maybe he didn't believe the likes of a shoemaker would ever make a curate. But he'd agreed to the reference. That was all that mattered. Sandy grabbed the podgy hand and shook it again. They both smiled and Sandy took his leave as a very happy man.

Once out of the provost's house Sandy hurried up the main street with his coat tails flying behind him, not in the least bothered by the curious glances from passers by. Back in his workshop he locked the door. Customers would have to wait. He'd an important letter to write. Retreating to the back of the shop he pushed a pile of shoes, boots and sandals to the far end of his bench and made space for his precious sheets of paper. Out came the big glass inkwell and the quill used for the shop accounts. Now he was ready to make a start.

After a few lines he began to realise that this was a real

challenge. However, he kept at it, and gradually the words began to take shape. By the time he went home for his dinner the completed letter was safe in his pocket, ready to be delivered come morning.

His wife Meg was busy in the kitchen. She looked up and smiled as he bustled in and hung up his coat on the back of the door as he always did. But before she could ask about his day he burst out with his news.

"Whit are ye on aboot?" She gaped at him. "Onyway, whit's a curate?"

"Lik a meenister."

"Dinna be daft. Ye're a time served journeyman wi yer ain shop, an weel respected in the toun. Why wud ye gie that up for somethin ye ken naethin aboot?"

He hadn't reckoned on this. He'd expected her to be pleased, even excited. "Luk Meg, ah ken this is a bit o a shock but think aboot it, ah can read an write wi the best o them, an ah ken my Bible as weel as the next. Trust me, ah'm weel suited for the post."

"Is that so?"

"Ay. An ah spoke tae the provost aboot my idea. He agrees wi me. He even promised me a reference."

"Has he indeed?" The words bounced back in Sandy's face. "Weel, ah'll hae somethin tae say next time ah see him." She banged a heavy plate down on the table. The sound seemed like an argument in itself, or a warning that he'd gone too far.

To prove her point she began to dish out a generous helping of lamb gigot and boiled potatoes. "See this? It's a guid bit o meat, an smell that rosemary, its fresh. Wud a curate dae as weel? Ye an yer fancy notions. Ma faither aye said it's best tae flee low an flee lang. Mark ma words Sandy, nae guid comes o reachin above yersel."

"Tak this awa." Sheriff Meiklejon had no appetite for breakfast this morning. He glowered at his usual plate of grilled ham and pushed it away.

The young serving girl hesitated.

"Stop starin at me lik an owl. Dae as ye're tellt and fetch up a tankard of ale." The big man half rose from his seat. "On ye go. I'm no in the mood tae wait."

The girl backed away and scurried downstairs while Meiklejon turned to take a second look at the letter which had arrived from his masters in Edinburgh. Its contents didn't please him, especially the warning of a visit from John Graham of Claverhouse, the man trusted by the king himself to oversee the ousting of rebel ministers and return southern Scotland to its normal law abiding self. No doubt Claverhouse would want to know how many vacant posts had been filled.

Meiklejon sucked air through his teeth. All he'd managed to do was stick a notice on the garrison gate. As far as he was concerned religion was best kept at arms length. Maintaining order was his forté. He knew how to do that and seldom heard any criticism of his personal take on administering the law in Clydesdale. This was different. He was about to have an inspection of a very different nature. In an unusual burst of honesty he wondered how he could avoid being found wanting. He leant forward to spit his disgust into the roaring fire and hear it hiss back at him.

Just then his clerk, Joseph Thrum, appeared in the doorway with another letter.

"Whit noo?" Meiklejon snapped.

Thrum stepped forward, laid the paper in front of his master then turned to go.

"Haud on," Meiklejon snapped.

"As ye wish, sir."

After a few lines the sheriff looked up and almost smiled. "The very thing. Bring the man in."

Thrum shuffled his feet. "He's no here, sir."

"So whaur is he?"

"Ah mmm, ah sent him awa. Ah cud see he wudna dae. He's jist a shoemaker."

"Whit aboot oor Lord? Wis he no jist a carpenter?"

Thrum's face reddened and he had the sense to hang his head.

"Since when did ye start makin decisions aboot here?" Meiklejon demanded. "Ye're here tae listen and obey orders. There's nae mention o thinkin for yersel, let alane decidin onythin on my behalf."

"Ah'm sorry sir."

"So ye're aye sayin." The sheriff glared at Thrum. They'd worked together for years but lately Meiklejon had sensed a change in his clerk's attitude. He suspected this minion might be interfering in matters beyond his remit. Meiklejon stood up. His bulk and height dwarfed the short, stout Thrum. He thumped his fat fist down on the tabletop.

Thrum jumped back. "Whit's wrang sir?"

"I'm no happy wi yer so cawed best. Frae noo on ye'll consult me afore makin ony decisions or ye'll find yer coat on a shoogly nail." The sheriff watched the man squirm. "Aifter aw they years it saddens me ta see ye abuse yer position."

"Ah'll try harder sir."

"Richt." The sheriff allowed his voice to soften a little. "Ye can mak a start by findin this Alexander Gillon and fetchin him back till I hae a word aboot this letter."

"But sir - " Thrum whined.

"Nae buts. On ye go an dinna come back withoot him. An dinna bang that door shut ahint ye."

Pleased with himself Meiklejon settled down to read Sandy's letter again. He'd hardly started when there was a tap on the door. He looked up. "Did I no tell ye - "

His words faded as a pair of dancing eyes set in a small, brown, wizened face peered round the door edge, then a dirty little figure in a raggedy coat slid into the room whispering, "Sam Galbraith, travellin man. Ah tak it ah hae the honour tae address the sheriff o Clydesdale?"

"Chris sake." Meiklejon sat up with a jerk. "Hoo did ye get in here?"

"Naebody notices me unless ah want them tae. Whae bothers wi an auld man, a mere naethin, slippin here an ther an hearin things? Things that micht interest yer guid sel."

"I doubt it." The sheriff scowled at the strange apparition bobbing in front of him. He reached across the table for his bell to summon the guard.

"Ah jist happened tae be in Lesmahagow last nicht. An whit ah saw, weel, me bein a law abidin citizen, ah felt the need tae come an tell ye." The old tinker smiled and showed an uneven row of yellow teeth. "Ah tak it ye're acquaint wi the name

Brotherstane?"

The sheriff's hand closed over the bell. "The man defied the law and wis dealt wi." Even as he said this he could hardly believe he was bothering to answer this ridiculous creature.

"Richtly so, sir. Richtly so." The old man crept a little closer. "An ah'm sure ye ken aboot the unfortunate death o that parteeclar meenister's wife. An hoo it brocht sadness tae the village."

Reading the tinker's expression, and guessing there was more, the sheriff waited.

"Mibbe ye dinna ken the lassie's settled in the graveyard ahint the kirk. No that she's daein ony harm ther. But aw the same it's defiance. Especially aifter ye issued the order flingin meenister an wife oot on their lug. Her man wis at her funeral. Oh ay. He's still aboot the village an bidin in a farm nearby."

"Is he indeed?"

"Seen him wi ma ain een."

"I tak it that's no aw ye've seen." Meiklejon began to see this interruption might be opportune after all. A half groat spun towards Gaby.

He caught the tiny silver coin then whispered, "Ah'm awfy hungry, sir."

The sheriff couldn't help laughing at the rascal's cheek. He lifted the bell and rang it several times.

Within seconds the door burst open and a guard rushed into the room.

Meiklejon pointed at his visitor. "Hoo did this slip by ye?"

The guard stared at Gaby. "Ah wis by the main door sir. Ah nivver moved."

"Wi yer een shut maist like," Meiklejon accused the red face. "Shame on ye." He turned to Gaby. "Awa doon tae the kitchen wi this man. Tell the cook I sent ye. Eat whit ye like. And nae slippin awa. I want ye back here for anither wee talk." He almost smiled with approval at the way this would-be informer squeezed the tiny coin in his hand and obediently followed the soldier downstairs for his promised meal.

About an hour later Sandy was hustled into the garrison, past the duty guard, and up the back stairs to the first floor. He was pushed along a narrow corridor to a door at the end. "C'mon." Thrum grabbed Sandy's sleeve, pushed the heavy door open, and propelled him into the room. "Here ye are, sir."

The room was large, lit only by one tiny window. Heavy tapestries of hunting scenes lined the walls, and the wooden floor was partly covered by a thick woven, patterned carpet, much marked by muddy footprints. A huge fire blazed in the corner and the light from the flames danced across the white plastered ceiling. The contrast between this flickering light and the darkest corners made the room seem alive. It reeked of authority, of coming and going, and orders, many orders.

Sandy hesitated and felt another push in his back.

"On ye go," Thrum hissed. "He asked tae see ye parteeclar like."

Almost overcome by the heat blasting towards him Sandy took a few steps forward. "Sir." He nodded politely to the bald head of a broad shouldered man sitting behind an oak table in the middle of the room.

"Ah, Maister Gillon." The sheriff looked up. "Come in, man. Come in. I'm richt sorry for no seein ye earlier." He waved a hand at his clerk, "We'll be fine by oorsels."

Thrum hesitated.

The sheriff's high colour deepened. "Whit did I say?"

Thrum bowed and withdrew, and the sheriff seemed content to wait till the reluctant feet stomped back downstairs.

Sandy tried not to fidget as Meiklejon sat back in his big chair and studied him through half closed eyes. He hoped he was making a favourable impression in spite of his unruly ginger hair which he guessed might be considered the wrong colour for a religious man. He knew his clothes were well past their best. But at least they were clean and well mended. Meg saw to that. Under the continuing stare he forced himself to stand up straight and to more or less meet that uncomfortable gaze without seeming challenging or rude.

"Weel, weel." The sheriff continued to stare. "I'm jist trying tae imagine ye rigged oot in some decent claes. Ye see this kinda post requires a gentleman, or as near as we can get under the circumstances." He lifted Sandy's letter from the pile of papers in front of him. "Ye write weel sir, and yer words are guid." A chubby finger stabbed at the letter. "And ye've plenty tae say aboot yersel."

Sandy dared to say, "Ah wis keen tae explain, sir."

"So ye did, so ye did." Meiklejon nodded. "And I see ye hae the approval o the provost himsel."

"He's a guid customer an kind enough tae support ma application."

"Ye're a shoemaker."

"Ah hae ma ain shop."

"Very commendable. And nae doubt profitable." The sheriff leant forward. "So whit maks ye think aboot takin up wi religion?"

"Ah've spent years at ma books an the Bible is nae stranger tae me. This seems lik a chance tae mak guid use o my learnin an alloo me tae be o better service tae ma fellow man."

"If I believe that I'll believe onythin, Maister Gillon. Still, ye said it withoot a blush, and at least ye sound sincere."

Sandy did blush.

The sheriff laughed. "I'm no criticisin ye. There's no mony can lie as weel wi a straight face. Noo whit aboot Scripture? Can ye quote frae the Bible?"

"Nae problem, sir. Wud ye care tae test me?"

"I'll tak yer word for it." It was Meiklejon's turn to flush. "Whit aboot a sermon ivvery Sunday? Ye'd need tae speak in front o folk an haud their attention."

"Ah've nae experience there, sir," Sandy admitted. "But ah'm weel enough versed tae mak a start. Lik ah said in ma letter ah'm a quick learner."

The sheriff shuffled in his carved chair. "Tae be honest Maister Gillon I hae a bit o a problem. I've mair than ane curate tae find at short notice. And then there's the quality o applicants tae conseeder. It aw taks time. Time I havena got."

"If ye're willin tae gie me a chance ah'll no disappoint."

"That's a richt moothfu. Noo, whit aboot Lesmahagow? Hae ye ivver been there?"

"No sir. But ah'm sure it's a fine place."

"Mibbe so. But the meenister in that village left his post raither sudden. And no in the best o circumstances. Somethin lik that can be a bit unsettlin when folk dinna unnerstaund the problem and listen tae aw kinds o tittle tattle. Ye'd need tae work at introducin yersel. It wudna be easy Maister Gillon. There's a few chainges in the way a kirk service is tae be conducted frae noo on, and I dinna suppose that'll gang doon too weel. Mind ye, there's a guid softener. The charge pays a stipend o twenty five pounds Scots per year, and a grand hoose wi a Glebe field. And since I'm a generous man there's a horse and trap on offer as weel. For the richt applicant that is."

A rap at the door disturbed them.

"Ye can see hoo busy I am." The sheriff looked Sandy up and down then pushed an important looking paper across the table. "Damn it. I need a curate and ye're here. Ay. Ye best sign afore I chainge my mind." He pointed to a large glass inkwell, and a well-worn quill among the clutter on the table. "On ye go. Put yer name on this paper. Ye can gie it a try."

Sandy signed at once.

"That's no aw Maister Gillon." The sheriff dusted Sandy's signature. "Ye'll need tae luk the pairt. On the way oot tell my clerk tae gie ye a credit note for a new coat, hat and breeches. And maybe twa linen shirts and white stockings wudna gang amiss. I dinna suppose we can dae much aboot yer ginger hair, so tie it weel back and maybe it'll no luk sae bad."

"Whit aboot new claes for my wife an bairn? That way we'd aw luk the pairt."

"Ay, weel." The sheriff nodded. "The coffers micht jist stretch that far. Mak sure it's guid sombre stuff, appropriate tae yer callin, naethin fancy. And mind I want ye ready and awa afore Sunday."

"This Sunday?"

"Come Sunday ye're in that village deliverin yer first sermon."

"Ah'll be ready tae travel in twa days. "

"Ye'd better be."

"Ye'll no regret this decision, sir."

"That remains tae be seen, Maister Gillon," the sheriff said slowly and lowered his voice. "I tak it ye unnerstaund hoo we're livin in difficult times?"

Round-eyed, Sandy nodded.

"Jist so. And ye'll be understaundin that I'm aifter a bit mair than jist the administerin tae yer flock. Yer eyes and ears must miss naethin. Lik I said, we hae difficult times tae deal wi, and yer help will be appreciated, indeed required."

"Ah'll dae ma best, sir."

"Jist mak sure it's naethin less. Noo on ye go." The sheriff sat back in his big chair and looked pleased as Sandy squeezed past the guard who was marching Gaby into the room for his second interview.

When Thrum heard the sheriff's decision he muttered, "Ye've done weel. He must be impressed."

Sandy beamed with pleasure and mentioned the promised credit note.

"If that's whit he said ah'll hae it ready by mornin."

"Thrum!" A loud summons came from above.

"Comin sir." The clerk scuffled about gathering papers from his desk. "As ye can hear ah've a difficult maister tae try an please."

Sandy treated the flustered man to a beaming smile and stepped into the street as if he was walking on air. He could hardly believe he'd pulled it off. From now on everything would be easier, better. He kept smiling all the way home. When he reached his own door he dusted his jacket then rattled the knocker. When Meg appeared he pulled off his cap and swept her a low bow. "Mistress Gillon. May ah introduce the new curate for Lesmahagow, officially appointed by the sheriff himsel."

She burst into tears and ran back into their tiny kitchen. He followed her, trying not to look too disappointed at her reaction.

She snuffled and refused to look at him. "Ah dinna want this." She sniffed again. "Ah like things the way we are."

"But whit aboot aw they hoors ah spend repairin boots an shoes? It's hard work an brings in a pittance. This new post will bring in a lot mair siller wi haurly ony effort."

"We dae weel enough."

"Listen Meg, ah'll hae a stipend o twenty five pounds, a hoose, a Glebe field, an a horse an trap as weel."

"Whit's the catch?"

"Nane. Ye'll see that in the mornin when ah get a letter o

credit for new claes. An no jist for masel, for ye as weel, an wee Isabel."

She looked up.

"Best o stuff."

"Whit aboot oor hoose, an the shop, an the repairs, an oor furniture?"

"Ah've had a word wi Henry Seaton. He wis a guid, reliable apprentice. He's a journey-man noo an mair than capable. Ah offered him the chance tae rent the shop an the hoose. He jumped at it. So there ye are, extra money frae him as weel."

"Is this true?"

"Ay. It's aw agreed. He taks on the repairs. We get on wi oor new life in Lesmahagow."

"But - "

"Nae buts. Ah've jist tae ask a carrier aboot movin oor stuff an we're awa. Hoo does that sound?"

"Unbelievable. But are ye sure it's really whit ye want?"

"Trust me Meg. Ah want it for us aw."

"In that case - " She stood up and hugged him.

From that moment life became one rush. Choosing new clothes, finalising things with Henry Seaton, packing their belongings, ordering a carrier, and all in two short days. It was little wonder that neither Sandy nor Meg had time for second thoughts. By morning the whole town was talking about the shoemaker. Many envied him.

Some wondered why he was giving up a good business to become a curate. One or two shook their heads at the very idea.

Meiklejon was in a good mood when he began his second interview with the old tinker. Not that he held back his usual threats. Not that he needed them, for Gaby told him everything he knew. The sheriff was grateful for these nuggets of information, but gave no hint as he dismissed the old ragamuffin with a final warning. "No a word aboot this. No if ye ken whit's guid for ye." He flicked another coin across the table and rang the bell for the guard.

Gaby caught the silver coin and had it in his pocket before the guard appeared.

"See him oot." Meikljon pointed at Gaby. "He slipped by ye

on the way in so keep a guid eye on him."

"Sir." The guard grabbed Gaby's collar and propelled him out the room and down the stairs. When they reached the bottom step he pushed the old tinker against the wall. "Hoo did ye git in here? Ah nivver saw ye an it wis ma watch. An ah dinna tak kindly tae lukin a fool."

Gaby tried to wriggle free. The guard closed his fingers round the scrawny neck. Gaby stopped struggling and put on a pathetic face.

"Ah'm tellin ye," the guard squeezed Gaby's throat. "Ah want tae see hoo ye got in here."

Gaby spluttered and tried to nod.

The guard released his grip but drew his sword. "Richt. On ye go. An nae messin."

Gaby led him along the darkest side of the yard to the furthest away stable then dived inside. From there he worked his way to the back stall where he stopped and pointed up at a narrow window set into the thick wall. Without any glass to give protection from cold and wind someone had hung a length of rough sacking across the space.

"Is that it?" The guard snorted.

Gaby grinned and climbed onto the edge of the wooden stall and tiptoed along the top till he reached the wall. The guard was amazed at this delicate balancing act, and even more surprised when the little figure ducked under the sacking and vanished.

"Here." The guard rushed forward. "Wait a meenit." He reached up to lift the end of the sacking and found a narrow, empty space, but wide enough for a nothing of a figure to squeeze through. "Weel, ah'm damned. The auld deil's no sae daft aifter aw." He stared at the narrow hole. "Ah'd best tell the blacksmith tae fit a bar across this afore we huv anither visit." With that he went down to the forge before going back to his guard post.

Out in the street Gaby scampered past several houses then dived into a side garden where he'd left his pack behind a row of redcurrant bushes. He slung the thick strap across his chest and congratulated himself. "A wee story tae the richt man an here ah am wi a fu belly an some siller tae jingle in ma pocket."

Once in the main street he walked up to the crossroads and stood for a moment then nodded to himself. Instead of following the Lesmahagow sign he went in the opposite direction, towards Hyndford Bridge and crossed the Clyde. There he turned left onto the Biggar road. "Ay," he grinned. "Best bide awa frae Maister Steel."

Chapter 6

"My that's bonny," Meg gasped as the horse and trap slowed to a halt at the top of Lanark Brae. Below them the Clyde valley was drenched in white blossom where the river rippled and sparkled through sweet smelling apple and plum orchards before deepening speed pulled it towards the distant city of Glasgow. Never before had she seen such a beautiful sight. But never before had she stood at the head of the brae so early on such a perfect morning.

"Ay, it's bonny," Sandy agreed. "An dirty auld Lanark ahint us. Sit back an enjoy the view while I guide the horse doon this twisted track." Not that he need bother. The horse had more than enough sense to lean in against the overhanging bank and slowly edge round the tight corners. All Sandy had to do was sit there while the horse did the work and soon the trap was rattling across the cobbles on the old stone bridge at the foot of the hill.

When they came to the first village Meg asked, "Hoo lang till we reach this Lesmahagow?"

"No afore midday," Sandy replied. "But it's a fine day. The time will easy pass wi plenty tae see."

Coming towards them were two carts loaded with vegetables for the town market. Rough, woven cages were piled at the front, some with hens squawking and poking their beaks through the spaces, some with silent rabbits, eyes round as if guessing what going to market might mean. Four fresh-faced women walked behind the carts. They were laughing and chatting, each one carrying a large basket brimming with more vegetables. What a sight they were! Hair tied up in coloured kerchiefs and the corners of their long, swinging skirts and sack aprons looped up they walked along scuffing little clouds of dust with their toes. Everyone nodded in passing. Meg smiled back and then turned to watch as they began the long climb up Lanark Brae towards the town she knew as home. Her smile vanished at the thought of her own life back there, so different to this journey into the unwanted and unknown. But a quick glance down at her little daughter sitting alongside told her another story. She squeezed the child's arm and Isabel grinned up, her face glowing with pleasure.

A few minutes later they reached a crossroads to read the word Lesmahagow cut into a wooden sign pointing to the left. Sandy steered the horse in a wide arc, past the sign, and they began to climb the opposite side of the valley. Almost at the top he stopped the horse for a rest and they sat there looking towards the church spire and chimney smoke of Lanark itself.

Meg sighed. "It's a fine sight."

"Ay. An better tae come."

Meg sniffed and said nothing. She closed her eyes and held on to the view while Sandy clicked the horse on. A few more steps and they crossed the brow of the hill to leave it all behind.

Now they were rolling past farms and fields where great tracts of land were criss-crossed with corn and barley already several inches high. Even the tiny shelters of farm workers, nestling at the edge of the road, had enough space to keep a few hens and grow their own vegetables. It was all very different to congested Lanark with its tight, dark vennels and constant noise. On they went through this pleasant landscape and Meg began to feel less anxious, to enjoy this new experience of riding along like a lady, admiring the scenery. On her left was the familiar outline of Tinto Hill, always a landmark from Lanark, but now so large and long it seemed to be coming with them. Other hills lined up beyond, one behind another, in different shades of green and purple, till they were too faint to see. It was a new experience to be in so much open space and feel such warm, sweet air slide past as they trotted through this beautiful morning. Meg took off her bonnet, laid it on her lap, and lifted her face to the breeze. She enjoyed this so much it seemed natural to unclip her hair and let it tumble down to gently wave around her face. Sandy glanced at her and smiled, and she smiled back.

After a while faint drifts of smoke began to appear in the distance.

"Is this it?" Meg's throat tightened.

"Ah think so." Sandy sounded excited.

Soon clusters of buildings appeared, nestling along the edge of a small, steep valley. Dense woods rose behind the village. As the trees gave way to the moor beyond mile after mile of heather and grass took over lending an untamed backdrop to such a gentle picture. On the horizon there was even a hint of the Ayrshire hills merging with blue sky and white fluffy clouds.

"Looks nice," Meg admitted and smiled again. "Ah wonder whae'll be waitin tae meet us."

"The sheriff never said."

Meg sat up straight, tied up her hair again, and crammed on her bonnet.

The small man in the wide-brimmed black hat, driving the fine horse and trap slowly along Lesmahagow main street drew several curious glances but no one seemed to realise who he was. They did notice the freshly laundered linen cravat covering his throat; the jacket and breeches must have cost a pretty penny too, and the woollen stockings were good quality, new like his polished shoes with their oversized buckles. He certainly made a tidy sight, as did the slender woman and young girl by his side. They were dressed in discreetly patterned grey dresses of good material with simple, dark bonnets hiding their hair, and soft woollen shawls in the same colour covering their shoulders.

Sandy stopped the trap alongside a group of villagers chatting by the open door of a bakehouse. He nodded towards them and touched the edge of his hat in greeting. "It's gie warm for travellin."

The nearest man looked up. "It is that. Hae ye come far?"

"Frae Lanark. Is this Lesmahagow?"

"It is."

"We've arrived then." Sandy smiled. "So whaur's the manse?"

"The manse?"

"Ay. My name is Alexander Gillon. Ah'm the new curate. The sheriff in Lanark has sent me tae live an work amang ye."

"Is that richt?" The man's face darkened. "Weel, Maister Gillon, if ah wur ye ah'd turn roond an gang back tae Lanark. An when ye get there be sure an tell the sheriff that Lesmahagow disna want a curate, new or itherwise."

Meg grabbed Sandy's arm and whispered, "Dinna answer. Jist drive on."

Sandy clicked the reins before the angry face could say any more.

"New curate indeed," Meg muttered.

"Maybe we jist spoke tae the wrang person. It'll be fine." Sandy pointed towards a church steeple above the roofs. "See. We're nearly there."

A few yards more and the street opened into a cobbled square bounded on three sides by rows of two storey houses. A general store was set in the middle, an inn and stable sat opposite. The fourth side was almost entirely made up by the church's wide, stone front. Meg pointed at the date 1140 inscribed in the carved arch above a pair of tight closed wooden doors.

"There wis an abbey here," Sandy explained.

"Wi monks and priests?"

"A lang time ago. Times hae chainged since then."

"No the only thing." Before Meg could say any more they heard raised voices followed by a burst of laughter. They both turned towards the sound. The inn door was wide open allowing some of the banter to drift into the open air.

A tall, broad shouldered man in rough spun grey breeches and jacket appeared in the doorway and glanced at the horse and trap. He seemed to like what he saw and came across the square towards them. He stopped beside the horse, stroked its muzzle, then looked up and smiled at them. "Ye've a fine beast there."

Meg stared at the handsome face partly shaded by a large, blue bonnet. A pair of warm, brown eyes studied her. They seemed friendly enough, although the gaze itself was steady and searching. It was a long time since a man had given her such an appraising look and she almost blushed.

Beside her Sandy nodded. "We're weel pleased wi him."

A big hand smoothed the muzzle again and the smile broadened. "If ye want tae bide pleased ye best gie the beast a drink. There's a watter trough jist alang frae the inn door. It's in the shade tae." He pointed. "See. Ower there."

Sandy obeyed.

The man followed the trap across the square. He seemed to guess that Sandy knew little about horses. "Jist loosen the reins," he advised. "Let the heid doon. He'll dae the rest."

Sandy obeyed and the horse gratefully leant forward to begin a long, cool drink.

While they all watched and waited the man asked, "Hae ye come far?"

"Frae Lanark, this mornin. We've come tae bide." Sandy leant forward and dared to hold out his hand. "My name is Alexander Gillon. I'm the new curate. Ma wife and daughter are wi me."

There was a slight hesitation then a firm grip in return. "John Steel. Ah hae a farm twa mile oot at Logan Waterheid." In spite of the set face there was the hint of a twinkle in the brown eyes. The big man doffed his cap to Meg. "Is this yer first time in the village, maam?"

She nodded then nudged Sandy.

He looked round the deserted square then said, "Is this the way tae the manse?"

John pointed to a narrow gap between the church and the next house. "Thru there. But slow like. It's a bit ticht an some beasts tak fricht. Aifter that doon by the graveyard wall, then left again. The manse is a few steps mair. It has a brass nameplate so ye canna go wrang."

"Thank ye." Sandy made to click the reins and move off, but John grasped the bridle. "Can ah ask ye somethin afore ye go?"

"Indeed."

"Ye say ye're the new curate?"

"The sheriff himsel sent me."

"An it jist ower a week since oor meenister hud tae leave."

Sandy coloured.

"Thur's been nae word aboot anither tae replace him. He left kinda sudden ye see."

"It wis sudden for us tae," Meg joined in. "Ma man wis appointed ane day an then tellt tae git movin mair or less the next day. Is thur a problem?"

John stared past Meg as if seeing something unpleasant on the wall opposite then glanced back at her anxious face. "Did the sheriff no warn ye?"

"Whit aboot?"

John scuffed the toe of his boot in the dust. "Ye mean ye dinna ken?"

"Whitivver it is - no." Meg sounded anxious.

"Weel ye shud. The meenister ye've come tae replace wis weel respected an a guid man. We aw liked him although whiles he cud be a bit strong willed. That's whit caused the bother. Ye see he spoke oot against the king an his nonsense aboot bishops in the Kirk. No jist that, he wudna sign some paper aboot it, alang wi refusin tae declare his loyalty tae the crown. Next thing a fu military platoon arrived tae force him an his wife oot the village."

Sandy remembered the sheriff's words about the previous minister's sudden departure.

"That's no aw. The lieutenant in charge got cairried awa wi his ain importance. He tormented the meenister's horse that much it bolted doon the street trailin the cart ahint. The edge o the cart smacked against a wall an the guid wife lost her grip. She fell aff." John looked away. "When we got tae her she wis deid."

Meg's hand flew to her open mouth.

"The lieutenant didna care. He ordered us tae gaither her up an put her body in the back o the cart. An then he made the pair man drive oot the village."

"For God's sake." Meg rounded on Sandy. "Whit hae ye gotten us intae?"

"Ah'd nae idea," Sandy insisted. "Ah jist happened tae see a notice aboot a post as curate here an applied for it."

"Withoot askin ony questions? Did ye no wonder hoo the vacancy came aboot?" John's voice and face echoed his shock. "Ye must hae heard aboot the trouble atween Kirk an king. Did ye no realise?"

"Ah didna think it wis that serious." Before John could come back at him Sandy said, "Ye've gied me much tae think aboot. But richt noo ah need tae get on an see ma family settled."

John nodded and stepped back and the new curate urged his horse towards the narrow close mouth.

A few minutes later the Gillon family stopped by a tall, stone fronted house. Sandy stared at the brass nameplate. "This seems tae be oor fine, new hoose."

It certainly was with many tall, elegant windows and a black panelled front door. Five broad scrubbed steps led down to the cobbles setting it apart and giving added importance. Paintwork was fresh, the railings along the front immaculate and well cared for. It was a big change from their tiny house in the vennel at Lanark.

Meg studied the impressive frontage. She was more desperate than angry. "Earlier this week ah wis in ma ain hame. Nae fancy ideas in ma heid. So wur ye, if ye're honest. Look at us noo. Pretendin tae be somethin we're no. An no jist that, we're in the middle o somethin we neither unnerstaund nor want. I'm tellin ye Sandy, this is aw wrang. We should nivver hae come."

"Please Meg. Dinna speak lik that. It's no as if we can turn roond an gang back." Sandy's fingers twisted the leather reins. "The sheriff wud lock me up for no keepin my end o the bargain. Ah wis a fool. Is that whit ye want me tae say?"

"Wis a fool? Naw, naw. Ye are a fool."

They sat outside the house in silence for several minutes before Sandy pulled a large key from his pocket. He studied it as if expecting some answer. It came unexpectedly when Meg snatched it from him and jumped down from the trap. She ran across the little yard to the front door of the manse, went up the five steps, and pushed the key in the lock. She turned it. There was a loud click. The heavy door swung wide and she disappeared inside leaving the door open behind her.

Sandy stared at the open space for a moment then slid down from the driving seat to tether the horse by the iron railings. As he turned from doing this he saw his small daughter, still sitting in the passenger seat, her expression hovering between uncertainty and fear. Any moment now there would be tears. He held out his arms and smiled. "C'mon Isabel. We'll go an see whit Ma's found. An ken whit, it micht be a nice wee surprise."

Isabel made no move.

"Ah think thur's a garden at the back o this hoose."

"A garden?" She leapt into his arms, hugging him as he carried her into their new home.

Meg was standing in the midst of a coloured pattern cast on the wooden floor as the sun streamed through the red, blue, yellow and green glass of the curved panel above the front door. She looked up. "Isn't it lovely?" Her voice was gentle again.

"Ay, it is." He set Isabel down.

Meg stayed there admiring the colours dancing across the

floor. Finally she whispered, "Richt or wrang, hae we ony choice?"

He shook his head. "Ah'm sorry. Ah didna think."

Meg sighed. "Ye're aye the same. An it's no as if ah didna warn ye."

He grasped her hand. She pulled him closer and they clung together in an unhappy huddle within the colourful mosaic of colour gleaming up at them from the polished floor. And then an excited, little voice rang through the empty house. "Come an see. Come an see. Thur *is* a garden."

That afternoon Wull Gibb, the carrier, stopped his cart before the big house, shielded his eyes from the sun and inspected the property. "My, my," he muttered. "Maister Gillon seems tae be goin up in the world." Out came the scrap of paper Sandy had given him earlier. Slowly he read *Alexander Gillon, the Manse, Lesmahagow*. He peered at the paper again. "An it's Alexander noo, no plain Sandy. A fine name for a fine address."

Crossing the little cobbled yard Wull stood on the bottom step to yank the bell pull. He heard it ring far inside the house then echo all the way back to him. No one came to the door. He gave another tug then glanced up at the empty windows and wondered if maybe he was too early. As he turned away the door opened. There stood the same pretty young woman, with the same anxious face he'd seen earlier that day. He took off his cap and said, "Mistress Gillon. Ah've brocht yer stuff."

She smiled at Wull and called into the house. "Sandy. The carrier is here."

Sandy appeared at her side. He too smiled. "I'll gie ye a hand tae carry in oor furniture." Running down the steps and across to the cart he grasped the edge of an overhanging table and began tugging at it.

"No lik that." Wull rushed forward. "Easy does it, Maister Gillon. Bide whaur ye are till ah get a firm grip."

Sandy obeyed and the table was safely lifted down.

"Richt sir." Wull took control. "If ye really want tae be usefu leave the thinkin tae me. Ah'll tell ye whit tae dae."

Sandy was soon puffing and struggling as Wull ordered, "Ower a bit. Naw. This way. Noo doon. Watch oot. Haud steady. C'mon lift a bit higher."

By the time the last piece of furniture was deposited in the hall Sandy's face was red with exertion, a fact which wasn't lost on the stalwart Wull, who'd enjoyed his brief roll as master. Now he took pity. "Richt Maister Gillon, ah think ye've hud enough."

"Not at aw," Sandy gasped. "If there's mair tae dae we best keep at it."

Wull grinned. "As ye wish."

Meg bustled about and seemed pleased to see her own things begin to make the house feel less strange, although the few pieces they possessed seemed to almost vanish in the huge space.

"This is a fine hoose," Wull commented as they finished their task.

Sandy and Meg smiled and Wull studied the unlikely pair now resident in such a grand place. He was about to mention their sudden change of fortune when Meg said, "Ye must hae somethin afore ye go, Maister Gibb." She led him into the kitchen where she unwrapped some bannocks and cheese then turned to lift a small, stone flagon and beaker from a basket on the floor. "An a wee drink." She filled the beaker with ale.

"Why, thank ye, maam." As Wull ate and drank he glanced at the husband and wife and wondered why neither of them looked happy to have escaped from their dingy vennel in Lanark to such a grand house. The fine horse and trap tethered outside was worth a bonny penny too. Somethin was nae richt, nae richt at aw. He lifted the mug to his mouth again and felt the strong ale revive him. Ah weel, it was nane o his business. He emptied the mug and wiped his whiskers. "Work lik this gies a man a richt drouth, so thank ye maam. Noo, if yer man jist settles up ah'll git on ma way an leave ye in peace."

Sandy fumbled in his jacket pocket and produced a little leather bag. He undid the thongs and took out a few coins. "As we agreed, ah think." He counted them into the carrier's upturned palm then added one more coin. "That's for being prompt. An of course, we're gratefu for yer help wi the furniture."

Wull pocketed the extra money and left with a cheery, "Guid day tae ye baith."

He was driving through the square when he looked across at

the village store and thought about some tobacco for his pipe. A quiet smoke and a leisurely drive back to Lanark seemed the very thing on such a nice day. He stopped the horse then jumped down and tethered the horse before heading into the little shop to make his purchase.

After the bright sunshine it was dark inside. His eyes took a few minutes to adjust. He peered into the gloom and saw a small, podgy woman with a raggedy green shawl draped across her shoulders. She was standing beside a broad, wooden counter with a well-scrubbed top. An elderly man in a white apron was on the other side. They stopped their conversation when Wull appeared.

"Fine day." He nodded to them both.

"Ay," the woman agreed.

Wull stood back to wait his turn. "It wis nice comin frae Lanark this mornin." He coughed and felt obliged to say more. "Ah'm jist on my way back an lookin for some baccy tae enjoy alang the road. On a day lik this it's grand tae be oot an aboot seein things."

"Whit kinda things?" The little woman's dark eyes flashed with interest.

"Oh, this an that," he teased.

The little woman turned and her fat, little fingers tapped Wull's ample waistcoat. "Ah'd like tae ken whit kinda things?"

He took a step back. "It wis only an observation, maam."

"Whit aboot?" She tapped him again and looked up at his red face.

"Jist somethin unusual aboot a job ah wis at." Aware this was only making matters worse he added, "Och mibbe it wisna sae odd aifter aw."

"Ah'll be the best judge o that."

Wull groaned. This must be the nosiest woman in the village. To make matters worse the Gillons' grateful thanks were still ringing in his ears.

"Lost yer tongue then?" The woman's sharp voice cut across his thoughts.

Trapped, he began his story. "This mornin ah lifted furniture frae a wee hoose in a dark vennel in Lanark an brocht the stuff here."

"Ye're a carrier. That's yer job. Ye're supposed tae cairry things."

"Let the man feenish," the shopkeeper cut in.

Wull acknowledged his support. "Whit ah mean is the address ah had fur delivery wis the manse."

Now the shopkeeper leant further across the counter and they both stared at the hapless Wull.

He had to continue. "When ah git here ah find a grand hoose, an the same man here as wis in the wee hoose earlier on."

"So?"

"At the start o the day that man wis a shoemaker. Mind ye, he's weel learnt. Aye at the books. He's guid at his job tae. Best mender in the toun. An he's aye willin tae write letters fur them as need it. Weel respected so he is. But that disna mak him a meenister. So whit's he dain in the manse? He tellt me the sheriff gied him the job. Ah cairried his stuff here, an he paid me weel fur ma work, even helped me cairry in the furniture. His wife offered me somethin tae eat an drink afore ah left. Vera civil, baith o them." Leaving it at that he stabbed a thick finger towards the tobacco jar. "An ounce o yer best black, an ah'll be on ma way."

"No afore ye tell us mair," shrilled the little woman.

"That's enough," the shopkeeper rescued Wull. "The man hasna time tae staund in here aw day."

Lifting his purchase Wull escaped into the street and hurried back to his horse and cart. "Funny folk here," he said, half to himself, half to the horse.

The horse snorted as if in agreement.

He chuckled. "At least ye're a sensible beast an mind yer ain business. Mair than can be said for they twa in ther." Wull unwrapped his new bought ounce of best black then filled his old clay pipe and lit up. Puffing thick smoke into the clear air calmed him. Soon he was his usual happy self.

Behind him the woman was already re-telling the story. And of course she was adding a little bit of her own to improve the flavour.

Later that afternoon John told Marion about meeting the man who said he was the new curate. "Name's Gillon. He seems freendly enough but raither anxious aboot his new post. His wife didna luk too pleased either. An their bairn wis jist starin aboot her wi een lik an owl. When ah tellt them hoo the meenister wis flung oot the guid wife seemed ready tae turn roond an heid back for Lanark."

"Hoo come this Maister Gillon's a curate an no a meenister?"

"Ah dinna ken. That's hoo he introduced himsel. Ah wis mair taen aback aboot him no kennin whit he wis comin tae. His wife insisted the sheriff hadna said a word afore he sent them."

Marion shook her head. "Nae doubt he has his reasons. But whitivver they are can wait. Ah'm mair interested in ma ain news. Ye see, ah heard that Reverend Peden's in the district. Come Sunday he's expectit tae hae an open air service on the moor ahint Auchlochan Hoose. They say he's a richt guid preacher. Since he's nearby ah thocht we cud gie it a try an miss oot on the new curate. Aifter aw, Maister Brotherstone did say chainged times wur upon us."

John nodded. "Aifter the past few days ah canna argue wi that."

Chapter 7

Early that first Sunday morning Sandy paced back and forward in front of the big, carved communion table in his new church. Above him rows of long, narrow windows sparkled in the morning sun and lit up the vast space. The black robe he'd found hanging in a back room was a good fit, and the heavy swish of the material helped him feel the part, and gave him the confidence to climb up to the pulpit. From there he had a clear view of the empty building, all the way to the main door. Soon the rows of dark pews would fill with villagers, curious about the new curate. A proper start would make all the difference. He adjusted the heavy robe, and felt the responsibility this brought, and for the first time in his new role Sandy closed his eyes to pray for guidance.

Opening his eyes again he tried to imagine all those upturned faces, eyes watching, ears listening to every word. This scared him and he prayed again, this time for courage, then climbed back down to resume his marching back and forward, rehearsing his first sermon.

Half an hour before the service there was still no sign of the beadle to ring the kirk bell. This was strange, for ringing the summons to worship was a must in every village and town. Sandy began to feel more anxious as the hands of the church clock crawled towards ten. No beadle. No sign of his congregation. When ten chimed across the village it was clear no one was likely to appear apart from Meg and Isabel, who were now sitting in a front pew looking as uncomfortable as he felt.

With only three people in this great barn of a place a deep silence took hold and held them. Here he was looking the part, willing to give his best, only no-one seemed inclined to come and find out. Or maybe he needed to make an announcement to the village, invite them to come? Ay. They needed tae be tellt.

Meg gaped as he tore off his robe, stumbled down from the metal steps and disappeared out the side door.

Back in the manse he headed for the kitchen, opened the larder door, and reached into one of the deep shelves where he'd stored his precious sheets of paper for writing sermons. He lifted one sheet and carried it to the big, scrubbed table, smoothed it flat then went back to fetch his prized travelling inkwell along with a fresh cut quill. He laid the inkwell beside the clean sheet of paper, lifted the brass lid, dipped his new quill in the thick, black ink and began to print:

Sunday service 10 o'clock
All welcome
Signed Alexander Gillon, curate.

He'd almost finished writing when Meg appeared with Isabel trailing behind her. "Whit are ye playin at?" she demanded. "Leavin us in ther by oorsels. An whit's this?" She leant across the table to read his notice.

"Ah'll pin it tae the kirk door."

"Dinna be daft. Naebody's been near the place since we got here. This Sunday's nae different. They've nae intention o comin this Sunday or ony ither Sunday. An dinna look at me lik that. Ye ken fine it's the truth."

"Ah thocht - "

"Oh did ye?" Meg cut him short. "When did this miracle happen?" In a softer tone she added, "We canna mak folk come if they dinna want tae." Turning away she busied herself unbuttoning Isabel's new, wool coat.

"Ah'll pin it up onyway." He searched out his work-bag to find a hammer and nail then marched round to fasten his notice on the kirk door. For the rest of the day he paced the house almost as restless and full of doubts as the previous occupant had been.

Meg watched him. She said nothing and the silence they'd felt in the church seemed to creep into the house and render them both helpless. Only Isabel was happy. She ran out to the garden to twirl back and forward on a thick rope swing below the big beech tree in the garden, loving this unexpected freedom and wondering what she could get up to next.

Meg put on her new grey dress and matching shawl, lifted her basket and set out for the village shop. Meeting a few villagers might just make a difference. She was determined enough when she set out but once she reached the shop door she wasn't so sure. She stopped, almost turning to walk back towards the manse, but the thought of those past few days spurred her on. A few more steps and she reached the shop door. Once there she forced herself to grasp the worn handle and turn it. The door opened. The little bell jangled above her head as she stared into the gloom. At the far end of a long, low room several women were clustered in front of a big, wooden counter. The clatter of the bell made them turn and all conversation stuttered to a halt at the sight of this new arrival.

Meg nodded. "Mornin ladies."

Faces stared at her.

She tried smiling.

No response.

She walked towards them.

The women stepped aside but no one spoke and she reached the counter in silence. She tried another smile at the elderly shopkeeper staring at her across the counter.

"Ay, Mistress Gillon?" His voice was as hard as his set face.

He did know who she was. And his expression told her she wasn't welcome. "A pound of ground oats, two butter pats, an six eggs, if ye please." It was an effort to keep her voice steady. It was worse having to stand there while butter was cut, patted, and wrapped, oats weighed out, then the eggs carefully placed in her basket. Well aware of every eye fastened on her, noting every detail, she stood very straight. At least they'd approve of her clothes. "Thank ye." She opened her little purse. "Hoo much is that?"

"One and fourpence."

She took out two bawbees and a bodle and offered them.

The man studied the coins then nodded.

"Ah'll awa then."

No reply.

There was nothing left to do but turn and walk back through the silent, hostile space. Although she wanted to make a run for it she forced herself to appear calm and steady till she reached the door. Hand on the handle she turned. "Guid tae meet ye aw." Somehow she even managed a last smile before escaping back into the street.

She clicked the latch shut behind her and heard a sudden surge of voices. No doubt heads were nodding, tongues wagging as those women shared every snippet of the last few minutes. It had been an ordeal among them, and the shopkeeper had been just as bad. She'd been wasting her time even trying to break through their barrier. Her legs began to shake. She leant against the rough stone wall of the shop for support and closed her eyes. It was all so different to back home in Lanark, among friendly faces, people she knew and trusted, people who liked her, who actually spoke to her. Already it felt faraway, like another life. And so it was, with no way to turn back the clock.

Standing there against the rough wall it seemed as if the stones were rejecting her, telling her to go away, she didn't belong. She thought of the one who'd caused all this to happen and anger took over.

Minutes later she stomped into the kitchen and found Sandy sitting at the big table, his Bible open, quite the picture of a dutiful curate.

"Whaur hae ye been?" He looked up and smiled.

"Dinna ask."

"Whit?"

She glared at him. "If ye must ken ah canna staund whit's happenin so ah decided tae dae somethin aboot it. Ah thocht meetin some o the folk wud help so ah went doon tae the wee shop. Mair fool me. Ah wis met wi naethin. No a word. No even a nod nor a smile. It wis worse than bangin ma heid against a brick wa." She dumped her basket on the table and burst into tears.

Sandy jumped up and pulled her towards his chair. She sat down with a thump and stammered through the whole story.

"That wis weel done." He squeezed her shoulders and kissed the back of her neck.

"No!" she wailed. "It wis terrible." Her eyes welled up again. "If ye'd seen them ye'd unnerstaund. It's nae use. We're no wanted here."

"It's early days yet," he replied. "Gie it time."

She sniffed and opened her mouth, but before she could utter a word he backed away. "Ah need tae - " He turned and was out the half open kitchen door into the hall.

She stared at the empty space and shook her head. "Ah ken whit ye need tae."

She flung her soft, grey shawl on the floor and stared at it, the finest she'd ever had. Today the cost of it spoke of the man who'd paid for it. Sheriff Meiklejon had known only too well what he was doing when he paid the Gillons' clothing bill, same as he paid for the horse and trap. As for this fine house and the Glebe field - he must be expecting a great deal back for all that. Sandy had been reeled in like some gullible fish. She blinked and looked down at her basket, sitting on the table where she'd dumped it. Instead of winning over a few villagers with her shop visit she'd had a clear warning that nothing in this godforsaken place would ever be right. She clenched her fists then banged them down on the scrubbed tabletop.

Sandy hurried into the tiny stable behind the house to hitch up his new horse and trap. He remembered John Steel mentioning the name of his farm. It wasn't far away and shouldn't be difficult to find, and the man seemed friendly enough. Maybe he wouldn't mind a quiet word.

After an hour of rattling along unmarked roads Sandy gave up trying to find Logan Waterhead Farm and turned back towards the village. Another idea gone wrong. He slowed the horse to a walk. There was no hurry to return, not with the mood Meg was in. The sun was warm on his shoulders, the breeze was gentle, daisies speckled across the soft spring green of the grass where contented cows and sheep were enjoying the fine day. Everything seemed idyllic but already he knew better.

A horse and laden cart came slowly towards him. He pulled in to the side to let it pass, and then realised the driver was the very man he was after.

John Steel stopped alongside. "Whit are ye dain oot here, Maister Gillon?"

"Lookin for yersel. Hae ye a meenit?"

"On a day lik this ah'll happily gie ye twa, or even three."

"Could ah hae a word o advice?"

"Ah'm no the richt man for that," John chuckled. "Ah've enough bother wi masel."

"It's aboot the kirk. It wis empty on Sunday. Ah wis hopin ye'd be there."

John frowned and shoved his cap back on his head. "Ah wis at anither service in the open air."

"Ootside? That doesna soond the richt thing at aw."

"We thocht so. We had a real meenister willin tae gie us God's word the way we like it. Nae harm tae ye Maister Gillon, whitever ye are ye're nae a meenister. Onyway, ah warned ye the ither day whit folk wud be like."

"But surely - "

"Luk, sir. If ah wur ye ah'd gang back tae Lanark an git on wi whitever ye did afore aw this."

"Ah canna," Sandy admitted. "The sheriff."

"Ye'll jist hae tae explain that Lesmahagow isna on wi a curate. Noo dinna git me wrang. Ah'm sorry if things are no workin oot. Ah'm sure it's far frae pleasant, but ye've only yersel tae blame. Why did ye no ask some questions afore takin on the post?"

"But the sheriff - " Sandy repeated.

"If that means whit ah think ye seem stuck atween a rock and a hard place. If that's true an ye've nae choice but bide here ye'll jist hae tae mak the best o it an put up wi an empty kirk. Mind ye, ah'd no let on tae the sheriff. Is that enough advice for ye?" With that John clicked the horse forward and left Sandy to make what he liked of his words.

Sandy turned and watched the laden cart till it was almost out of sight. Twice in one day he'd heard more or less the same thing, first Meg, now John Steel.

The horse began cropping the grass. Sandy leant back in the driving seat and stared into the distance, seeing himself reading that notice on the garrison gate. Why had he ever thought it was a good idea to leave being a shoemaker? After all, he'd been the best one in Lanark, everyone said so. He could even see his old work-bench, laden with scrappy old boots and shoes and sandals needing attention. The thought of tackling them appealed. But this was out of reach. Now he was a curate, whatever that was. One thing for sure, he was an unwanted stranger in a strange village. It was little wonder he preferred to be out here where fields were green and hedgerows bulged with warm, vibrant life, so different to the cold resentment that seemed to have taken hold of the village, even his own wife.

In the trees nearby crows flapped and cawed and argued, much like the confusion in his own head. The constant noise and his own questioning took him further inside himself, mulling over the whys and wherefores of how he had ever allowed himself to imagine he could be a curate. He was so engrossed with all his justifications and regrets he didn't notice the breeze grow stronger and begin to swirl as the air cooled. The clouds thickened and darkened. Still he didn't notice. The first raindrops didn't matter, but within minutes he was all too aware of water dripping from the wide brim of his new hat, soaking his shoulders and running down the back of his good jacket. His breeches stuck to his skin. He began to worry about his new clothes; maybe they'd shrink.

The rain grew heavier, turning to hail with hard, little stones bouncing off his nose and stinging his cheeks. And now he seemed to be moving through this icy curtain. He blinked and realised the horse had set off on its own. The trap was rattling through the puddles and potholes, jarring and shaking him. He hung on and didn't mind, for the beast seemed to know where it was going, and this was neither the time nor the place to argue about who should be in control.

When he drew into the stable behind the manse he was desperate to rush into the house, to dry off. But he'd a trap to unhitch, and a horse to rub down, to settle and feed. By the time he'd done all this he was almost warm again, his clothes no longer clinging to him, and all the physical effort had cheered him up.

Meg was sitting by the fire, knitting. She looked up at the scarecrow who burst into her kitchen. "God's sake," she gasped. "Ye're soaked thru. Whaur hae ye been?"

"Oot for a drive. Ah didna ken it wud rain. Onyway, ah needed tae think."

"Ye're a bit late wi that." She put down her knitting and crossed to the kist by the door. She lifted the lid and took out a blanket. "Here. Aff wi yer wet claes, wrap up in this."

While he undressed she bustled into the scullery and came back with a bowl and some hunks of bread. "Noo sit doon for somethin tae warm yer inside." She bent over the simmering pot and filled the bowl with fresh cooked vegetables in a rich marrow bone stock.

He sniffed the vegetables and felt better, and then he saw her expression. "Ah'm sorry," he began.

"Ah'm weel past hearin that word," she snapped. "Eat up yer soup while ah see tae yer claes. No that ye deserve it."

The next Sunday there was still no beadle. The kirk bell was silent again. But just before ten chimed on the big clock the outer door creaked open a few inches. Five elderly villagers crept in to sit in a back pew. Peering round the vestry door Sandy saw a congregation of five plus Meg and the bairn. Seven was a start of sorts, but he didn't know whether to be relieved or disappointed. Two Sundays ago the church had been crammed with more than three hundred to hear Lucas Brotherstone's parting words. Today five villagers seemed an affront.

Little did Sandy guess but another Sandy had stolen his congregation. Alexander Peden was in the district. His reputation and speaking ability drew crowds wherever he went. The village had learnt he'd be preaching on the hill behind Auchlochan House that very Sunday, so who'd want to sit in the parish kirk before some nonentity of a shoemaker pretending to be a curate when one of the Kirk's great men was nearby?

Straightening his new black robe Sandy stared at the tiny group of faces. Like Lucas Brotherstone a few weeks ago in the same pulpit, he had the same thought of maybe saying nothing and just walking away.

Without daring to glance at Meg and Isabel, marooned in an expanse of empty pews, he forced himself to speak. "Freends." His voice was far from steady. "Welcome tae oor first service thegither."

The few faces at the back of the church showed no reaction although they did sing out the hymns as if these words at least meant something. The next two Sundays were the same with the same group. It was plain they didn't want to be there. Why? he wondered. Why come? Not being brave enough to confront them and ask he was left guessing at possible reasons, none of which he wanted to explore. Instead of enjoying his new role, he dreaded it.

The six lonely days that followed each service were just as bad although he did try to reach out by walking round the village, passing the time of day, appearing friendly to anyone he met. No-one refused to speak to him but their brief, guarded answers gave him no chance of any conversation. *If only*, he thought. But they knew he was a shoemaker. Once a shoemaker always a shoemaker. He even wondered if sneaking back to Lanark was an option, but the thought of the sheriff's reaction put a stop to that. He had to watch Meg's resentment which only made him ashamed of his own stupidity. They spoke less and less, and every day little Isabel grew more lonely with no one to play with, nowhere to go but the big garden behind the manse.

One morning a carrier on his way to Dumfries stopped by the manse with a letter for Meg. Within minutes she was waving it in Sandy's face. "It's frae ma cousin Lizzie in Lanark. She seems tae ken mair aboot this place than we dae. Go on, read it. See whit's really happenin. The folk here are stravaigin aboot the countryside each Sunday an no comin tae the Kirk. They're makin a fool o ye an need tae be tellt braw plain that kirk attendance shud be proper, an no this nonsense in the open air. At the next service ye need tae mention the sheriff's name an say somethin aboot yer empty kirk."

Meg's cousin was well informed. For the past few Sundays the villagers had indeed chosen a grassy hillside instead of their usual hard pews.

Sandy's heart sank as he read the letter. He thought about it, argued against Meg's advice, and did nothing.

Two weeks later there was still no change in church attendance. He gave in. At the start of the next service he announced, "Tell those missin frae the kirk that oor king will look ill upon such a denial o their maister."

Before he could mention the sheriff an old man stood up and called out, "Weel, Maister Gillon, Sunday aifter Sunday ah've sat here listenin tae yer fine talk. But that's aw it is. Whit ye've jist said maks me wonder if ye even unnerstaund yer ain words. Oor King's up above, no a mere man on a gilded throne. Ye speak aboot denial. Weel, tak a guid look at yersel for ther's yer answer." With that he stepped into the aisle and limped towards the outer door.

Unable to reply or even defend himself Sandy could only watch while one by one the others silently left their seats and followed their spokesman.

"Ah've lost them aw," he whispered as the great doors clanged shut.

Meg glared up at the pulpit, "Ay. An time the sheriff kent aboot it."

"Ah'd raither no."

"An if he finds oot whit's been happenin here an ye're no lettin on? Ye'll need tae chainge things. Meet they folk heid on, let them see ye hae the law ahint ye. Ye cud write a carefu letter explainin the problem an askin for some help." Her face softened. "Ah'm sorry it's come tae this."

Sandy nodded and slowly climbed down the pulpit steps to the flagstone floor.

He looked so miserable Meg left her seat and came towards him. "We canna go on lik this." She stopped in front of him and threw her arms round his neck. He hugged her back and for a moment everything felt right between them.

Knowing it wouldn't last he made the most of it and pressed his face against her soft skin, to breathe in her own special scent, and try not to think about that letter.

John Steel's absence from church was complicated. He'd nothing against Alexander Gillon as a man. He'd taken to him that first day in the village square, although he did wonder how a shoemaker could claim to be a curate, let alone the sheriff's chosen man. And how did a sheriff have the authority to interfere in Kirk affairs? This was unheard of and bothered him. But the memory of Elizabeth Brotherstone's body lying in the gutter near the church was the real reason for staying away. Rather than face this demon it had been easy to follow Marion's suggestion and attend Sandy Peden's open-air service. He even took the family with him.

The reverend's ability to take scripture and connect it with ordinary life was uncanny, and John could relate to every word. Then there was sitting outside, enjoying the fresh air, so different to the confines of a cold, stone building. In spite of doubts about where this might lead he went along to the next meeting, and the appearance of another travelling preacher. He even enjoyed the excitement and the secrecy of something with a whiff of danger about it. He could see how Marion was carried away with the experience. The boys approved. He could hardly blame them, for now they could sit on sweet smelling grass watching birds twitter and dive above their heads instead of fidgeting on a hard bench, with nothing to do but stare at blank walls and listen to some black-robed adult droning on about doom and gloom.

When the sheriff read Sandy Gillon's careful letter he wasn't so much enraged by the villagers' defiance as afraid for his own job. The old tinker had given him a warning and he'd done nothing. If his masters in Edinburgh found out there would be trouble. He had to act quickly. A list of culprits was needed. He had to look as if he was in control of his district.

Thrum was summoned and given a leather bound book with a list of every property in and around Lesmahagow. Against each property he was told to record the names of any church dissenters. "And dinna come back afore ye've got them aw," Meiklejon warned as Thrum stumped away on his unwelcome mission.

John was carting hay to the stable when Thrum led his pony into the yard. He looked up at the little man. "Ay?"

Thrum nodded and took his book from the pannier bag. He opened it, ran his finger down a long, spidery list then said, "Is this Logan Waterhead?"

"Ay."

"An ye're John Steel, owner o this farm, an twa ithers nearby?"

"Whit's it tae ye?"

"Naethin at aw, sir. Ah'm here at the sheriff's biddin."

John stiffened, "Ah mind ye noo. Ye came wi yon paper for

the meenister."

"In that case ye'll be aware o ma authority."

"Whit are ye aifter?"

"Ah need tae ken yer intentions."

"Whit intentions?"

"Ye're a member o the kirk here?"

John nodded.

"Will ye be comin tae the kirk this Sunday?"

"Whit's that got tae dae wi onythin?"

"The sheriff wants tae ken."

"Whit for?"

Thrum frowned. "Tae remind ye that Kirk attendance is nae langer a maitter o choice."

"Since when?"

"Since oor lawful government said so. The sheriff wants ye in the kirk this Sunday. An no jist this Sunday but each an ivvery Sunday hereafter."

Marion appeared beside John. She glared at the little man. "Hoo can we when we've lost oor meenister?"

"Ye hae a perfectly guid replacement, carefully chosen by the sheriff himsel."

"The man's nae mair than a shoemaker."

Thrum puffed out his cheeks. His little round mouth opened and shut and he seemed at a loss to answer.

"It's no as if we've onythin against the man," Marion added. "But his way is no oor way. The sheriff needs tae unnerstaund this an send us a real meenister, no some excuse lik a curate."

"Highly unlikely," Thrum sniffed. "Onyway, ah'm no paid to express opinions, gie explanations, or even unnerstaund the reasons for ma orders." He sniffed again. "Ah'm only a poorly paid clerk sent oot wi a list o names, an orders tae come back wi an answer against each and ivvery name. But ah'll gie ye a piece o advice, unoffeecial like, an freendly offered. Speakin oot can land ye in trouble. The sheriff's a great believer in makin an example, if ye tak ma meanin."

Marion flushed.

"Ye need tae unnerstaund the sheriff has his maisters. He's only cairryin oot orders. These orders come frae some powerfu men that govern this country. If ah wis ye ah'd think long an hard afore steppin beyond the law." With that he snapped the book shut and stuffed it back in the panier. "Guid day." He turned his horse round and led it away through the close.

John stared after the clerk. "So noo we're bein black listed. Whit next ah wunner?" He almost said more then thought better of it and lightly kissed Marion's cheek. "Ah weel, at least the sun's shinin."

"The sheriff is no gonna like this," the clerk muttered as he underlined more and more names. Even when he decided to stop for the day and seek lodgings at the village inn his temper wasn't helped by the stable lad's reluctance to accept his horse.

After that the innkeeper tried to tell him, "The place is fu."

"Whaur's the crowd?" Thrum demanded. "An afore ye gie me ony excuses, whitever ye say will be reported back tae ma maister the sheriff."

"Wud a wee room in the attic dae?" the innkeeper suggested.

"So long as it's clean." The clerk was exhausted by the hostility he'd endured all day and could hardly be bothered arguing with the man.

As if to make amends the innkeeper provided a good meal and Thrum went to bed in a better mood. Maybe he'd eaten too well, or maybe it was that third mug of ale, for try as he might sleep was not to be. He spent most of the night reliving the difficult interviews he'd had. Come morning he was desperate to finish his task. He rose early, breakfasted, and pressed on. Two more pages of names and he'd be back in Lanark.

Late that night Thrum arrived to find his master lounging before a crackling log fire, boots off, waistcoat undone, quite at ease. He didn't even bother to look round when his clerk stumped into the room.

Feeling the blast of heat and staring at all this comfort the weary little man thought of the past two days. Resentment almost choked him. "A lazy big lump so ye are," he muttered. "Loungin there while ah'm left tae trail the country wi yer damned book." Scowling at his master's ample back he banged the book of names down on the oak table. "Here's whit ye asked for."

The sheriff swung round.

His clerk pointed to the record book. "Ah asked them yer question, jist lik ye said. An ah noted it doon exactly. It's aw ther as best ah cud manage. Ye'll no like it. But thur's naethin ah can dae aboot that."

The sheriff glowered, but said nothing, and made space on the table to open the book. Joseph Thrum watched his master's eyebrows rise at the list on the first page. His frown darkened by the second. Several more pages were flicked through before he looked up. "Did ye tell them that bidin awa frae the Kirk is no an option?"

"Jist so sir. But these folk seem set on defiance."

The sheriff began to count the underlined names. "If aw this is true these village folk seem raither wayward in their habits."

"Ah've aready said, sir," Thrum bridled.

"Ay, so ye did," the sheriff mused. "It luks lik a wee lesson micht be in order." He lapsed into silence.

Finally Thrum broke the silence with a loud cough and dared to say, "Sir. Ah'm deid tired an stairvin hungry. It's been a long job an no vera pleasant."

"Awa ye go then." The sheriff flapped his hand. "But mind I want ye back here first thing in the morning."

"Ay sir. Guid nicht." The weary clerk banged the door shut and clattered downstairs, relieved to escape from his master. Well aware that something unpleasant was brewing he hurried along a dark vennel towards home muttering to himself. "First yon tinker wi his tale aboot the meenister, an then the new curate's letter aboot kirk attendance. Whitivver's goin on in yon village it'll hae tae stop afore Commander Clavehoose hears or he'll be ower here kickin up dust an blamin the sheriff. An nae doubt ah'll git the blame." Thrum held his tiny lantern in front of him and scuttled on through the darkness, longing for a proper meal and a rest before his own fire.

Home at last he gladly allowed his wife to help him out of his dusty clothes and fuss about heating his slippers. Supper smelt good. He began to feel more like himself again.

"Does the sheriff no appreciate yer hard work?" his wife asked as she boiled up hot water in the big kettle.

"In a word, no." For the first time in all his years as clerk to the court Thrum gave in to a desperate need for sympathy and told her where he'd been and why.

"Ah'm glad we dinna live in Lesmahagow," his wife admitted when he finished his story.

"Ay," he sniffed. "these folk are in for a shock. Mind ye," he said grudgingly, "ye hae tae admire their defiance."

"An much guid it'll dae," his wife retorted as she rubbed his aching back.

When Thrum arrived in the morning he was greeted with, "Leave yer paper work the noo. Awa and fetch the lieutenant."

"Ah passed him on the stairs, sir. Will ah shout aifter him?"

"Naw, naw. It's Claverhoose's man I'm aifter. At the garrison across the street. Run and tell him I'd be pleased tae offer a spot o breakfast if he'll gie me some time for a wee discussion, private like."

"Whit aboot?"

"Nivver ye mind."

"Whit if he asks?"

"Ye say nowt," Meiklejon growled at his clerk. "A sore trial so ye are, Joseph Thrum. As for last nicht, speakin lik that ahint yer maister's back will no dae. Jist mind yer place or ye're oot o here the meenit I find anither clerk."

"Ah meant nae offence, sir."

"So ye keep sayin. Noo get movin in case we miss the man."

Thrum grabbed his coat and hurried over to the garrison where Claverhouse's platoon was based.

The lieutenant did indeed ask, "Whit aboot?" especially when he heard the invitation included breakfast.

"Ah'm no at liberty to say," Thrum blustered, "but it's likely tae be worth yer while. Oor cook does a guid breakfast."

Garrison fodder was not of the best; neither was the lieutenant averse to furthering his own interest. He lifted his jacket, buckled on his sword, and was out the door, taking two steps at a time down the rickety stair.

"A meenit, sir." The little clerk stumbled behind.

The lieutenant ignored him.

The little man broke into a run and caught up with the soldier as they reached the sheriff's apartment. "Wait sir," he wheezed. "Ah need tae announce ye." With a sudden lunge he pushed past the tall figure and called out, "Lieutenant Crichton frae Commander Claverhoose's platoon, as ye requested, sir."

Thrum was dismissed and retreated downstairs. Sitting down at his own desk surrounded by piles of documents and papers he felt less resentful. This was where he belonged, where he was master, where he kept diligent records of all aspects relating to the garrison. Meiklejon would be out his depth in this room. Not that he appeared to appreciate his clerk or ever bothered to give him a compliment. Any supposed slip ups were pounced on, any failings noted and pointed out, and Thrum took many an unjustified tongue lashing. Indeed, this overworked, downtrodden clerk could be said to be sheriff Meiklejon's right arm. But only Thrum knew that.

Taking off his moth-eaten old wig he hurled it across the room. "Whit am ah supposed tae wear this for? Meiklejon an his fantoosh ideas." He glanced up at the ceiling and thought about the sheriff entertaining his guest. "Mair lik a pair o rats in a sack. Ane as bad as the ither." He grinned to himself and picked up his quill to scratch across the parchment sheet in front of him.

Upstairs in the overheated room Lieutenant Crichton stood to attention before a well spread breakfast table. His heels clicked. "Sir!"

"Lieutenant. Guid o ye tae come." The sheriff waved his visitor forward. "I'm richt pleased tae see ye. Here. Sit doon. Forget aboot formality." Turning towards a half-open door at the other end of the room he shouted, "Fetch anither plate o ham and some eggs. There's a hungry man here waitin tae be fed."

Moments later a huge steaming plate was set down before the soldier. Better than the barracks and no mistake.

Meiklejon watched the soldier's hard eyes light up. He pushed a tankard of ale forward to accompany the meal. "I've sent for ye somewhit special. But eat up, I dare say it can wait till ye skite some o that hunger aff yer face."

Crichton obliged and wolfed into the plentiful selection. Finally he sat back to wipe his whiskers. "Ye were sayin, sir."

Meiklejon nodded. "I ken ye're Clavers' man but I'm sure

whit I hae tae say wud meet wi the guid commander's approval."

Crichton hesitated as if he sensed a favour about to be asked, for this large figure in the fur trimmed doublet didn't look the type to give away a free breakfast, or anything else for that matter.

"No long ago," Meiklejon began, "ye were required tae oust yon rebel meenister at Lesmahagow."

"We accompanied yer clerk ower wi some document then dealt wi the meenister's defiance."

"Jist so." Meiklejon leant closer and lowered his voice. "Since then I've appointed a curate tae replace the man."

"Ane ye approve o this time?"

"Goes withoot sayin. But I've had word he's no gettin much o a welcome."

"That's unfortunate."

"Ye cud say that," Meiklejon admitted. "My curate has the kirk mair or less tae himsel. At least so it says in this letter." He pulled Sandy's letter out from under his great pewter plate. "The man's at his wits end and asks for some help tae rectify the matter."

Crichton said nothing.

"Aifter news lik that I had my clerk visit every hoose and steadin in the parish tae check oot kirk attendance."

The book of names was thrust under Crichton's nose. Row upon row of underlined names stared up at him.

"Evidence, lieutenant, evidence," the sheriff growled. "Each name wi a line drawn under it represents absence frae the kirk. Under the present law that amounts tae deliberate defiance against me, the government, and the king himsel."

"Whit did ye hae in mind, sir?"

Meiklejon lifted a rolled up parchment from the table. "I want ye tae tak this notice, ride ower tae Lesmahagow wi yer platoon, and post the thing up in the village square. Mak a bit fuss while ye're at it and draw attention. Aifter that jist withdraw."

"It's no in my nature tae withdraw."

"Alloo me tae explain." Meiklejon tapped the rolled up parchment. "I'm a fair minded man even when provoked. This here is the final warning. If they folk choose tae ignore this notice and bide awa frae the kirk next Sunday they'll regret it." He tapped the lieutenant's arm. "That's whaur yer special expertise wud come in handy."

"Whit aboot yer ain men?"

"I'd prefer - "

"This tae be handled by professionals." Crichton smiled.

"Not at aw." The sheriff shuffled uneasily. "There's naethin amiss wi my command." He shuffled again. "This garrison draws on men frae aw ower the district. Some come frae that parteeclar village and micht no hae the stomach for the kind o persuasion that micht become necessary."

"If it's a guid clear oot ye'r aifter, jist say so." Crichton nodded. "It's nae problem tae mak an example o as mony miscreants as ye want. Rest assured ma men will no shirk their duty. Ma commander has a commission frae the king tae clean oot the Kirk. Yer suggestion will suit him jist fine."

"I'm glad tae hear it."

"If ye'll alloo me tae say so, sir, a final warnin's mair than they deserve. Mibbe ah cud tak the platoon tae the village an round up a few o the names on yer list. A guid whippin an a few nichts in the tolbooth shud hae the rest runnin back tae the kirk."

Meiklejon looked at the pile of official papers on his table then back at the lieutenant. "Lean furrit a meenit."

The two heads came closer and the sheriff whispered, "I'm inclined tae think there's naethin wrang wi appearin tae gie a man anither chance, especially when ye mean exactly the opposite."

Crichton sat back in his chair and nodded.

"Here's tae us." The sheriff turned to the large jug by his side and refilled both tankards.

Chapter 8

Later that morning Lesmahagow main street rang to the clatter of heavy hooves before the platoon shuddered to a halt in front of the manse. The lieutenant jumped down then crossed to the front door. He rang the heavy bell several times but there was no response. He tried again. The door opened and Meg Gillon gasped to see an armed soldier on her doorstep.

Crichton wasted no time. "Whaur's the curate?"

"In the back garden."

Crichton turned away and disappeared round the end of the building.

Meg slammed the door shut and ran through the house to warn Sandy. She was too late. By the time she opened the back door Crichton was marching down the garden path towards an unsuspecting Sandy. She almost called out then thought better of it and simply stood where she was to watch.

Sandy was trying to tackle a corner at the foot of the garden where grass was almost waist high. He was using a sickle to slice through the tall fronds. This was a new experience and he was finding it difficult to swing the curved blade in a steady arc. When he heard the footsteps crunch on the gravel path he laid down the heavy sickle and turned to greet his visitor. Relieved to be interrupted he smiled a welcome, then saw the red uniform.

"Ah tak it ye're the curate." Crichton barked the words out like an order.

Sandy nodded. "Can ah help ye?"

"It's the ither way roond," Crichton snapped. "Ye wrote tae the sheriff aboot yer empty kirk."

"Ah didna want tae bother him. But ah'd tried ma best and - "

"No guid enough." The lieutenant cut him short. "But dinna worry ah'm here tae sort it oot." He turned and marched back up the path.

Sandy groaned, dreading what that arrogant figure might do. Whatever happened now he'd be to blame.

The platoon returned to the square where Lieutenant Crichton made a great show of nailing up his notice to the church door. He soon had an audience. It was all going to plan. He pointed to the announcement. "Read this and tak note. It's a parteeclar notice aboot kirk attendance in this village. The sheriff kens ye've been stravaigin aboot the country listenin tae renegade meenisters which is unlawfu. Ye shud be locked up for it. But the sheriff intends giein ye anither chance. Frae noo on ye'll be in that kirk ivvery Sunday. Ony back slidin an the fu force o the law comes doon on ye."

No one spoke.

Crichton treated the crowd to a long stare then remounted his horse and slowly led his troops back down the main street in a grand show of military strength.

Gavin Weir witnessed the whole performance in the square and joined the cluster round the notice.

"This is no lukin guid," said the man beside him.

Gavin nodded and thought of the last time he'd seen a military presence in the village. That had been about the minister; now the whole village was involved.

Head buzzing he turned to leave and saw a familiar cart trundling across the far side of the square. "Stop. John. Stop." He chased after the cart.

John waved and drew in to wait till Gavin caught up with him.

"We've jist had a mounted platoon here in the square."

John nodded. "They came by lik rats oot a trap, shoutin at me tae move ower. As if ah could dae onythin wi a loaded cart."

"Ay. But listen, thur's mair. Yon lieutenant whae caused aw the bother for the meenister, posted up a notice aboot oor kirk attendance. The sheriff seems tae ken we've been goin elsewhaur an noo he's orderin us tae be in the kirk on Sunday or else."

"Or else whit?"

"The lieutenant didna spell it oot but the threat's plain enough. The meenister's conscience turned oot tae be a hard maister for him. Noo we seem tae be heidin the same way. No that my faither sees it that way. Ah'm dreadin tellin him whit's happened."

"He's certainly a man wi his ain opinion," John admitted.

"Tell me aboot it." Gavin shook his head. "Ah'll awa an gie him the guid news."

John watched the young man go and thought about Marion and how she'd react. She enjoyed the open-air meetings. Like her father she wouldn't be pleased about going back to the kirk, especially with the new curate in place. Instead of a stop off at the inn he sat where he was and tried to work out the best way of avoiding an argument when Marion heard his news.

And argue she did, letting him know she was determined to ignore the notice. Finally she resorted to one of her sweetest smiles. "Come on admit it, ye'd raither be ootside, listenin tae a real preacher an no shut up in the kirk wi yon pair excuse for a preacher."

"Ay. But ah dinna want tae end up in jail."

"Ah wudna think the curate's likely tae tell on us. Ye said he seems a quiet kinda soul."

"Ay. Vera civil. "John said. "But we need tae think a bit mair aboot this. Jist mind the pair man's been rattlin roond an empty kirk for weeks. Mibbe he cudna staund it ony longer an tellt the sheriff whit wis happenin."

That evening Marion's family appeared at the farm. There was none of the usual gossip or family banter. Her father went straight to the heart of the matter. "We're here aboot yon kirk notice. Ah say we ignore it."

The others looked at one another but no one spoke.

This encouraged Tom Weir to go further. "The next preacher meetin is at Kypewater. It's weel oot the way."

John frowned. "But whit if the sheriff finds oot an sends the military aifter us?"

"We go onyway."

John shook his head. "It cud git dangerous."

Tom Weir shrugged. "We tak a few muskets alang wi us."

"Here, here," Marion turned to her father. "This is gettin oot o hand."

"Naw, naw." Gavin stopped her. "Faither's richt. If we dae

go tae that meetin we need tae be ready tae defend oorsels. Jist in case like."

"Cud we no jist go tae the kirk?" Rachael Weir reached out to touch her husband's clenched fist.

"Ye're no unnerstaundin," he said firmly.

"Ah think ah'm seein it aw weel enough." She patted his arm. "C'mon Tom. Think aboot it. Ye ken ah'm richt."

Tom looked flustered and turned to the circle of watching faces as if seeking support.

After that everyone pitched in. On and on it went with John suggesting caution, Rachael agreeing with him while Gavin and Marion veered one way then another. Not that it mattered. Tom Weir's mind was made up. He refused to budge and kept going till the talking stopped. "That's settled then." The old man looked round the table then sat back looking pleased. Rachael glared at him but said nothing. The others avoided looking at each other.

The sheriff's notice seemed to work. When Sandy Gillon climbed up to the pulpit on Sunday he could see at least fifty faces staring up at him. He felt excited at the prospect of a real audience instead of booming his voice off bare walls as he'd done for the past few weeks. And then he noticed the set expressions and brittle eyes. Bare walls were preferable to this and the words he was about to utter froze in his mouth.

Just then the church door swung open and Sandy forgot his struggle to speak as every head turned to watch a red-coated figure stride down the central aisle towards the front of the church.

Face flushed with importance Lieutenant Crichton stopped below the pulpit then swung round to face the congregation.

Determined to assert himself Sandy leant over the pulpit edge. "Sir. Oor service is aboot tae start. An may ah remind ye this is God's hoose."

Crichton spun round and scowled up at him. "An it's no as fu as it shud be."

Sandy indicated the number of occupied pews. "Today is a promisin start."

"Ah dinna think so." Crichton stared at the silent observers.

"Whaur's the rest?"

No-one spoke.

The soldier banged a black, leather bound book down on the front pew then glared at his silent audience. "Write yer name in this book. That way we ken whae's here. If ye canna write ask Maister Gillon tae oblige."

"This is no whit ah had in mind," Sandy tried to object.

"It's whit ye've got." With that Crichton marched from the building, the only sound his boot spurs ringing on the flagstones.

No one coughed. No one spoke. No one moved. Finally a young man in a back pew stood up. "Will ah close the big door afore ye start the service, sir?"

Sandy didn't answer. His thoughts were outside, beyond the village, willing those out there at any illegal meeting to remain hidden. Closing his eyes he whispered, "Them absent frae the kirk this day need yer protection, Lord. Misguided they may be but keep them safe. For ma part ah confess my responsibility for their plight and beg yer forgiveness."

Every word was clearly heard, his admission accepted, blame apportioned, but no one spoke out to condemn, nor left the building.

"Sir?"

Sandy blinked at the speaker.

"Will ah shut the door?"

"Thank ye." He straightened his robes and like Lucas Brotherstone a few weeks ago wished he was anywhere other than where he was right now.

"There's too few in there for the size o this village," Crichton announced to his platoon outside the church.

"Dae ye want a hoose tae hoose search?" his sergeant asked.

"Waste o time." Crichton pointed to the ridge of moorland beyond the village. "We'll tak a look up there an likely catch a wheen at some meetin wi a rebel meenister."

Gelled into action the dragoons thundered along the main street in a flurry of colour and speed, making a great show, though there was no one to see them pass.

Once away from the village they followed a rutted track and

the horses settled down as they began the long climb towards the moor. About half-way up they stopped by a densely planted birch wood and stared out over the Nethan valley.

"We'll skirt roond here," Crichton told the sergeant by his side. "An informant said there's a hidden gully no far frae here. Jist richt for a secret meeting. Go quiet noo. Surprise is whit ah'm aifter. Ah want tae catch these rebels in the act then thur's nae debate aboot whit they're up tae." He winked at his sergeant who remained impassive and passed the order down the line. This type of work was not to the sergeant's liking, nor the politics, nor even the lieutenant, but he knew his place.

Leaving the gravelly track the horses jumped a low hedge, picked their way up the grassy slope beside the birch wood then continued climbing till just below the brow of the hill. There the column of riders turned away from the birches towards more mixed woodland that spread down the side of the hill to the Kypewater Burn.

At that moment they were seen, and the watcher signalled to those gathered in the little valley beyond.

The preacher abandoned his prayer and pointed towards the waving figure. "Soldiers approach. Ye must look to yer ain safety my freends."

One or two were defiant and muttered, "If it's a fight they're aifter - "

John stopped them. "Listen tae the preacher. Think aboot the women an bairns. Scatter as quick as ye can. A few of us will try an heid aff the danger."

"Whit if ye're caught?" the preacher asked.

"We'll no be. Onyway, we'll no go quietly, we've brocht oor muskets."

"Whit? I thocht ye came here in peace, no itchin for trouble."

"Ay," John admitted. "But richt noo that peace is tempered wi caution."

"I'm no happy aboot this."

"Neither am ah," John agreed. "But better unhappy as deid."

"I still counsel a peaceful retreat."

"Look sir." John sounded exasperated. "That's whit we intend. A few o us men can let oorselves be seen an draw the troops. If the rest split up an heid in different directions there's a chance o escape. If the military follow us intae the wood it's easy tae lead them a dance then disappear oorsels. They soldiers are no local men. They've nae local knowledge. Trust me, arms will only be a last resort." He turned to the crowd. "Git movin afore it's too late."

Within seconds all that remained was trampled grass and a small knot of armed men.

The preacher stepped forward as if to join them.

John shook his head, "No sir. On ye go."

"I must support ye."

"Kindly meant but think aboot it. If they catch us we're jist peasants, mair a nuisance than ony importance. A fine or a jail sentence is oor likely option. As a declared fugitive an rebel preacher it's the end o a rope ye'll git. Naebody here wants tae see ye swing so jist dae as ah ask an keep yer heid on yer shoulders whaur it'll dae mair guid."

They shook hands then the minister was off through the bushes to the Kypewater burn where he splashed across the narrow shallows then up the steep slope towards the moor itself. Soon he was out of sight among the scrub.

John shook his head. "Ah thocht he'd nivver go. C'mon, we've wasted enough time. Intae the wood afore they troopers arrive."

"Then whit?" Wull Gemmell asked.

"We wait till they're richt close then mak a noise tae attract their attention. We can draw them in amang the trees. That way we'll hae them."

"The preacher thinks ye're leadin them a dance then disappearin. Is this no mair lik an ambush?"

"A wee chainge o plan," John said. "Whit the meenister doesna ken canna hurt him, or bother his conscience."

Wull grinned. "Ah micht hae guessed."

John had the grace to look away as he spoke to the others. "Aince amang the trees a horse canna turn as easy. That's when it's time for yon game we played as bairns. Mind hoo we had the hunter an the hunted? Some up trees, some in bushes, an then yin darin tae try an escape? This time we'll turn it roond. It's the hunter we're aifter."

"Ay," chorused a dozen voices as they vanished among the trees.

Marion and the boys were on their way back to the farm by a little used path. John had little fear of their discovery. She was quite at home on the moor, or in the woods, and well understood the importance of cover. The boys would enjoy the excitement but follow their mother's direction. The worry was that those returning to the village might be seen or even blunder into the approaching horsemen.

"Whit hae we here?" Crichton reined up when he saw a group of young girls coming towards him.

The girls stopped and stood with shawls clutched tight to hide their Bibles.

"My, my ladies." He edged his horse closer. "Whaur are ye off tae?"

"The village sir," one girl whispered.

"Whaur hae ye been? An why are ye no in the kirk richt noo?" Silence.

"Ah'm waitin," he threatened. "An my patience is runnin oot."

Another girl spoke up. "We were oot for a walk. Daein nae harm, sir."

Crichton's eyes narrowed. "By yersels?"

No answer.

"As ah thocht." He turned to his sergeant. "Order twa men tae line up these strays an keep them secure while we move on tae catch somethin worthwhile for the sheriff. He'll be happy tae mak an example. Unless ah'm mistaken we've got haud o some Covenanters."

Two of the girls began to cry. Others remained silent but ashen faced. Taking a lead from the lieutenant's attitude a soldier tweaked one of the girl's shawls. She dropped her Bible and screamed. The sound carried into the wood where John and the others were hiding. Now they knew how close the troopers had come; Gavin made to run forward.

"No yet," John hissed. "Bide still."

The soldier tried again. He poked the terrified girl forward with the tip of his sword. She stumbled and fell in front of his horse. "Richt ma beauty." He reached down to lift her clear of the ground then swing her back and forward like a doll.

The other girls ran forward, surrounding the horse which took fright and reared up. The soldier dropped his victim, trying to regain control while one of the girls jumped forward and pulled her friend clear.

The sergeant heard the commotion and stopped. He turned, took in the situation at a glance, and trotted back down the line to lash out at the culprit. "Let that be a warnin. Haud the captives secure. That's yer order. Dae ony mair an ah'll hae ye on a charge afore Claverhoose himself."

Returning to the front of the line he took his place beside the lieutenant.

Crichton shook his head. "Ease aff man. It's only a bit o sport."

"That's as may be sir. But it's no hoo ah wis trained tae behave."

Crichton flushed. "Weel Maister Morality, ah'm ivvery bit as keen on discipline as the next man but some fun against a daft lassie hardly merits yer concern."

The sergeant said nothing and Crichton's flush deepened.

They trotted along in silence till the track came over the breast of the next hill. Below them stretched the most perfect, unexpected, green valley, a circular bowl of flower speckled grass with a wooded lip so private that even Crichton felt like a trespasser. And yet according to his information many feet regularly crept to this spot to take part in unlawful worship. In spite of himself he almost approved. No wonder these rebels thought themselves safe in such a hidden corner. "Thank guidness," he said aloud, "there's aye somebody willing tae speak up for siller." He pointed at a large patch of newly flattened grass, "Ah think we've jist missed some company."

There was a shout from the wood beyond. Crichton spun round. Edging his horse towards the trees he drew his sword. Another shout had him picking his way through the bushes and into the wood itself. Low swinging branches brushed his helmet and held him back. He pushed on. The branches drew closer. He pulled them aside with one gloved hand, and clicked the reins with the other while edging further into the deepening gloom.

"Watch oot, sir." The sergeant made no move to follow. "It's no wise tae proceed withoot proper formation."

"We're aifter peasants, simple peasants, unarmed and on foot," Crichton sneered.

The sergeant sat still. The other men took one look at their sergeant and stayed put.

High in the branches John watched the advancing horseman. His heart pounded as he glanced down at Wull hidden deep in the broom bushes. Wull was his chosen decoy to lead the troops into the centre of the trap. Success would depend on the speed in his feet and his ability to weave and twist as he ran. When they were children Wull had always won this game. John hoped he'd lost none of his skill.

The lieutenant came closer. The hidden watchers stayed absolutely still until the unsuspecting horse and rider passed Wull's hiding place. John signalled to Wull. A sharp snap of dry twig filled the quiet space. Crichton wheeled round as a shadowy figure broke cover. Digging in his spurs he gave chase. The fugitive twisted among the trees, racing as if in blind fear, then seemed to stumble, almost fall. The soldier was nearly upon him. It was a convincing performance. Crichton only saw a man fleeing in terror. "Got ye!" he screeched and leant forward to strike with his sword.

A solid body dropped from the overhanging branches and landed on the lieutenant. Winded by the impact Crichton had no chance to react, and a deft smack under the protective metal helmet rendered him senseless so quickly he'd no idea what hit him. Helpless as a baby he lay there while Wull rolled him over to bind up his wrists and ankles.

The sergeant heard nothing of this other than the sounds of the lieutenant giving chase. Quiet returned. No triumphant whoop of success. Maybe the idiot was stuck in the undergrowth. He'd be in some temper if he was left to claw his way back out. Against his better judgement the sergeant waved the men forward and began to pick a way into the wood.

He peered round as his eyes adjusted to the gloom. Nothing moved, then the ears of his horse pricked up. The sergeant raised a hand in warning. The men behind him stopped. Uneasy within this shadowy world of green they waited a few moments.

Everything seemed quiet and still. Too still for the sergeant's liking. He listened and heard nothing, not even the lieutenant's horse up ahead. This bothered him and he sat a moment before moving forward again. Behind him the soldiers picked their way round tree trunks and bushes. Still no sign of Crichton. They were about to turn when one of the men waved to the sergeant and pointed to a little grove on the left. There was the lieutenant's horse quietly cropping the grass.

"Chris' sake." The sergeant stared at the riderless horse. "The eedjit's fallen aff. Serve him richt if he's hurt himsel. But whaur is the man?" Just then dark shadows seemed to materialise out of the trees. Understanding instantly, he roared, "Ambush!" and made to turn his horse.

In the same instant a strong hand laid hold of his bridle, another relieved him of his sword, and a voice said, "Bide still."

The voice was civil enough but he knew to obey. Anyway, there was little choice with a battery of muskets and pistols now aimed at their heads.

The sergeant signalled surrender and jumped down from his horse while his men did likewise. There were no heroics, no resistance. Within seconds the entire platoon was stripped of their arms and trussed up like chickens for market.

When Crichton opened his eyes he thought he was in a dark green cave full of giants. He blinked, tried to focus, then blinked again. They were still there. Giants with the longest legs he'd ever seen. He shook his head. Impossible. His vision improved and he began to realise he was looking up. That's why they seemed so tall. They were men. But who were they? Why were they surrounding him? And why was he lying flat on his back? He tried to rise. His whole world became a spinning circle of faces, legs and green leaves, multiplying and dancing, merging then separating with flashes and zig-zags in bright colours. Holding his breath made no difference. The swirling circle engulfed him, swallowing him as surely as a fish takes bait. "Chris' sake." He groaned, falling forward and vomiting into the long grass. He lay there, gasping with the effort.

It was several minutes before he tried to sit up. That's when he felt the tight binding round his arms and legs. He rolled about struggling, then saw his men sitting in a neat row, trussed the same as himself. Some missing pieces of an embarrassing jigsaw began to come together. He'd been well and truly had. "Chris' sake." This time it sounded like an apology for his own stupidity.

John hunkered down beside him. "Feelin better?"

Crichton stared and recognised the face. "Ye'll pay for this."

"Mibbe. But ye asked for it." John signalled to the strongest man in the group who grabbed the heavy soldier as if he weighed nothing. Crichton was then carried to his horse and flung over its back like a wounded steer.

The sergeant watched this. Despite his own predicament he almost smiled.

"Richt." John nodded towards the captives. "We'll tak this lot back tae the village."

"Then whit?" Wull asked.

"Jist wait an see."

They came out of the wood to find the two soldiers who'd been left to guard the group of girls. The soldiers gaped at the sight of their comrades as captives and offered no resistance.

"Renegades!" Crichton shouted as he hung across the horse's back. "Ye shud aw be in the parish kirk. No oot here breakin the law."

John turned towards the protester. "Whit aboot yersel lieutenant, makin a meal oot o chasin simple villagers?"

"Release me at once. Ah'm here on the sheriff's orders."

"Mibbe ye came on his orders," John replied, "but ye'll go back on oors tae tell him hoo ye tried tae strike needless fear an terror intae helpless folk for nae reason ither than yer ain enjoyment."

Crichton kicked his legs in frustration and the horse lunged forward.

"Tak care," John advised. "Ye're scarin the beast. If ah let go the reins he'll be awa wi ye hangin on lik a trussed chicken. Ye never ken whaur ye micht end up."

Crichton stopped struggling and snarled, "Very weel, ah'll tak yer message tae the sheriff. The sergeant ther's my witness. Noo untie me."

John made no move.

"Whit else dae ye want? We cairry nae gold."

"Whit we're aifter is mair valuable than that. Thur's naethin beats a guid lesson. An ye'll git ane when we parade ye in front o the village."

"Ye wudna dare."

"Jist watch us. But dinna fret, we're no cruel men. Aince doon the main street will be enough afore ye're awa back wi that message ye've promised tae deliver."

Crichton's cheeks scuffed the hairy flank of his own horse as a reminder that he'd never looked such a fool. And the thought of his commander's reaction to this fiasco was worse than anything the sheriff was likely to say. Feeling like one of his own victims he bumped along cursing John and his friends.

Slowly the procession returned to the village with some of the girls running ahead to spread the news. This time the soldiers didn't ride in a high and mighty column along the main street, swords glinting, demonstrating their authority but walked alongside their horses, hands tied behind their backs trying not to bow their heads in shame.

To their surprise there were no insults from the villagers only a burst of applause at the sight of John leading the lieutenant's horse with the hapless individual slung across its broad back like an old sack.

Crichton almost wished he'd been shot on the moor or hanged in the wood. At least his face was turned inwards, away from the watching faces. But he still heard the applause. Try as he might he couldn't help imagining what he must look like. For the first time in many years tears stung his eyes.

As they passed the square where people were lingering after the service there were gasps of surprise and embarrassment from those who'd given in to the notice and attended church. Sandy Gillon stood open-mouthed at the top of the church steps, not so much at the lieutenant's treatment - he'd probably deserved it all - but the thought of the consequences was terrifying.

When the procession reached the Lanark road John called a halt. "From here on ye're free." He turned to the sergeant. "Ah'm relyin on ye tae see this officer keeps his word. Ah wudna like him tae forget his promise atween here an Lanark."

There was a garbled oath from the figure still dangling across the back of his horse.

John grinned. "Maybe ye cud vouch for him?"

The sergeant coughed then nodded.

"Dinna forget tae mention hoo yer leader came here tae flaunt the law an brow beat us pair villagers. An dinna forget tae mention hoo we were kind enough tae forgie sic wickedness an alloo him back tae his maister wi nae mair than a dent in his pride." John gave Crichton's horse a whack.

The beast took off. It galloped down the road with its helpless passenger roaring as he bounced up and down against the hard leather saddle.

The soldiers' bands were slit. They were allowed to remount. The erstwhile rebels stood back. John shouted, "Ye'd best git on afore yer lieutenant disappears."

Relief plain on every face the dragoons charged off although the sergeant did hesitate long enough to give John a salute before spurring after his runaway leader.

Chapter 9

"Am I hearin richt?" Sheriff Meiklejon's temper was about to break. "Are ye tryin tae tell me these fine mounted troopers were helpless as bairns against mere peasants?"

Lieutenant Crichton's silence was answer enough.

The bald head shook with disbelief. "We're talkin aboot Lesmahagow villagers. Simple country folk, no some cut throat band. I thocht ye were supposed tae be professional? Yer words, no mine, when we had oor last wee talk."

Crichton's face was scarlet. "We were taen by surprise."

"Surprise?" Meiklejon banged a fat fist on the table then leant forward to grip the wooden edge. "That sir, is an understatement. Mair fool me for ivver thinkin ye were up tae the job. I shoulda stuck wi ma ain men. They'd hae seen thru sic a simple trick. Here I wis thinkin we micht dae business. Ay. Mair fool me."

"It wis unfortunate," Crichton whispered.

"Naw. Unbelievable," Meiklejon spluttered. "Commander Claverhoose needs tae ken aboot this, hoo ye managed tae mak a fool o yersel, the military, even masel."

"Ma report is on its way tae the commander."

"And whit kinda picture did ye paint for yersel?"

"Ony shortcomin has been mentioned. Rest assured sheriff, my service record bears scrutiny. Ah hae several commendations."

"I'm mair concerned wi yer performance here which cudna be ony worse."

Crichton stepped back as if stung.

"Tae put it bluntly sir, yer coat's on a shoogly nail. Get oot my sicht afore I dae somethin we micht baith regret."

Crichton retreated, shutting the heavy door behind this tirade. On the way downstairs he met the captain of the sheriff's own platoon who gave him a knowing grin. Laughter rang out of the stables, following his every step. He tried to maintain a steady pace as he walked along but once inside his own garrison pretence was abandoned as he dashed up the narrow, twisted, wooden stairs, taking three steps at a time in his desperation to reach his own tiny cubicle at the end of the men's dormitory.

He flung himself on his straw pallet and curled up like a dog in disgrace. Still in full uniform and boots he knew he looked ridiculous but didn't care. All he wanted was to shut out every thought, every emotion. It was no use. The blame factor was too strong, and he knew it. The sheriff would make sure commander Claverhouse had every last detail, none of which he could explain, not properly, and certainly not to Clavers' satisfaction.

His head pounded, each beat repeating the word *idiot*. Like a resentful child he buried his face in his pillow and bit into the rough cloth. Then the tears came. He pushed further into the pillow and stayed there till his duty sergeant rapped at the door, then rapped again. Finally the door opened. "Sorry tae disturb ye, sir. But the day's orders. The men are waitin."

Crichton turned slowly and blinked at the figure in the doorway. The sight of the man's familiar, disciplined shape made him sit up. The two men eyed each other, one quietly awaiting instructions, the other wondering about his chances of remaining in charge. Crichton sighed and swung his legs over the edge of his bunk to place both feet on the rough wooden floor and stare at them. The shiny black leather of his well-polished boots stared up at him. He could almost see his reflection with its expression from childhood, his I-am-in-disgrace look. Or was it changing, moving towards the need to grasp whatever saving grace might be offered?

He stood up and tried to smooth his crumpled uniform. "Richt sergeant, if the men are ready we'll ride ower yesterday's route. At least some o it." He didn't mention Lesmahagow but the name hung there. "A patrol aroond there micht alloo us a better unnerstaundin o the challenge we faced yesterday."

"Ay sir." The sergeant nodded. "Whit happened yesterday wis nae mair tae the men's likin than yersel, even though ane or twa did gie a smile at ye danglin across the back o yer horse."

Crichton flushed.

"I wudna hae liked it aither," the sergeant admitted. "But mind, the men didna get aff easy themsels. They were mair than a bit discomfited, an weel aware hoo bad it micht luk. An nane

118

o us wants a bad report goin in aboot this platoon."

"I'm glad tae hear it sergeant."

The thought of their commander's wrath was having its collective effect.

"Cud ah add a word o advice, sir?"

Crichton nodded.

"Whit happened yesterday micht hae been avoided wi a wee bit caution. Enthusiasm is aw vera weel, an necessary in every guid soldier, but rashness can whiles become self indulgence."

"Ah hear ye." Crichton's colour deepened.

The sergeant saluted and Crichton followed him downstairs to confront the assembled men.

At a shout from the sergeant each foot sought a stirrup as the troop mounted in unison. They made a fine sight astride the beautiful, strong animals, each one washed and brushed, their metal and leathers polished. The sergeant and lieutenant inspected the line together. Crichton tried to remain impassive, careful not to glance down at the black hide of his own horse and relive the embarrassment of rubbing his face against those shiny hairs just a few short hours ago.

Raising his hand he gave the signal for off.

At the return salute the lieutenant breathed more easily.

The lieutenant was barely down the stairs before the sheriff summoned Thrum from his papers and ordered him to pen a letter to Commander Claverhouse.

Thrum's normal frown darkened as he scraped away at his master's words.

"Whit's up wi ye this time?" the sheriff growled.

Thrum said nothing and wrote on.

"Did ye hear me? Ye're no usually ahint at comin furrit."

Thrum laid down his quill and pushed the letter towards his master. "If ye'd jist sign, sir."

"I said, whit is it?"

Thrum coughed. "Is this a wise move, sir? Wud it no be better tae handle the maitter yersel? Ye're weel able. Surely it wud be a guid way o showin yer maisters hoo weel ye run yer ain command."

"Mmm. As ye ken I'm no yin tae shirk frae my duty but this

unfortunate happenin merits takin anither way furrit. It's a pair day if we canna rely on the support we shud hae frae the great and the guid. Them above us seem tae think themsels beyond fault and dinna expect criticism frae us lesser beings. In this instance I conseeder it my duty tae let Commander Claverhoose ken aboot that eedjit o a lieutenant. Richt noo he'll hae nae idea o the truth. He'll be readin a report that hasna even a noddin acquaintance wi whit happened at Lesmahagow. Weel, a few words frae masel shud pit him richt." He grabbed the quill and signed with a flourish. "Noo awa and fetch the courier. I want this delivered withoot delay."

Thrum sighed. "Richt sir."

"And the man's tae tell Clavers that I require a response in person, and no jist some written reply."

Although it was a long ride over difficult and wild country the courier had been warned to keep going till he reached the commander's comfortable quarters in the Black Bull Inn at Moffat. Well aware of the sheriff's temper the man did exactly that, and a few hours later John Graham of Claverhouse was surprised to receive the flustered and exhausted courier. He was even more surprised by the sheriff's angry letter. He took another read of his lieutenant's report then laid the two accounts side by side. They were about the same incident. That was the only similarity.

The commander was due to make a visit to the sheriff. Maybe the tone of this letter suggested it should be sooner rather than later. In recent weeks Clavers' superiors had been hinting that progress seemed a little slow against the rebels. Maybe this would be a chance to quash that notion with some decisive action. He'd take two men with him and set out on the ride across country to Lanark.

The sun was shining in a clear sky as they left Moffat but once they'd picked their way down Greenhillstair's winding path the wind changed and clouds appeared. As they passed through the narrow gorge leading to the Crawford Valley the sky darkened, a sign of what to expect. Here they crossed the upper reach of the river Clyde. Finally the storm broke, bringing driving rain, sometimes even hail, to batter against their frozen faces. From now on it would be a difficult journey across the miles of moorland where the wind swirled and surged with little hindrance. Visibility was almost nothing but Clavers seemed to have an innate ability to head in the right direction. Secure within his thick riding cape the commander set a fast pace, his two companions struggling to keep up.

It was another two hours before Clavers made a stop at Redmoss, a remote farm he'd often passed when responding to reports of secret rebel gatherings.

The farmer heard the horses champing in his muddy courtyard and peered out of his byre. "Luks lik the military." He turned to warn his son who was mucking out the cow stalls, "thur aye aboot these days. But in this weather?"

The leading horseman dismounted and in spite of the cloak, hood, and driving rain the farmer recognised his important visitor. "Chris' sake," he groaned, "it's Claverhoose himsel." He rushed out to meet the great man, hurried the group into the shelter of his barn, called his son to see to their horses then ushered the three dripping travellers across the yard and into the warmth of his kitchen. "Here sirs, gie me yer cloaks tae dry aff. Sit doon, sit doon by the fire. Ah'm sure ye'd like a bite tae eat." He signalled to his wife who began to heat soup and slice a ham intended for their own meal. Finally she added a few bannocks from the hot griddle by the fire.

The farmer asked no questions. No conversation was offered other than mention of the weather. Clavers had a fearsome reputation but his behaviour was impeccable. Gradually the farmer and his wife began to believe they were not in trouble.

As soon as he'd eaten Clavers pushed back his chair, stood up and placed three coins on the table.

"Nae need sir," the farmer protested.

"Every need." Clavers nodded. "We arrived unexpected like, and ye did weel by us. It's only richt tae thank ye."

Following the commander's lead his two companions nodded their thanks and followed him to the door. Once open rain drove through the space to soak the flagstones beyond. The three men pulled their cloaks tight round and stepped into the courtyard to wait while the farmer ran to the barn for the horses, and then held them steady while his visitors mounted up.

Clavers nodded again and disappeared into the storm.

Back in the house the farmer's wife was staring at the silver coins left on the kitchen table. She looked up when he came in. "He gied us three quarter merks. He mair than paid his way withoot bein asked. He canna be as bad as they say." She held out the coins to her husband.

"Dinna be fooled lass." The farmer shook his head and pocketed the money. "There's mair tae thon yin than meets the eye."

Despite the bad weather and the rough ground to be covered the horsemen made good time and arrived at Lanark Court House by evening. Hesitating only to see his men into the main garrison and issue instructions about his sweating horse Clavers headed for the sheriff's private quarters.

Two heads were in earnest conversation when the commander swept in to interrupt them. "Here I am Meiklejon, as requested. And mair than willing tae deal wi yer problem."

Meiklejon jerked round in his seat by the fire and peered at the figure in the dripping cape. "God's sake Claverhoose, it's yersel."

"Whae else?" Clavers laughed and took off his sodden hat with its bedraggled white feathers. He laid it on the table in front of him where it immediately created a small puddle.

Meiklejon stared at the water beginning to drip off the edge of the table. "I didna expect ye sae quick."

"Why no? Yer letter wis explicit."

"The fact is," Meiklejon began then stopped as if nonplussed. "Mibbe I wis a tad hasty wi my summons. And noo I feel guilty for causin ye tae ride oot in sic foul weather."

"Yer letter mentioned the need for haste and yer courier made it braw plain I wis tae come in person. Surely the situation hasna chainged since this morning?"

"No," Meiklejon admitted. "The situation hasna chainged."

"It's mair the manner o dealing wi it." A clipped voice cut across the sheriff's stumbling speech.

Meiklejon looked at the speaker then back to Clavers whose face was as tight as a spring. "A moment sirs," he gasped, "I'm remiss here. Perhaps ye twa gentlemen are no acquaint wi ane anither. Forgive me." He turned to his visitor who'd been watching from a chair by the roaring fire. The dancing light showed his amused expression as Meiklejon said, "George Ross, Lord Ross of Hawkhead, may I introduce John Graham of Claverhouse."

"Sir." Clavers bowed. "I've heard o ye."

"Likewise sir." The visitor nodded.

Clavers took off his heavy riding cape, flung it over a chair then subjected his Lordship to a long, hard stare. "I must confess surprise at seeing ye here in Lanark. We're thirty miles frae the city and I believe ye're currently charged wi keeping the law in Glesca. Whit are ye daeing oot here and awa frae yer important duties in these dangerous times?"

Lord Ross sniffed. "Pressing family business necessitated this journey. Since I'm here it seemed only polite tae pay my respects at the door o a fellow law enforcer." George Ross, a thin, pale-eyed man of middle age, bland expression and very expensive, brightly coloured fashionable clothing raised an eyebrow. "Does that explanation meet wi yer approval John Graham?"

"I jist wondered why ye'd seen fit tae come awa when ye hae sae much tae luk aifter. Glesca's a fair trading centre and a magnet for them set on stirring up trouble. The businesses and merchants must rely on ye safeguarding them and their profits."

"Just so," George Ross replied. "But rest assured the city is under proper and lawful control for my deputy is mair than able. My absence is unavoidable but I hae nae fear on that score. Whit aboot yersel? Yer reports aboot rebel activity in these parts are much discussed in the privy council these days."

"I didna realise ye were amang yon pack o esteemed rogues."

"Recently appointed and honoured tae join them. There's much tae learn aboot the richt way furrit. Much tae learn aboot this country and hoo it should be governed for the benefit o us aw. I dae my best tae listen as weel as offering advice as and when it's sought."

"Nae doubt."

Lord Ross nodded as if this was a compliment. "So far only suggestion I've made has been weel received and conseedered." He waited for further comment. None came so he added,

"There's been much mention o yersel and yer work. Several council members seem weel disposed tae show some appreciation o yer diligence on behalf o his majesty. Ye're weel in there on aw accounts. Indeed there's been mair than ane whisper aboot inviting ye tae join us. Mibbe we'll soon be sitting roond the same table."

Clavers did not reply.

Lord Ross smiled and a heavy silence hung between them. Finally the noble lord said, "The sheriff tells me ye're charged wi raither special responsibilities in these pairts."

Clavers stiffened. "Frae the King himsel. But I'm sure ye're aware o that frae the privy council."

"They seem tae think it a stalwart challenge."

"Dealing wi rebels is aye a challenge." Clavers turned away to address Meiklejon. "If ye'd be guid enough tae spell oot whit's required I'll get on wi it."

The sheriff looked even more uncomfortable. "Like I said. Things hae altered somewhat."

Lord Ross cut in on the sheriff again. "At least the interpretation has slightly changed."

Clavers turned back to Lord Ross and fixed him with cold, unblinking eyes. "I understood frae the sheriff that my assistance wis required withoot delay. Here I am. Ready and willing as they say, although it looks lik a wasted journey and nivver sae much as an explanation." With that he stepped towards the sheriff. "I dinna enjoy riddles. So jist tell me dae ye or dae ye no require my intervention ower the fracas at Lesmahagow? Yer written words indicated a problem, and ye did stress that time wis o the essence."

Meiklejon found his own letter thrust under his nose. He edged away. The commander pressed forward, and the retreating sheriff felt the rolled up paper slap against his chest. Clavers' fine-featured face jerked closer and the darkening flush of his rising temper suggested more to come. Meiklejon drew back. The rolled up paper followed him. This time it pushed harder. "Weel?" Clavers demanded. "I'm waiting."

"Lord Ross has jist explained."

"No he hasna," Clavers hissed. "Something's changed. Ony fool can see that. But ye're no telling me why. So whit are ye up tae, or hae ye gone soft on whit can be construed as rebellion?"

"Of course no."

"Let me remind ye that my lieutenant wis made a laughing stock by these rebels. The way I see it he wis mair or less kidnapped. No jist him but his platoon as weel. In my book that maks a fool o the law and merits immediate attention."

"As far as I can gather," Lord Ross's voice was level and reasoning, "yer man suffered no actual bodily harm. Surely that must be taen intae account?"

"Are ye implying there's nae harm in defying monarch and government, no tae mention making a fool o the military?"

"Not at aw." Lord Ross's tone slid into silky persuasion. "In this instance I merely suggested tae the sheriff that mair effective means micht be employed."

"Lik whit?"

Lord Ross sighed as if wearied by the commander's slowness. "Ye must be aware there's mair than ane way tae skin a cat."

"So ye say." Clavers' voice rose. He half turned as if to leave. "I'm a professional soldier, no a political animal. I dinna appreciate this needless bandying wi words. Speak plainly or I'll be aboot my ain business and leave ye baith tae yer ain devices."

"Please commander, come ower by the fire and sit doon." Meiklejon tried to assert his authority. "Here at Lanark we're grateful for yer efforts, and the special attention ye've afforded us so far. Yer assistance has made a difference on several occasions. Please sir, hear us oot."

George Ross nodded and indicated a chair by the fire.

John Graham looked at them then slowly crossed the room and sat down opposite.

The sheriff poured out his best wine, and offered a goblet to both men. "This misunderstandin is ma fault. In the heat o the moment I wis in a rage aboot whit happened tae yer lieutenant." He sighed. "A fine man but a mite unfortunate."

"I'm weel aware that the man behaved like an eedjit so stop toadying tae me." The commander viewed the stout figure through narrowed eyes.

Meiklejon tried again. "Perish the thocht, Clavers. I'm only tryin tae explain. My first reaction tae the news wis the need for a guid lesson, wi maybe a year or twa hard labour, or even a hanging." He paused and looked uncomfortable. "But while I wis waitin for yer arrival I've been fortunate enough tae hae a wee word wi my unexpected visitor here."

"And?"

"I'm beginnin tae think I didna need tae write yon letter," the sheriff said lamely.

Clavers glared at the sheriff. "I wish ye'd come tae that conclusion afore sending it. I've plenty duties needing my attention and I dinna tak kindly tae high tailing across miles o God forsaken moors in a storm for nae guid reason." The commander emptied his goblet and banged it down on the table. He stood up. "I'll tak my leave o ye baith."

"Och no, Clavers. Please. Hear us oot. It's tae yer advantage as weel." Meiklejon held out the big, silver wine jug. "Here. Hae a drop mair while ye listen. And if ye approve o whit ye hear we can talk some mair ower a guid meal. I'm sure my garrison cook can come up wi somethin tae yer likin."

Clavers sat down again, looking through dark brows as if sizing up both men, then suddenly his grey eyes lit up and sparkled. He laughed out loud. "So, whit are ye up tae?" He waved a hand at Lord Ross. "Ye're an experienced advocate and nae doubt capable o mony an intrigue. I've heard a few stories aboot ye. As lithe as an eel frae aw accounts. Still that goes wi the territory I suppose. And ye'll need aw yer wits and mair tae survive the privy council."

"The noble lords are certainly a diverse bunch." George Ross was pleased to smile, an almost genuine smile this time.

Tension eased. The sheriff felt confident enough to speak more plainly. "Lord Ross wis pointing oot that loss o money, or property, maybe stock confiscation, even personal possessions micht be mair effective as a punishment than imprisonment or a simple hanging. It also shows hoo the law is capable of mercy. At least it wud meantime. Mibbe a hangin cud come later."

"And hoo dae ye propose going aboot it?"

"My clerk has a full list o dissenters and troublemakers. Wi this tae help us there's a guid chance we micht secure some confessions or witnesses tae testify against the rascals whae broke the law as weel as being responsible for yer lieutenant's discomfiture."

"And then?"

"We round up the guilty. Bring them tae Lanark. Lock them in the tolbooth for a few days afore a trial whaur yer guid sel can sit as the justice. Aifter aw ye're mair senior tae mysel, and also hae that special authority frae the king himsel."

Clavers nodded.

The sheriff turned to Lord Ross. "Maybe ye cud delay yer return tae the toon and assist. It seems opportune when ye're also a senior justiciary, and available so tae speak."

"When's this tae tak place?" Clavers asked.

The sheriff grinned. "Within hoors ma clerk can be oot amang the farms and cottages roond Lesmahagow lik he wis a few weeks ago. This time he'll no be askin questions aboot kirk attendance he'll be makin an up tae date valuation o each property. A guid assessment will surely assist yersel and his lordship in arrivin at a fine appropriate tae each misdemeanor."

"Indeed," George Ross agreed. "Surely it's only richt that the state receives due recompense." He emphasised the word *due* and smiled again at Clavers.

This time the commander smiled back. He didn't like this man. Nor did he trust him. But neither was he getting much monetary support from his royal master who expected results on a shoestring, never mind ignoring proper provision to maintain men and horses. If handled carefully this could be the very thing to ease this problem and see the men kitted out properly. And there was the growing stabling bill. Two months had passed at Moffat without any payment being made. The blacksmith was far from happy to continue shoeing horse after horse for nothing. Not that Clavers blamed the man. Working like this left him feeling ill done by with lords and masters dishing out orders and expecting him to function on little more than a song and a prayer. He stared at the two men sitting beside him. Worth the watching, the pair of them. But all the same. Clavers sighed. "I think we're beginning tae understand ane anither."

Lord Ross's mouth twitched and Meiklejon looked relieved.

"Whit aboot my expenses?" Clavers asked.

"Understood," Meiklejon nodded.

"But realistic," Lord Ross added.

"As always," Clavers snapped back.

"We're agreed then?" Meiklejon looked from one to the other. They both nodded.

Another goblet of wine was poured, this time to toast the venture.

Chapter 10

Dawn was still brightening when a loud rap came to the door of Logan Waterhead farm. Breakfast barely underway, Marion was turning bannocks on the griddle by the fire when this knock made her stop and look anxiously at John, who was leaning against the corner settle to pull on his work boots.

John signalled *stay where you are*. There was another hard rap. "Haud on. Ah'm comin." He crossed to the door. The top and bottom bolt slid back. The door was pulled open.

"Quick." Gavin's white face appeared. "We need tae git awa an hide somewhaur."

"Whitever for?" John stared at him. "It canna be that desperate."

"It is." Gavin grabbed his arm. "Ye canna bide here. No aifter last Sunday. The sheriff's sendin his clerk an a fu platoon aifter us. It's the tolbooth if they catch us."

"Hoo dae ye ken?"

"A freend frae Lanark wis in an ale hoose last nicht an heard a trooper boastin aboot the plan tae come aifter us in the mornin. He wis here only meenits ago warnin me."

As if in reply there was a flurry of sound at the bottom of the farm track and the drum of approaching hooves.

John pushed Gavin away. "Slip ahint the byre an doon by the low field. They'll nivver notice."

"But - "

"Jist dae as ye're tellt."

Gavin scrabbled across the cobbled yard and disappeared behind the white walled byre as the first horse cantered through the close.

John stepped out and closed the house door behind him. He straightened his shoulders and watched the official deputation arrive to fill his cobbled courtyard with sweating beasts. Behind them trundled two big carts. He nodded politely and started to say, "Guid mornin," when the words died on his lips. Astride the first horse was his recent prisoner, the lieutenant.

The front hooves of Crichton's horse clattered against the doorstep, close enough for him to lash out at John with his riding crop.

John staggered sidewards with a huge red weal rising on his temple.

"Sir." The sergeant drew up beside his officer.

The lieutenant hesitated then held back his second strike. "Tie this rebel up. Fling him in the back o yon cart."

"Are ye here on proper authority an no exceedin orders lik last time?" John called out as his arms were thrust up his back and lashed with strong cord.

Thrum pushed his horse through from the back of the line. He held up his black book. "Listen here, Maister Steel. Yer name's in this book as a Kirk dissenter. We also hae a signed statement aboot yer pairt in the rebellious assault on His Majesty's troopers last Sunday."

Crichton grinned. "Ye canna deny it."

John said nothing

"Please yersel," Crichton taunted. "It maks nae difference. Yer defiance goes afore ye an condemns ye. Wi a bit o luck we micht even manage tae swing yer feet aff the ground."

"No!"

Crichton turned to see Marion appear in the doorway. Her face was ashen. In her hand she clutched the knife used to flip the bannocks. He scowled at her. "Bide whaur ye are maam or ye'll be joinin this felon in the tolbooth." Dismissing her as of no further interest he jumped down from his horse and walked away to supervise John being dragged towards the waiting cart.

Marion stared at Crichton's broad back. This man seemed to think it was his right to invade her world and do whatever he pleased. She edged down the steps. The knife in her hand glinted in the pale dawn light as she passed close by the sergeant's horse. "Easy lass." He leant over to grasp her wrist and stop her in her tracks. A further squeeze forced her fingers open enough to release the bone handle of the knife. It slid to the cobbles and rattled harmlessly into the gutter. Marion struggled to pull free. The sergeant tightened his grip. "Ye're lucky the lieutenant husna caught sicht o that blade. If he thocht it wis meant fur him he'd jist lift his pistol and fire at ye. Trust me. I've seen whit he can dae."

Just then the lieutenant called out, "Fetch ma horse ower. We're finished here."

"Sir." The sergeant released his grip and Marion stepped back while he turned his own horse and led the other across the courtyard to his master.

Within seconds they were all gone including John. She was alone in the middle of the yard listening to the cart wheels rumble away down the track. Minutes ago she'd been preparing breakfast, now her world was falling apart. She bent down to pick up the knife and grasped the bone handle so tightly her knuckles gleamed white. She looked at the blade with its sharp edge and let fly with as a hard a throw as she could manage. Without a real target and no proper aim the blade hit the house wall, rang against the hard stone then dropped into a muddy runnel by the doorstep. She stared at it. The smell of her own fear and rage filled her nostrils. It might have taken hold but a small voice behind her called, "Ma? Whit's wrang?"

Johnnie had slipped out behind her and hidden behind the water trough where he'd watched his big, strong father being tied up like a chicken and bundled away by the soldiers. Da hadn't fought back. And the Da he knew could do anything.

Marion scooped up the frightened child and carried him back into the house. Right now her feelings didn't matter. Johnnie needed a hug and all the reassurance she could give. Once in the kitchen she sat down on the big settle, wrapping her arms around him and holding him tight. He shivered then snuggled into her warmth. They stayed like that a few moments then his wise little face looked up. "Ah didna like they men."

"Neither did ah." She tried not to cry.

"Ah wis feart when they tied up Da an taen him awa."

"So wis ah," she agreed. "But we'll help ane aither till he comes back. That way it'll no seem so bad."

"William's still sleepin. He disna ken onythin."

"We'll no tell him," Marion said. "He's too wee tae unnerstaund. Onyway, we need tae - "

There was a loud rap at the door.

They both sat very still.

Another rap, then another.

Marion smiled at the child and carried him to the chair by the fire. "Bide there." Trying to appear confident she marched to the door and yanked it open.

"Mornin Mistress Steel. It's me again." It was the nuisance of a clerk, the very one who'd been there with the troopers.

"Whit dae ye want?"

"Tae feenish the sheriff's orders." Thrum stuck his foot in the fast closing door. "C'mon maam. Open up, ah need tae mak an inventory o yer place."

"Whit for? Oor stuff is oor ain. Aw bought an paid for. Naethin tae dae wi onybody else."

"No if the law's been broken." Thrum pushed hard and managed to open the door further. "Ah warned ye the first time ah wis here but ye wudna listen."

This seemed to defeat her and she stood aside.

Thrum straightened his jacket and marched into her kitchen. Without another word he started his prowl, going round the room, looking, lifting, examining, and writing in his little black book, then whispering to himself and writing again.

"Dae ye need tae dae aw this?" Marion followed every step.

"Oh ay." Thrum bustled out of the kitchen and inspected every room with Marion still on his tail. Page after page of the clerk's book was filled with lists of her personal possessions.

"Happy noo?" she asked when they returned to the kitchen.

Thrum shook his head. "This is only the stert, Mistress Steel. Ah said inventory an ah mean inventory. There's still yer byre, yer stable, yer oothooses, yer animals."

Speechless, she could only follow and watch while he went through every nook and cranny, inspected every stook of hay, counted every hen and chicken. "Nice place," he kept muttering, "worth a bit o siller." Finally he seemed satisfied and closed his book. Then came another shock. "Ah've a note here that twa ither farms belang tae Maister Steel."

"They're baith tenanted."

"They still need tae be inspected as a Steel possession."

Marion stepped in front of him. "Is there nae ither way?"

"Naw. Ah hae orders which ah must obey. Ah dinna ken the reasons for them but it luks lik the sheriff wants tae ken Maister Steel's worth. The cost o bein a rebel disna come cheap these days."

Marion gasped.

"It's no lukin guid for yer man. But he's no alane. Ah've a guid few ither calls tae mak." Thrum stuffed his book into his saddle-bag and untethered his pony. "Guid day mistress. And mind hoo ye go frae noo on." With a quick nod he clambered onto the beast and clattered through the close while Marion tried to work out what all this meant.

Joseph Thrum was having a difficult morning. It hadn't been easy confronting that young woman so soon after her husband was dragged away. But orders were orders, especially when they came from the sheriff. Anyway, she should have guessed something like this would happen after such defiance. No doubt it would be the same reception at the other farms he had to visit. Mind ye - he blinked at the thought - he'd hae paid guid money tae see yon high and michty lieutenant trussed up an strung across the back o his horse. He crammed his official hat tighter on his head and smiled to himself while his pony picked its way down the stony track towards the next farm on his list.

On market day Lanark was bustling with people. Market stalls at the top of the high street were in full swing, trestles loaded with fresh vegetables while in the auction ring an assortment of beasts were being eyed up and bargained over. Street hawkers wandered through the crowd offering trays of sweetmeats, bright coloured ribbons, and all kinds of enticing nonsense to tempt the unwary. The inns were busy serving those who could afford refreshment while the vennel howfs catered for the less particular, or those with less money in their pockets.

The sun was shining. The air grew warm. Already the stink from the steaming middens was wrinkling a few genteel noses while others dabbed at a nosegay or sniffed at a square of linen soaked in lavender. Just a normal market day until Lieutenant Crichton appeared at the bottom of the high street and attracted attention when his platoon ploughed through the congestion.

A couple of farm carts loaded with men trundled along in the centre of the soldiers' formation. Many townspeople stopped their business and craned their necks. A few followed the cavalcade to the main entrance to the garrison jail where a crowd gathered to watch the military line up and wait while Lieutenant Crichton dismounted then went in by the little side gate.

A moment later he was out again, ordering the carts to be unloaded. Fifteen weary looking men stumbled, fell, or were pulled from the carts. The big gates swung open, the men were hustled through, then the gates clanged shut again.

"Whit's up?" came the call from the back of the crowd.

"A load o prisoners," said those at the front. "Thur nae local."

Just then one of the watchers spied the town deacon hurrying towards the tolbooth. "Mornin, sir. Ye're in a big hurry on such a fine day."

"Ay." The deacon barely broke step. "Terrible times we're livin in when country folk indulge in civil disorder."

"Whaur wis this, sir?" the man persisted.

"Lesmahagow. Ye'd think they'd hae mair sense oot there. Noo that the rascals are caught the sheriff has tae lock them up an then deal wi the maitter."

Someone in the crowd laughed.

The deacon wheeled round. "It's nae laughin maitter. It's serious enough for Claverhoose himsel an Lord Ross frae Glasgow tae be sittin on the bench alang wi the sheriff." The deacon shook his head and strode towards the garrison gate leaving the crowd staring after him.

Meanwhile the Sunday rebels, as they'd been labelled, were manacled and secured to wall rings in a basement cell. A tiny, barred hole high up in a corner admitted the only light and air from a world beyond the thick, wet walls. Crouching in this gloom the men tried to ignore the scuffles in the filthy straw around their ankles. The rancid stink didn't bother them much. Most of them were well used to mucking out their byres. Fear of what might come next was another matter, and each man began to worry about the consequences of the adventure they'd joined in so willingly.

John stared up at the distant square of light and cursed his wilfulness. He'd enjoyed kidnapping the lieutenant and then humiliating him so publicly. It had seemed right at the time, and his friends had joined in easily enough. But all the same. Angry tears welled up and his head sagged. He pressed his cheek against the cold, wet wall and then, like Lucas Brotherstone before him, he began to realise that whatever he felt, in the end it would make no difference. Heart first mind second had proved a trial for that young man. Now it was proving the same for John Steel.

He stood in silence for a long time and then almost without thinking he began to hum. Not a psalm nor a hymn but a rhyme he'd almost forgotten from childhood. The sound made him feel better. He tried again, louder this time. Others picked up the tune and repeated it. But third time round the thought of where they were and why surged back, and everyone grew quiet again.

Each morning the captives were given a miserly bowl of gruel and a single ladle of water. These strong men were used to good food and plenty of it. Hunger set in. They began to weaken. They were not allowed to exercise, but forced to stand there, tethered like one of their own beasts. Cold and miserable they listened to the constant drip of dampness and scuffling in the straw. At night this seemed to grow louder, as if the walls were whispering against them, triggering dark thoughts, torturing them with fears of what might happen next. Worst of all, time seemed to stand still with never a mention of their fate.

On the fifth day the cell door was flung open and their burly jailer announced, "Time tae move gentlemen."

No one asked where or why. They stood quietly as he loosened the chain to each ring then waved them forward. "Line up ane ahint the ither. When ah say walk, dae it. When ah say stop, ye stop."

After tight confinement and lack of food many staggered as they took their first steps in days. John's father-in-law tripped and fell over. John had to lift the old man and push him up the rough steps to the next level. Even then Tom Weir could barely walk and John half carried him along the narrow passageway, up three steps, and into a long, dark guardroom with no windows to the outside. Two guttering sconces made it just about possible to see. They also cast unreal, dancing shadows along the walls.

"Bide here," their jailer ordered. "Listen for yer name. When that happens step furrit an ye'll be escorted up there." He pointed to a metal studded door at the top of several stone steps. "Somebody important wants a word wi ye." Climbing the rough steps he disappeared beyond the heavy door while the captives shuffled and tried not to look as anxious as they felt.

At last marching feet approached. The door swung open. Two dragoons in full dress uniform stood to attention. One called out, "Gemmel."

There was no response then one of the prisoners asked, "Which ane?"

The soldier retreated, consulted someone in the corridor beyond then returned to shout, "James."

James Gemmell struggled up the steps, disappeared into the narrow corridor and did not return. The men in the chamber strained their ears but heard nothing. Time passed. The two soldiers returned to announce, "The ither Gemmell." A pause. "William."

Wull took the same route as his brother.

Gradually each man in the line was summoned.

Finally it was John's turn. He climbed the steps. Beyond the metal studded door he was jostled along a narrow corridor to stop before another closed door.

"Wait." One soldier opened the door, climbed up a further stair then called back to his companion. "Bring him up."

As John climbed the light came closer and the air grew sweeter. The door at the top was open. Stumbling into sudden brightness he had to blink a few times before he was able to make out a large, well furnished room with long windows admitting welcome sunlight. An ornate desk in the centre indicated this room belonged to a man of importance, accustomed to comfort. Tapestries covered the walls. A settle and several chairs grouped near a blazing fire suggested a place of discussion, a sociable room with an air of refinement for receiving guests, not where a prisoner would be interrogated.

John was marched across this room to a carved door in the opposite wall. The soldier did not knock nor open the door but leant against the wood and listened. A few moments passed then there was a muffled call, "Bring in the prisoner."

The soldier opened the door and pushed John forward.

He found himself at the foot of another set of steps, ten wooden slats, like a short ladder.

"Up!" The soldier's bayonet reminded him.

At the top was an open trap door showing a square of light. Up he went and stepped onto a polished wooden floor. Confused he looked round to find rows of faces staring at him. The sudden change from being one of a crowd in dank, dark privacy to becoming the centre of attention unnerved him. Uncertain of what would come next he waited till his escort pushed him towards a marked spot on the floor.

He took his place and quickly realised he was in the courthouse. In front of him was a long, polished trestle table. Behind this sat three official looking men. The grandest one presided in the centre. In front of him lay a hat with an enormous white plume. Elegant elbows, covered in the best of blue velvet, rested on the table. A freshly laundered white cravat with an ornate lace frill adorned the throat, and a pair of white hands with long, tapering fingers were clasped as if in prayer. Here was a fine gentleman indeed with shoulder length reddish hair brushed till it shone, coiffed and curled at the bottom providing a complimentary frame for a pale, delicately shaped face, almost on the verge of being feminine. The clear, grey eyes with their piercing stare, was the only give away as to what lay behind this refined façade.

On the right side of this frippery sat a rather different individual, obviously important by the look of him. Dressed in a dark, leather jacket with a less than pristine cravat knotted below his massive face, he seemed very much the part of law enforcement. The uncertainty in the dark eyes told another story, constantly flicking here and there, taking everything in, missing nothing, yet every now and again resting on the flamboyant cockerel beside him.

On the left side sat another gentleman, a little older, and dressed in a coat of ornately decorated, bright green material. A length of matching silk was carefully twisted round his thin neck, and his waistcoat buttons gleamed like polished silver. A bit of a dandy at first glance. However, like the first grand gentleman, something about his bland expression and still, dark eyes was a warning.

These three men and the military array lined up on either side, were in stark contrast to John's filthy appearance. A fastidious man by nature, and one who appreciated good worsted cloth, he felt a mess and knew he looked dreadful in his present state.

Looking to the side John saw the little clerk who'd visited the farm.

The clerk nodded then announced, "Maister John Steel, farmer frae Logan Waterhead, by Lesmahagow, in the county of Lanark." He then went on to read out a lengthy charge relating to the previous Sunday.

"Whit hae ye tae say aboot this charge?" asked the grandest gentleman of the group.

"We'd nae choice," John kept his voice steady, his face as calm as he could manage.

"Explain sir." The shaped eyebrows arched. "We'd be delighted tae hear yer reasons for sic disobedience against the crown."

"Sir," John plunged in. "Whit happened is doon tae ane o yer so cawed law enforcers. He's a platoon lieutenant so mibbe ye ken whae ah mean. He's a man wi scant respect for onybody but himsel. The way he behaves tae his innocent victims, ay victims, has nowt tae dae wi common decency. Of course he'd say thur no innocent an that entitles him tae deal wi them as he pleases. Weel it disna. No accordin tae the law. It aw began when this lieutenant wis sent tae oust oor meenister frae his charge. Insteid o mindin his orders he cudna resist showin aff an frichted the reverend's horse that much it taen aff wi a fu ladin cairt ahint it. Meenits later the meenister's wife fell aff the cairt an hit the cobbled street. When we got tae her she wis deid."

"Enough!" Crichton leapt to his feet. "Sir, I must protest and refute ivvery word this rebel utters. It's naethin but libellous rubbish and shud be struck frae the court's record."

The grand gentleman turned to the public benches and stared

at the red-faced soldier. "The prisoner has mentioned nae name and yet ye jump up tae deny the accusations. Forgive me for saying, and I may be wrang, but such an outburst micht be construed as a tad suspicious."

Crichton looked stunned, shook his head and sat down again.

The grand gentleman acknowledged the soldier's co-operation then swivelled round in his seat to face John again. In a pleasant voice he said, "Prisoner. Ye may continue."

Encouraged by this John picked up where he'd left off. "No content wi whit he'd done the lieutenant even forced the pair man tae drive awa frae the village wi his wife rolled up in the back o his cairt lik an auld carpet."

The audience began to murmur.

Unsure if it was approval or anger John kept going. "Tae mak maitters worse, that same man has continued in like vein, abusin ordinary folk for nae guid reason. Whit we did wis forced upon us when he wis scourin oor countryside lukin for folk tae arrest withoot a by yer leave or seekin oot ony proof. Is that hoo the law shud operate?"

"Nae mair." The fat man sitting on the right of the grand gentleman stood up and banged his fist on the polished table. "It's a pair day when a prisoner is allooed tae openly abuse the law lik this and tell sic lies."

The grand gentleman neither turned his head to the side nor raised his voice. "Sheriff, I'll decide whit's heard or no heard. If ye feel aggrieved by whit's being said, or hoo I conduct this court ye're free tae remove yersel and wait ootside."

The fat face paled. The mouth opened and shut. The huge bulk sat down with a thump then glanced furtively at the other gentleman. No encouragement was forthcoming.

"Please." A ringed hand waved at John. "Continue."

John nodded. "The lieutenant an his men hud captured a wheen lassies an wis ill treatin them. A few o us heard thur terrified screams an decided we hud tae dae somethin. When we got tae them the troopers wur taen up wi tormentin thur captives an no payin attention. They wur easy caught an tied up. An it's no as if we hurt them. We jist mairched them doon the village main street tae show the lieutenant an his men the error o thur ways."

The murmuring grew louder.

The grand gentleman clicked his fingers and directed a soldier to quieten the audience or remove them from the court. He waited till the noise subsided then nodded to John. "Weel Maister Steel, ye've had a mair than adequate hearing. Mibbe some wud caw it a rant." The voice was silky. "In case ye've forgotten yer appearance here is due tae wilful law breaking alang wi a personal attack on an officer representing His Majesty. As for kidnapping a hale platoon, ye've aready admitted that. If we add aw this thegither we hae a maist serious offence tae consider."

There was a gasp from the audience.

"At no point in yer interesting and colourful tale did ye mention ony recourse tae official assistance in rectifying yer problem. Dare I suggest that shud hae been the proper path insteid o whit happened. Indeed, ye seem tae consider yersel above sic niceties. Let me remind ye this is a law abiding country whaur neither oor gracious King nor his government countenance sic behaviour."

John opened his mouth as if to argue.

"Ye've had yer say, sir." The grey eyes narrowed. "Plenty o it. Noo, wi yer forbearance, I'll hae mine."

John winced and began to wonder if his tirade had simply been an opportunity to dig himself a deeper hole.

"In fairness tae ye I suspect whit took place wis nae mair than whit seemed a guid idea at the time." The grand gentleman spoke as if having a private conversation with John. "In my experience that signals the mind o a fool whae acts withoot recourse tae proper thocht. In future I'd advise ye tae think a bit mair afore embarking on yer fanciful notions. That way ye'll save yersel a deal o trouble. Unplanned as yer actions micht hae been they're still treasonable, never mind the affront tae a government officer, though I dare say he'll recover. As his commander I look tae his well-being, which I dae for each and ivvery man I command. John Graham o Claverhouse taks these duties very seriously indeed, and whit ye did merits the severest punishment." The grand gentleman paused and nodded towards the crowd cramming the courthouse benches. "However." He turned his gaze back to John. "I'm prepared tae afford ye His Majesty's generosity. I am also extending the same privilege tae yer band of rogues."

"They're no ma band. An nane o them are rogues," John burst out.

"I trust ye jest Maister Steel." Clavers smiled coldly. "When questioned earlier the ither prisoners seemed tae think ye were their leader."

This time John did not fall into the trap.

Clavers smiled as if reading his thoughts. "Ye and yer freends hae an unfortunate attitude tae authority which must be punished."

The other finely dressed gentleman glanced at the commander and nodded.

Suddenly John understood. He'd been duped. His friends had been duped. The great and the good, supposedly sitting in judgement, were not averse to bending the law to suit their own ends. He could almost guess that money was about to be mentioned. It would be a fine, a crippling fine, probably the amount agreed by those three gentlemen beforehand. And yet this public spectacle had been set up to suggest justice being dispensed in a fair and proper manner.

The finely modulated voice cut into his thoughts like wire through cheese. "Are ye listening Maister Steel? Ye seem a mite distracted."

John reddened at Clavers' astuteness.

The voice continued, "Ye appear the only authority amang this rabble. If that isna the qualities o a leader, weel?"

John swallowed his reply.

Seeing this Clavers waved the clerk to the table. "Read oot the inventory and we can arrive at a proper judgement."

The clerk opened a black book and began rhyming off familiar items. John gasped as he heard his entire property, stock, even personal possessions revealed to the court.

The commander now looked directly at John, "As ye see, we've taen the trouble tae dae a thorough check afore yer appearance here."

John felt sick.

"Ye're the prime mover in this unfortunate incident. An example needs tae be made. However, since I am extending His

141

Majesty's clemency tae ither prisoners by imposing fines as a penalty I feel obliged tae dae the same wi ye raither than the imprisonment ye certainly deserve. It will be a fine. But severe enough tae bite intae yer reserves. I think the amount must also act as a warning against future behaviour. Or mibbe ye can afford tae fling awthing awa on whit ye seem tae consider a maitter o principle." His fingers drummed on the table then the clerk was summoned for a whispered conversation with the grand gentleman.

Clavers turned to his two companions. They both nodded. Clavers sat back in his chair and studied John.

John stared back at the elegant face.

The commander kept him waiting. The silence in the courtroom wrapped round them all. Everyone stared at the central judge and his prisoner.

Finally Clavers lifted both hands from the table and held them towards John as if extending an invitation. "John Steel, I find ye guilty as charged. However, on behalf o his gracious Majesty I intend tae lace this judgement wi clemency. On this occasion I merely fine ye but I also advise ye tae think lang and deep aboot yer behaviour. If ye appear in court again there will be a lang custodial sentence waiting for ye. The penalty on this occasion will be three hundred Scots pounds, twenty bags o best meal, three milking cows, four stirks, and a black horse."

The audience muttered while Clavers sat back and nodded to his two companions, who appeared to agree with his judgement.

"When is this due?" John asked.

"Everything must be ready by 11o'clock the morn." Clavers smiled. "I'll be there mysel tae supervise proper collection. Ye're noo free tae leave and mak necessary preparations. He nodded to the soldier standing behind John, "See Maister Steel oot the building."

John was hustled down the short, wooden stair, back into the well-furnished room where lieutenant Crichton was waiting. "Thru that door, doon the hall, and ye're ootside." He pointed to the open door. "A lucky man so ye are, Maister Steel. But mind hoo ye go for ah'll no be far ahint."

John had the sense not to reply. He hurried across the room and down the hall to the main doorway. Seconds later he was in the busy street, part of the milling crowd going about its normal business, unaware and uncaring of what had happened in the courthouse.

He had began to walk away when a voice called out, "John. Ower here."

He whirled round and saw Gavin in the doorway of a howf on the opposite side of the street.

He pushed through the crowd to the young man,

"C'mon. Oot o here." Gavin grabbed John's arm. "Ah've horses waitin at a stable at the bottom o the high street."

"Whit aboot the ithers?"

"Long gone. C'mon. We can talk on the way."

Together they walked down the busy street and into the little wynd which led to the stable. And there was Juno, tethered, saddled, and ready to go.

"Ah thocht ye'd enjoy ridin her back hame," Gavin said. "Did ah dae wrang?"

"Far frae it," John smiled. "In fact ye've gied me an idea. Hae ye ony money on ye?"

"Marion made me bring a fu bag in case we hud tae pay tae git ye oot the court."

John took the money-bag and crossed to where the stableman was flicking hay from one stall to another. John pointed at Juno and whispered something. The man nodded, laid down his rake and went into a stall at the back of the building. He brought out an old, black horse. After further conversation he harnessed the beast then handed John the reins. John nodded and opened the leather bag to count out several silver merks into the man's open palm. The man pocketed the money while John led the old beast out to the cobbled wynd.

He winked at Gavin. "If ye wur in the court ye'd hear that pairt o ma fine is a black horse. Weel, here it is. An ye'll mak sure my Juno is naewhaur tae be seen when yon grand gentleman appears in the mornin."

Gavin grinned while the stableman scratched his head, mystified why anyone should ask for an old, done beast, and be prepared to pay over the odds for it.

The moment hooves rang in the close Marion and the two boys

were out the house, and down the steps to pull the tired man from his horse. She pressed her face against John's filthy cheek, and her fingers traced the dark lines circling his brown eyes. "Thank God," she whispered, "ye're hame."

The boys clung to his legs while Gavin remained on his horse and looked embarrassed at the fuss.

"Easy, lass easy." John kissed her. "It's no ower yet." He tried to sound confident. "Ah've a big fine tae pay in the mornin. Noo whit aboot Gavin, the lad's due some supper."

Marion turned, "Sorry Gavin, ah forgot aw aboot ye."

"So ah saw." He laughed. "Dinna worry aboot feedin me, ah'm awa hame. Mither will need help wi faither's tantrum ower his fine. Noo mind, ah'm takin Juno awa wi me and stablin yer new purchase ready for the mornin visitors." With that he took the old horse into the stable, removed the harness and settled it down before coming back for the precious Juno. He nodded to them both and led her away, his cheerful whistle drifting back as they disappeared into the dark.

"He's a thochtful lad," John whispered and hugged Marion again.

"Ay," she agreed, clinging to the rank figure as they stumbled into the house together.

"A real bed," John whispered, "Ah've been dreamin aboot it."

"No afore ye strip and wash."

The big wooden tub was trailed out and placed in front of the fire where Marion had two large pails of water sitting snug against the burning logs. "Richt. Git oot they filthy claes while ah fill the tub, an then we'll try an scrub some o that dirt aff."

Glad to be rid of his stinking clothes John sank into the soothing warmth of clean water and felt some of the past few days begin to slip away.

Layer after layer of grime was scrubbed away, his skin bright pink before Marion was satisfied. "Richt. That'll dae. Oot ye git."

He patiently stood to be dried and wrapped in a thick towel then offered a bowl of the best vegetable soup he'd ever eaten. Finally he was guided through to his own bed, and Marion was left to gently tuck him up like the sleeping child he became as soon as his head touched the soft feather pillow.

Despite his weariness John was up before dawn to make sure everything was ready for collection. Beasts were tethered in the yard, meal bags neatly stacked against the wall, money counted and bagged, waiting in the front room.

Prompt at eleven a great number of horses thundered up the track.

As soon as he heard them John ordered Marion and the boys to remain indoors.

"But - " she protested.

He pushed them into the kitchen, banged the door shut then hurried through the close to stand at the entrance before the troopers arrived. He stayed put and they were forced to pull up in front of him. "Ah wudna come ony further." He pointed into the courtyard. "The beasts are takin up maist o that space. If ye ride in wi sic noise an fuss the pair things will rampage aboot wi naewhaur tae go. Ah dinna suppose ye want them damaged."

Crichton glowered but Clavers took no offence. He was in high humour this morning. So far they'd visited several farms and collected more than two thousand pounds Scots as well as impounding many possessions. A fruitful morning and the due proportion of all this would go a long way towards paying the commander's mounting military debt back in Moffat. "Let it be," he warned his lieutenant. "Indulge him this time."

Crichton remained silent.

Clavers smiled as if paying a social visit, "Lead us tae the impounded items till I check that everything is prepared according tae my judgement."

John led them into the yard where the beasts were inspected. Clavers took great interest in the quality, looking in ears and slapping rumps before demanding that two of the stirks be exchanged.

John made no protest.

Another two were paraded out and duly chosen. The milking cows, however, met with instant approval.

"Ye keep guid stock Maister Steel. But whit's this?" Clavers frowned at the sight of the black horse. He pointed at the bony rump. "Is this the only black horse?"

John nodded.

Clavers turned to the two nearest troopers. "Check oot the stables."

They returned a few minutes later. "Nae ither black horse, sir."

Clavers' mouth formed a little round 'o'. "Indeed." He shrugged then ordered John's hard earned silver to be counted once more before issuing a receipt.

The ordeal appeared to be almost over.

Just as he made to leave Clavers smiled and asked, "May I trouble ye for a drink o yer guid milk? A sample so tae speak?"

"Ah'll fetch it masel." John went into the milkhouse, lifted a tankard and walked through to the cool parlour. He was ladling the milk into the tankard when Clavers' elegant figure appeared in the doorway. "Ye're a singular man John Steel." Clavers stepped closer.

John sniffed what had to be sweet lavender from the finest gentleman ever to grace his tiny milkhouse.

"Wi a bit mair practise ye'd mak a worthy adversary." Clavers spoke as if this was a genuine compliment.

"Ye hae me ther sir."

Clavers chuckled. "Still, an agreement is an agreement. And a black horse is a black horse."

John kept his face straight and said nothing.

"Did ye really think I'd be taen in by a simple switch?" Clavers chuckled again. "But mibbe a few days in yon dark hole has dulled yer wits. As if sic a wealthy farmer and guid stockman wud mak space for a pathetic auld beast." Still smiling he accepted the tankard and drank down the milk. "Excellent, as I expected."

"Thank ye."

"Ay. Ye'd mak a worthy opponent." Clavers sounded almost regretful. His voice dropped to a whisper. "Or better still, a guid freend."

"Sir?"

"Think aboot it." The tankard was thrust into John's hand. Clavers strode back into the yard barking out orders and was immediately engrossed in seeing the bags of meal loaded. Even the old black horse was tethered to the rear of a cart. Finally the commander seemed satisfied. He turned towards John. "Guid day Maister Steel. My regards tae yer wife and family." The proud figure remounted his horse and led his entourage through the close.

John stared after them. "Strange man," he whispered to himself. "An dangerous." This revelation disturbed him more than the loss he'd just suffered.

Chapter 11

"This is a fine catch, sir." The young captain riding beside John Graham of Claverhouse sounded rather pleased.

"Ay Blythe," Clavers nodded, "and easy done."

"They needed dealin wi oot here," Crichton growled.

"Not at aw. The law is oor maister and says they're entitled tae a trial."

"They dinna deserve a trial. We ken thur guilty. Whit else wur they daein oot here on the moor but indulgin in illegal worship? They need tae be stopped."

"That's whit we're here for," Claverhouse laughed. "Ease up man. Jist because ye had yer ain tail tweaked the ither day."

"It'll no happen again." Crichton flushed and turned his wrath on the fourteen bound prisoners stumbling along in front of him. He edged his horse forward then leant down to grab the neck of the nearest unfortunate. "Hoo does this feel? A wee taste o whit's comin in a day or twa." He laughed and swung the man clear of the ground.

"Sir." The sergeant riding alongside glared at him.

Crichton glared back, dropped the prisoner, and the convoy moved on through the dust towards the town of Strathaven.

Strathaven was a pleasant town nestling in the midst of a wide green plain. It was a warm evening at the end of May. Birds were singing. Nature seemed full of hope and promise. The commander felt likewise as the platoon rode into the Common Green and reined in to wait while captain Blythe started shouting for billets in the name of the King. Townspeople attracted by the fluster and colour drew back and hurried away. No one wanted the hassle of feeding and stabling the troopers with little chance of a thank you let alone payment for their trouble. There were sympathetic glances for the prisoners, but no kind word, nor criticism.

After a short search Blythe found a dark, airless store behind the main bakehouse in the centre of the town.

"Ah dinna want yer prisoners in there," the baker protested. "It's ower wee a space for as mony men. An whit aboot feedin them? Ah canna afford tae dae that."

"Wheesht man," Blythe warned. "The King's men are entitled tae mak use o yer property in dangerous times. Ye wudna want tae refuse, wud ye? Onyway, thur's nae need tae feed them. A sniff o yer bakin is aw they need."

All fourteen were hustled inside and left with neither food nor water till morning, and all the time tormented with the inviting smell of baking bread.

Clavers and his officers retired to an inn at the top end of the Common Green. Glad of the rest they removed their helmets and armour, and called for ale to toast the day's success. "And better tae come," the commander shouted as he kicked off his boots.

There was a rap at the door. A soldier poked his head in. "Sir. This lad has somethin ye micht want tae hear."

A small boy was pushed into the room. He stuttered and stammered then burst into tears, sobbing until the commander lost patience. "Tak him awa till he's mair sensible." The soldier dragged the child away.

Captain Blythe rose from his seat by the fire. "May I see intae this, sir?"

"Whitivver." Clavers waved him away.

The soldier was outside the inn thrashing the boy with a belt.

"Here, here." Blythe laid a hand on the man's shoulder. "Whit's he done?"

"Made a fool o me for a stairt."

"He's only a bairn and scared witless. Leave aff. I'll see tae him."

The soldier released his victim and shuffled off swearing.

The child looked even more terrified as the captain knelt down beside him.

"Weel, young man." Blythe smiled and lowered his voice. "Whit hae ye been up tae that's caused aw this fuss? C'mon, I'm no lik yon soldier." He tried to sound persuasive. "Ye can tell me."

The boy stared down at his bare toes then whispered, "Ah didna dae nuthin, sir." He flinched as if expecting a blow. None came. This seemed to give him enough courage to look up at the captain. "Ah wis jist bringin a message tae Maister McAllister at the stable."

"And did ye gie Maister McAllister his message?"

The boy hid his face again.

"Here. Tak this." Blythe held out his own fine linen kerchief.

The boy peeped through his fingers at the white cloth.

"Go on. Wipe yer een."

The child wiped away his tears before politely handing back the kerchief.

"Better?"

The little head nodded and a pair of large, round eyes solemnly regarded the adult kneeling by his side.

The captain waited a few moments then tried again. "Are ye no for tellin me aboot Maister McAllister?"

"He's a freen o ma faither. He often comes tae oor farm. He's a nice man."

"I'm sure he is."

"Ma faither heard aboot some kind o meetin at Loudon Hill the morn. Somethin tae dae wi the hill preachin folk. Maister McAllister's brither wis the meenister here afore he wis put oot his kirk. Faither thocht Maister McAllister shud ken aboot the meetin. He sent me tae tell him. When ah got ther he wisna in the stable. Ah wis jist askin the blacksmith whaur he micht be when yon ither soldier grabbed me an taen me alang the road tae the inn. Ah havena done onythin wrang. Ah'm only dain whit ma faither said." The child scraped his toes back and forth in the dust then looked up, his eyes full of defiant tears. "That's the truth, sir."

"I'm sure it is." The captain smiled broadly. "On ye go, then. Awa and gie Maister McAllister his message."

The child gaped at him then turned and raced into the crowd thronging the Common Green.

Blythe watched him go. He could hardly believe his luck and hurried into the inn to tell Claverhouse the good news.

"Fine man, jist fine." Clavers rubbed his hands in delight. "Ye've done weel. Loudon Hill ye say?"

Blythe nodded.

"We'll ride oot in the morning and keep that appointment.

Maybe even join in the prayers." Clavers raised his goblet to the dutiful captain and thought of the sport to come.

"Thomas Douglas is comin tae preach at Loudon Hill next Thursday," was the first thing Wull Gemmell said when he met John on his way back from market.

John was surprised. He'd expected Wull to complain about their time in the tolbooth.

"Jist shows ye, the meenisters are determined."

"Mibbe so." John pulled a face. "But Maister Douglas isna showin much common sense pickin Loudon Hill tae huv a service. It's far too open, an weel kent, an too easy reached frae Strathaven. An Thursday's market day, even mair folk aboot. In a busy toon folk talk, word gets roond, an the wrang ears hear. Whit if the law gits wind?"

"Some folk dinna care. In fact some are sayin it's time tae tak on the law."

"Whit aboot us? We got locked up an fined for oor trouble. It'll be a long time afore ah mak up ma losses. Worse than that ah feel guilty aboot leadin ye aw on."

"Dinna fash yersel." Wull shook his head. "We wur willin. Naebody forced us. An we're nae alane. Ithers are oot ther, jist as willin tae come furrit an say whit they think aboot king an government."

"An git locked up for thur trouble?"

"Mibbe no. Ah've heard talk aboot an army."

John stared at Wull.

"Ay. Tae march on the capital an mak the government back doon."

"Chris' sake, Wull. Ye're scarin me. That canna be richt. An army needs thoosands. Thoosands willin tae pit their life on the line."

"The meenisters are showin the way," Wull argued. "That's a stairt. Luk at Maister Brotherstane. He's oot ther dain his best tae spread the word."

"Haud on a meenit," John shook his head. "That yin's raither different. We baith ken he's no exactly himsel these days. He wis a bit odd afore the loss o his pair wife. Noo his heid's turned wi aw kinds o nonsense."

"John. That's no fair."

"Ay it is. Ah hud tae deal wi him. Ye dinna ken the half o it. An whit aboot the men that murdered yon archbishop on the road tae Saint Andrews a few weeks back? Thur heids wur mair than turned. Whit richt thinkin folk shoot an auld man in front o his dochter then force her tae watch while they slice him up lik a piece o meat?"

"If ye mean Archbishop Sharpe, ay, it wis terrible. But mibbe he had it comin."

"Tae be murdered? Ye soond lik yer ain heid's been turned."

"Is that so?" Wull stiffened.

"Ay. Ye're no thinkin straicht. It's no as if Sharpe wis a naethin. He wis an important man, an pairt o the government. We wur lucky oor case wis by wi afore the news reached Lanark. Claverhoose wud hae seen it as a golden opportunity tae dae his worst. We'd still be locked up for they say the murderers are Presbyterian folk lik us. Except they're no lik us."

"Ay, weel. Mibbe they did gang a bit far."

"Naw!" John's voice rose. "Way ower far. An dinna imagine the king will dae nuthin wi fanatics lik that on the loose. He'll hae his government chasin aifter them tae mak sure somebody pays the penalty. Luk at the harm they'll bring on the rest o us. Ah'm tellin ye, whit happened tae us at Lanark is naethin compared wi whit's roond the corner. If the law disna catch up wi they murderers we'll aw suffer."

"Whit aboot aw the harm Sharpe did?" Wull insisted. "He wis supposed tae be a Christian leader. Love thy neebor didna come intae it when he ordered torture for ony that disagreed wi him an his fancy notions. Some o the stories ah heard dinna bear repeatin. He wis a murderer in his ain way, an got awa wi it time aifter time. Whitivver they men did they did it wi the best o intentions. Archbishop or no he had tae be stopped."

John gave up before they both said something they'd regret. "Ay weel, mibbe so. Noo, whit aboot this meetin at Loudon Hill? Ah tak it ye're meanin tae go?"

"Whit aboot yersel?"

"Ah'll think aboot it."

"No like ye." Wull finally smiled. "Ye're usually first in there an nivver mind whit happens next."

Since their arrest and appearance in court John and his friends had struggled to pay their fines. The law had tightened its grip and they felt obliged to obey the court order about church attendance. Sandy Gillon had a full congregation every week and hated having to face the rows of resentful faces. As for being a curate, he wished he'd never heard the word, and yet he too felt obliged to act out his part as expected. It was all about Meg and the bairn. They had to be protected against the wrath of the law. This meant Sandy had to convince the sheriff that he was a sincere man, trying to do his duty in difficult circumstances.

Despite John having been locked up, and then the crippling fine, Marion still hankered after the hill preaching. But each time she mentioned the meeting at Loudon Hill John would say, "No the noo lass." Tonight was her last chance to persuade him.

At supper she chose her words carefully. "If we dae go tae Loudon Hill we need tae be extra carefu." She made it sound as if they had discussed the matter.

John stopped eating and looked up.

"They say this Thomas Douglas is a guid preacher." She moved the food round her plate. "Faither's keen tae go. He says he's fed up listenin tae yon curate's drivel ivvery week."

John frowned. "Yer faither has a short memory. He didna dae vera weel in the Tolbooth, an whit aboot his fine? Does he want mair o that?"

"He says times are chaingin, an no for the better."

"He's richt ther. We're a lot worse aff aifter yon fine. An ah didna exactly enjoy bein shut up in yon stinkin cell for days on end."

"Ah ken, John. Naebody's mair sorry aboot it than masel. But it still disna seem richt tae jist gie up."

"Gie up whit?"

"Oor beliefs. Whit's wrang wi listenin tae the meenisters when they dare tae speak oot against whit's happenin?"

"Whit aboot breakin the law again?"

"Faither thinks - " She tailed off.

"My, oh my." John's tone softened. "Whit's tae be done when ma ain wife is set on followin her faither an declarin hersel a rebel?"

She reached across the table and squeezed his hand.

He sighed. "If it's that important tae ye."

"Can we go?" Young Johnnie had been eating his supper and listening intently to the adult conversation.

John glanced at the excited little face then back at Marion. He sighed again and poured himself a full beaker of ale from the jug on the table while Johnnie sat smiling and swinging his feet.

Next morning the family was washed and dressed, breakfast eaten, picnic packed in the big, straw basket, beasts seen to, even the hens fed before daylight stole over the fields. Johnnie could hardly eat his breakfast. William remained half asleep until he saw the trap being pulled into the yard. That woke him. He began dancing about in front of his father.

John lifted him into the trap. "C'mon. Oot the way or ah'll never git Juno harnessed."

Johnnie clambered in beside his brother while Marion laid the food basket between their feet then climbed into her own seat beside John. And then they were off, rattling down the track. John thought of the day ahead and hoped he wasn't making another mistake.

On the Strathaven road they met carts, traps, people on horseback, even groups walking out from the town. There was little doubt where they were going.

John frowned. "Ower mony folk for ma likin. Mibbe we shud turn back."

Marion squeezed his arm. "We canna turn roond noo." She waved as her brother Gavin and his wife Janet came up behind them. "Goin oor way?" she called as they drew level.

"Us an half the countryside," Janet replied.

"Whit aboot mither an faither?"

"Awa an hoor ago. Faither cudna wait."

"Aye the same." Marion smiled and looked round at the other faces. She saw no hint of anxiety only excitement and anticipation. All the same, something brought Lucas Brotherstone to mind, and what had happened to him. And here she was encouraging her own husband to go down the rebel road. It wasn't as if they hadn't suffered already.

And then there was that grand officer who'd come to the farm to take away their best beasts and bags of hard earned cash. He'd been a right dandy, with his fancy ways, and fancy manners, and fancy hat with its huge, waving, white feather. And yet he was the one who seemed to upset John more than anything else.

She also thought of Sandy Gillon preaching away each week, convincing nobody. She guessed he knew that himself and yet she liked him as well as feeling sorry for him. So much had happened in no time at all, and none of it seemed real any more. And she could sense danger lurking close by. That did worry her, although she still said nothing about turning back.

The procession of carts grew longer, all moving towards the looming shape of Loudon Hill. Common sense sang in John's ear warning about the need to go home. He thought about it, glanced at Marion's excited face, thought again, then clicked the horse into line behind the last cart.

John Graham of Claverhouse wiped the remains of his good breakfast from his whiskers, pushed back his chair, and shouted, "Blythe, Gordon, Crichton, Pate, ootside. Raise the prisoners. Hae the men mount up. We'll awa and see if we can bag a few mair inmates for the tollbooth."

His officers rose as one. To leave their meal unfinished was a scant price to pay for keeping their commander in a good humour.

While the platoon was organised Clavers leant against the inn door enjoying the morning sun. "A rare day for a chase," he observed to the innkeeper hovering close by.

The man nodded.

"Mibbe we'll manage a clearance o these religious dissenters afore long and return oor country tae its lawful state."

The man nodded again.

"Whit are ye cringing for?" Clavers eyed him up and down. "Ye did weel. Last nicht's mutton pie wis jist whit we needed, and plenty o it. Ay. Yer service wis mair than adequate. I'd be pleased tae call again. Ye'll be hoping for some payment nae doubt?"

The man didn't dare answer.

"By richt I'm aboot the King's business and entitled tae assistance and hospitality as required."

The innkeeper's face fell.

"But here ye are." Clavers drew out a small leather pouch. Several silver coins rattled on a table-top. "John Graham seeks nae favour and never ignores guid service." Turning on his heel he was away across the common green to join his men while the innkeeper scrabbled to lift his hard earned cash.

The trumpet sounded. The prisoners stumbled out. The troops moved forward, and the town breathed a sigh of relief when the horses trotted up the narrow main street, then wheeled right at the top, onto the Darvel road towards open countryside.

Progress was slow because of the prisoners and Clavers soon lost patience. "This'll no dae. It's worse than driving cattle." He pointed to a farm up ahead. "We'll leave this lot ower there wi a few men on guard while we press on."

A few moments later the farmer at High Drumclog had an unwelcome surprise when he was ordered to give up his barn as a temporary jail. Four dragoons were left guarding the building while the mounted troopers set off at a brisk pace towards the massive outcrop of volcanic rock known as Loudon Hill.

As they drew closer to this landmark Clavers shouted, "Sergeant. Tak twa men, skirt roond the hill. See if there's onything o interest on the ither side."

The scouts set off and returned in no time. "There's a crowd gaithered aboot twa miles yonder."

"Is there indeed? Hoo mony?"

"Three hunner. Mibbe mair. Men, women, an bairns. There's a long line o carts at the bottom of a slope ahint the hill. It's a big gaitherin. The biggest ah've seen," the sergeant admitted.

The commander looked thoughtful. "Rounding them up micht tak a while."

"No if they're deid," Lieutenant Crichton suggested.

Captain Blythe winced.

"Nae quarter, sir?" Crichton winked at the captain's horrified expression.

Blythe turned towards the commander. "Dinna forget we're

only a hundred and fifty strong, sir. Somewhit ootnumbered, if the scout's report is true." He paused then added, "I suggest caution wi women and children present."

Clavers laughed. "They're ripe for the picking."

"I still think we shud be careful."

"Look man," Clavers snapped. "We're here wi instructions tae bring this pairt o the country intae line. There's too mony roond here see fit tae ignore the law. This wee sortie cud be a guid chance tae teach these dissenters a lesson they'll no forget."

Blythe scowled at the smirking Crichton then turned again to his commander. "Whit aboot nae quarter, sir?"

"Did I say onything aboot that?" Clavers swung round in his saddle and faced the captain.

"I thocht I heard."

"Aw ye heard wis banter atween Crichton and mysel. Forget his prattling. Mind my orders. I'm here tae enforce the law and I tak my duty seriously. Sometimes it isna very pleasant but I never stray beyond the law nor its limitations. Discipline has aye been my watchword. There's nae need tae think itherwise." He nodded at Blythe then turned back to the sergeant. "Whaur are these law breakers?"

"Aff tae the richt, sir. Ahint the hill. We cud hear them singin."

"Singing." Claverhouse snorted. "We'll soon hae them singing a new tune."

On the slope beyond Loudon Hill, the preacher Thomas Douglas was about to begin his sermon before the assembled crowd. Opening his Bible he fingered the verse intended as his theme when a single musket shot rang out. Every eye turned in the direction of the sound. No one moved. As the echo died a lookout ran down from a ledge above and shouted, "Mounted troops comin this way."

Unlike the preacher at Auchlochan a few Sundays ago Thomas Douglas was defiant. He held his Bible to his chest and faced his congregation. "So far ye've heard yer preachers speak aboot the theory, the need for resistance, the reason why. Weel, my freends, noo's the time tae dae it. Wi God's help this day can be remembered and revered. But only if we remain resolute. Prepare tae resist."

Within minutes the congregation was transforming itself into an army of fifty horse and two hundred foot with a variety of firearms, swords, pitchforks, and stout sticks.

One of the Strathaven gentry assumed overall control and shouted for village groups to form up with a leader in charge of each group, ready for action. John Steel found himself pushed forward as captain of the Lesmahagow men. This was the last thing he wanted but there was no time to argue. Meanwhile the women grabbed the children and ran down beside the carts.

The mounted troopers drew their swords and galloped towards the crowd gathered on the slope. At the foot of the slope stretched a wide expanse of boggy ground. The mud looked so soft it seemed almost a liquid. The platoon juddered to a halt and a sergeant was ordered to ease forward and test the ground. After a few steps the front legs of his horse began to sink. He quickly pulled the beast back, turned and trotted back to the waiting line.

John Graham looked impatient. "So?"

The sergeant shook his head. "Nae use sir. We canna cross here. No if we want tae keep the beasts safe."

John Graham frowned and signalled for the platoon to take up a stance along the edge of firm ground facing what looked like a military format of at least two hundred foot, and a double flank of mounted men. This would be no hunt and harry encounter of helpless peasants.

"Numbers are no everything," Clavers muttered. "The men are weel trained and experienced. It shudna be that difficult."

"Ay sir," Blythe replied but looked as if he doubted it.

"While I'm deciding oor next move ride doon tae the edge o the soft ground and tell that rabble tae lay doon their arms in the King's name. Say that the women and bairns can go free."

Blythe and the sergeant rode to the edge of the bog then the captain called across to the men opposite.

Three men stepped forward from the massed ranks on the other side. One dressed all in black shouted, "We're aboot tae spend time listening tae the Lord's word. Wud ye care tae mak passage across and join us? If ye come in peace ye'll be richt welcome."

"We're here tae uphold the law. Naething else. Whit ye're

daeing here is treason against His Majesty. Surrender in the King's name or it'll go ill against everyone gaithered here." Blythe went on, spelling out the commander's terms.

The black figure held up a defiant arm to the sky and cried out, "We surrender only tae the Lord's will."

Blythe stared at the man. "Is that yer answer?"

"Nae ither. Tell that tae yer maister and see whit he says."

Blythe groaned and rode back to repeat the message.

"The Lord's will." Clavers laughed then looked at Crichton. "These peasants seem tae agree wi ye aboot nae quarter."

Blythe groaned again.

Clavers studied the line opposite and picked out John Steel's figure astride a fine black horse which rightly should have been handed over as part of his fine. He was obviously one of the leaders. Clavers didn't like the thought of such a capable man against him. Still, he was part of a rabble. Nothing to worry about.

John looked at the rows of soldiers then back towards Marion with both boys held tight. He raised an arm. She returned his greeting. The boys waved too. When he looked again there was the commander astride a fine black horse. "Nae as guid as ye lass." He patted Juno's neck. "Jist as weel ah hid ye or yon fine gentleman wud be sittin on yer back richt noo. Luk at him, dressed lik a peacock an attractin even mair attention wi that fancy, feathered hat. If ah hadna seen whit he's capable o ah'd be thinkin him nowt but a dandy."

Thomas Douglas began to sing the psalm:

> *In Judah's land God is well known.*
> *His name in Israel Great.*

Voice after voice joined in, each one adding force to each word. John felt the swell of this sound rise in the clear air and shivered with excitement at their conviction.

On the other side of the swamp the words circled the soldiers' heads, as if reminding them whose side God was likely to be on. The horses began to wrestle and fidget and agitate the troopers.

Clavers could see the effect this was having and roared, "Fire!"

A few harmless shots whistled across the wet space, hitting nothing. The seventy sixth psalm continued to swell in volume.

Clavers turned to the soldiers on his left. "Enough o this nonsense. We need tae get across. Start picking yer way ower."

The front line clicked their horses forward. The first few steps were fine but once in the soft moss they began to flounder on the moving surface. Pulling hard on the reins made matters worse. The horses took fright, lunging and jumping, trying desperately to kick themselves free of the mud sucking round their legs, and pulling them down. The more they kicked the more the beasts sank into the cloying softness. Terror took over. The riders lost control, their only thought now to save themselves, to find a way back to firm ground.

The rebels ran out from their ranks then jumped from one grassy tussock to another till close enough to fire their pistols at close range. This done they simply jumped back the way they'd come, leaving several troopers dead or dying while their horses thrashed and floundered in the boggy space.

The troopers lined up on firm ground gaped at these hill folk. It seemed as if they did have God's protection. How else could they find a foothold where none seemed to exist? Those expected to take the next step forward looked at each other. The same message flew between them.

Clavers saw their expressions and roared, "Halt!"

Marion's father, watching all this, could hold back no longer. He spurred his horse and swung sideways to avoid John's attempt to stop him. Once clear of the front line he slowed his horse and allowed it to pick its own way through the boggy morass. Eyes on both sides watched the old man and his beast edge forward with no stumble or slip in the soft mud. The whole thing seemed uncanny. Time seemed to stop as Tom Weir passed the half sunk bodies of men and horses.

He'd almost crossed the boggy space when the spell broke. A trooper dropped to his knees and took careful aim. His musket rang out. The shot hit Tom's horse in the centre of its chest. Both front knees buckled. Stunned by the impact the horse's big, brown head dropped forward. The mouth opened in a long scream, the heavy body arching back with all four legs flailing and churning up the mud as Tom pulled on the reins, trying to hold the animal steady. But the pain spreading from the bullet, and the pull of liquid earth sucking at each leg was too much.

Tom hung on as the wounded horse found enough strength to lurch clear of the moving surface. The front hooves flailed. Mud flew around the beast as it managed to reach a circle of thick rushes. Perched on this tiny island the terrified animal wobbled as the rushes moved under its weight, then seeing firm ground only a few feet away the beast leapt the remaining space into a line of waiting swords.

Sharp revenge rose, cutting through the air and descending on man and horse. Pistols fired. Swords jabbed forward, were pulled out then plunged in again.

The sight of Tom Weir being hacked to pieces galvanised the dissenters. When their leader raised his arm no-one hesitated. Shoulder to shoulder farmers, labourers, shopkeepers, tradesmen and lairds stepped forward as if they knew exactly what was expected of them. Not a word was spoken, their determination louder than any threatening roar. Before them the mounted enemy sat transfixed as if accepting inevitable retribution was upon them. Unable to fire a single shot, the soldiers stared as so many men walked across the boggy ground as if by magic.

Once on firm ground all this was forgotten when the rebels charged. There was a ragged volley of musket fire, then another. Noise and sulphur-smelling smoke blinded friend and foe as the surge forward became relentless. This the troopers understood and thought of escape.

Clavers saw his men twist their horses' heads. Again he roared, "Halt!"

None heard or obeyed.

Two further shots rang out from the rebel line. The cautious Blythe and Clavers' young trumpeter fell dead at his side. Experienced in battle, and no coward, Clavers knew who the shots were meant for, and accepted the truth of the situation. It was time to withdraw.

He reached down for the platoon's flag now covering the young boy. Whatever else this commander might do he'd no intention of leaving the colours behind. He rolled it up and held it in one hand. With the other he grabbed the reins of Blythe's good horse and made off with it galloping alongside his own charger. Mistakes could be rectified later. But only if he was alive.

Any soldiers who had the chance to escape took it, but many died where they stood as the rebels swept forward.

A farmer in the advancing rebel line saw the commander leave and galloped after him. With a longer stride his heavier farm animal almost reached Clavers' horse. It came close enough for the farmer to lunge forward and send his long sword into the heaving flanks. If he thought this would bring down the beast he was disappointed. The frenzy of pain had it galloping faster even though blood was streaming from the gaping wound. The horse kept going for a further mile before dropping dead, almost disemboweled.

Clavers leapt across to the riderless horse he held alongside to continue his flight without interruption or pursuit.

There were few in Strathaven who guessed that the figure high tailing through the town was the same commander who'd swept out so proudly that morning. At Hamilton he halted long enough to change horses then pressed on to reach Glasgow and the safety of the city gates closing behind him before nightfall.

Claverhouse was forced to endure a difficult evening with Lord Ross who welcomed him in his official role as Glasgow's current guardian. His host frowned when he heard the news. "No been a guid day for ye Clavers. I dare say yer superior officer will be less than happy tae hear aboot this."

"Unexpected and unfortunate."

"Indeed it is." Lord Ross nodded. "And aw the mair so when that parteeclar officer happens tae be the Earl o Linlithgow."

"Whit's that got tae dae wi onything?"

"Weel, I hear he's no overly fond o yersel. Finds ye a bit o a handful; the way ye're inclined tae speak yer mind."

"Whit's wrang wi telling it lik it is?"

"Naething at aw." Lord Ross nodded again. "I'm a great believer in straicht talking masel. Mind ye, gie Linlithgow his due, he does admire yer ability as a soldier. He's mentioned ye mair than aince at council meetings. And it's no as if yer attempts tae preserve law and order in the south goes unnoticed."

Clavers blinked but said nothing.

"But jist mind the guid earl has also seen the king whispering in yer ear." Lord Ross sniffed as he imparted this information. "A guid few private conversations by aw accounts. Jist yersel and his majesty, yer heids thegither lik the best o freends. Ah've nae doubt ye gied the royal ear yer conseedered opinion wi the best o intention. And ah've nae doubt his majesty appreciated whitivver ye said. Aw the same, there's some micht interpret it anither way, and become jealous aboot yer new closeness tae the royal personage. Quite the favourite it seems. Linlithgow's words, no mine."

"The earl's got it aw wrang." Clavers stiffened. "I merely dae my duty for my sovereign. If he wants tae speak privately whit else can I dae?"

"Ay weel, them aroond oor monarch are talking aboot ye as a rising star. If I wis ye I'd tak care. Yon earl is a powerful man. He micht see this wee incident as his chance tae criticise ye and dent yer shine a tad."

"A report is a report. I hae naething tae hide."

"Jist so." Lord Ross smiled. A row of sharp teeth appeared. His voice dropped to a whisper. "Mind ye, that report needs tae be weel conseedered, ivvery word written wi the utmost care, while keeping within the spirit o truth, if ye ken whit I mean." Lord Ross was relentless. "Noo hoo aboot a bit supper and a sit by the fire? Jist the twa o us? It's wonderful whit can be discussed ower a guid meal. We micht even discover we've mair in common than we thocht."

"If it's nae trouble." Clavers only just kept his temper. Ahead of him lay more discomfort. His meal would be accompanied with more baiting and unwelcome advice.

Late that night the commander wrote his report. And he took note of his Lordship by hinting that some stories of the encounter might appear a trifle exaggerated, although he did venture his opinion that this event might signify the start of wider rebellion.

After a flourishing signature he re-read every word. He paused, read again, then laid down his quill to stare into the guttering candle. Pictures of the day's events came and went, some clearer than others. Maybe he should have paid attention to poor Blythe. He'd been an exemplary, sensible officer, well able to assess situations and how they might unravel. Clavers had listened to him before and been glad of it. Why not this time?

As for that damned bog. Without it the rebels would have been easy meat. Or would they? He dusted his words, and read them a third time before folding the thick paper. He stared at it a moment, then held a candle flame over a stick of wax and allowed it to drip along the join and seal the report. Just to be sure he pushed the raised pattern of his signet ring into the soft surface. There on the waxed impression was his badge, the laurel, the tree of victory. He'd just had his first real fight in Scotland, and unlike his earlier successes in France and Holland, it had turned out an utter defeat. No doubt this would suit Linlithgow. No matter. It had to be admitted, the consequences faced. He rolled up the parchment, stuck it in a canvas bag then called down the stairs for a dispatch rider.

Ahead of Clavers lay a restless night, full of recrimination. But there would be no outward hint of his real feelings, not in the current political climate.

Chapter 12

The echoes of battle had faded away leaving the gentle sigh of a summer breeze across the hillside. Bird song and pastoral sounds were everywhere along with a faint but growing hum of large flies sensing a feast nearby.

Five men were missing from John's new-formed contingent. Now he must search for them across what should have been a fresh, green field instead of an abused space for the dead, the dying, the struggling, and the victorious. Debate or argument had little meaning here with man heaped on man and beast, friend and foe in deadly embrace. The sight and smell would linger long and be difficult to forget.

Within minutes he spotted three of his men, injured but sitting upright, being tended by their families. After a quick word he walked on, forcing himself to turn over any body in his path. On the edge of the bog he found the fourth man, a hole larger than a man's fist in his forehead, mouth gaping with his last defiant shout, eyes still staring in surprise or wonder. Had he known it was more than the enemy he was rushing to meet? John knelt beside the contorted figure to gently close those awful eyes. Further over he found the last one, the village blacksmith, frozen in agony from sword and shot. Again he knelt and closed the accusing eyes then turned to go back, to make his report, and discover the price paid as others came forward with their casualty lists.

A few hours ago he'd persuaded himself to keep going, telling himself it would be fine. Now he felt an idiot. He should have turned his cart when he had the chance instead of joining that line of other carts. Heart over head had taken him to Loudon Hill.

On the other side of the field Gavin and Janet Weir wandered among the strewn bodies searching the area where they'd seen Gavin's father fall among a forest of flashing swords. When they did come upon him they found two cavalry men heaped across his chest like ghastly sentries. Had they enjoyed their revenge? The satisfaction must have been brief. Even as they cut and maimed and killed, the power of hate had been about to retaliate as another hand came forward to claim them in the same cruel way.

The young man and woman managed to pull the soldiers clear but the sight of the old man's bloody corpse was too much. His remains were hacked, full of shot, clothes and body in tatters, blood still seeping from deep head wounds. Ashamed of her reaction Janet covered her face and tried to hide her tears. Already she was trying not to breathe in the rising stench. Several minutes passed before she had enough control to be her practical self again and unfasten her long, blue cloak. "Richt Gavin." She held it out.

He nodded and knelt to drape the cloak over his father's body. There was enough cloth to tuck under. This allowed them to roll the body out of sight in the dark folds of cloth without touching it, or giving in to the constant urge to turn away and retch.

As they stood up Gavin caught a glimpse of John in the distance. He shouted and waved. John saw them and hurried towards them.

"It's faither," Gavin explained when he saw John stare at the tight rolled bundle on the ground.

John nodded. "Ah'll gie ye a haund tae cairry him back."

Together they lifted the awkward bundle and carried it across the field and down to the waiting cart.

Marion and the two boys were there, faces chalk white, eyes full of all they'd seen and heard. She pointed to the bundle being lifted over the tail-board of the cart. "Johnnie, William. Tak a guid luk. Aw that's left of yer Grandpa is in that cloak. He died believin he wis daein richt. In truth he wis nae mair than a bairn, imaginin he could tak on the world. Ithers here will respect him, name him as a martyr, a hero in battle. Respect." Her words came in great gulps. "It wis his ain impatience taen ower. An luk whit happened."

Gavin and Janet stared at each other.

Some of the women nearby tut-tutted and looked away.

John put his arms round Marion. "Yer faither wud ken whit ye meant. Like enough he'd agree wi ye." As he spoke he thought of his own father and how he'd seen nothing of him since the first charge began. Turning round he asked Gavin, "Hae ye seen ma faither?"

Gavin shook his head but Janet pointed towards a group gathered around the preacher. "Ah heard yer faither say he wis worried aboot his brither. He went ower there tae ask aboot him."

"On ye go," Marion urged, "we can wait."

Hurrying towards the noisy group John saw a strange mixture of the well-dressed, the rough, and the raggedy, in wild discussion around a red-faced young man who was shaking his head and waving his arms in frustration. John drew closer and heard the young man say, "Ah nearly hud him."

"Ye did weel," many voices reassured him.

"Ah'd haud o the bridle but he jerked awa. Ah'll hae him yet though," the young man insisted.

"Ay," they all agreed. "Ye'll git anither chance."

"Whit's this aboot?" John asked the nearest man,

"He nearly captured Claverhoose. He's William, the youngest Clelland frae the mill at Burnfoot. He's desperate tae prove himsel for the cause."

"Much guid it'll dae him." John shook his head and turned away to continue looking for his father. As he did he almost bumped into a group carrying a badly wounded man. One of the carriers was Wull Gemmell. He stood aside and watched them lay the man on the grass.

Wull looked up and smiled at John. "Guid tae see ye."

"An ye." John returned the smile.

"Some day, eh?"

"No a guid yin for him." John pointed at the gasping figure.

"No hoo he sees it." Wull said. "Keeps repeatin he's assured o glory in heaven. Name's William Dingwall. Ane o the nine."

"Nine whit?"

"The yins that did awa wi Archbishop Sharpe. Dingwall claims he gied the last sword thrust."

"So." John's voice hardened. "He admits feenishin aff a defenceless auld man, an then expects gratitude an glory in the aifter life. Chris' sake, he's worse than a common murderer."

"He fought weel the day. Noo he's dyin. Can ye no hae some thocht for him?"

"May he rest in peace," John retorted. "Aifter whit he's done, ah doubt it." With that he walked away leaving Wull staring after him.

Eventually he found his father kneeling beside his fallen brother. He gently touched the bowed shoulder. "Ah'm sorry. Ah didna ken uncle Tom wis missin."

"Hardly surprisin in aw this confusion." Robert Steel looked up with tears in his eyes. "Whit a misery we've brocht on oorsels."

"There's some think it worthwhile."

"That kinda thinkin is beyond me," the older man admitted as he took off his heavy jacket to lay it across his brother's body.

Just then John's cousin Davie ran towards them. "Is that faither? Let me see."

Robert Steel pulled back a corner of the thick cloth to expose the still, white face.

Davie knelt beside the body. To both men's surprise he began to pray, "Mighty Lord yer servant kent weel whit he wis daein, mair than willin tae gie his life for this just cause. It's us here need yer assistance, lest we be found wantin."

John could have smacked the words out of him and ground them into the dirt but a look from his father warned him to leave alone. Neither said a word as the young man prattled on. Neither tried to stop his flood of words as they carried Tom Steel's body back to join the one already waiting in the cart.

"Ye've paid dearly," someone said as they passed.

"Ay," Davie replied in a brittle voice. "But oor pain is worth it for the enemy's defeat."

John shook his head and they struggled on with their heavy load.

Davie was still muttering while they loaded the cart. John tried to ignore him and busied himself by lifting a folded tarpaulin from the front to cover both bodies with the heavy cloth.

A crowd had gathered round the preacher Thomas Douglas.

Now he made the most of it. "Ye'll mind my words tae trust in the Lord and staund firm against oor enemy. It wis mair than justified. Look hoo he came tae oor aid in this time o need and gied us oor victory. From this day king and government will need tae tak note and realise that Scotland is set against their evil ways."

There was a roar of approval.

The minister nodded. "As for oor fallen brithers we must haud their memory close tae oor hearts and nivver forget their selfless gift tae oor cause. But we canna stop aifter sic an effort and sacrifice. We must move furrit tae gaither mair support, mair strength. We need tae send oot tae freends far and wide. Tell them aboot oor success. Invite them tae join us. And we need tae dae it afore the enemy guesses whit's happenin. Aince oor number swells tae a real army we can speak wi authority and bring aboot the chainge we aw want."

Robert Hamilton, the son of a local landowner, stepped forward. He'd acted as overall leader and saw his chance to seize the moment and move the cause forward. "Tak heed o the Reverend. If we dae as he says we cud hae thoosands supportin us in nae time. So up an awa. Spread the word. Gaither in oor brithers in arms. Oor victory here shud persuade them tae rise agin the government. Wi a proper army we can heid for Glesca an mak the city faithers listen tae oor demands. Oor time is come gentlemen. The country will agree wi us. Mak guid use o it."

Again the roar went up. Blue bonnets flew in the air.

"Whit d'ye think?" John's father asked as they stood by the cart listening to all this excitement.

John shrugged. "We'll hae tae feenish whit's been stairted here. Claverhoose ran awa this time but yon man's nae coward. As far as ah cud see he'd nae choice. But rest assured he'll be hell bent on revenge, as weel as repairin the dent in his reputation. Aince he reports tae his superiors he'll hae nae difficulty gainin permission for whitever reprisal he wants. Jist think o the back up he has compared tae us. In nae time a professional army will be on oor tail wi ivvery intention o dain awa wi us. As for this lot an thur victory chant," he said bitterly, "they've nae idea."

"Yer heid's rulin yer heart this time," the older man said.

"Maks a chainge," John admitted. "Whit aboot the ithers in the family?"

"Yer brother William is likely tae join, an yer cousin Davie is there aready. Ye saw hoo he reacted ower losin his faither. If push comes tae shove ah micht feel obliged tae think aboot it masel."

"No ye'll no." John glared at his father. "Marion's faither and yer ain brither are lost. If Davie, William, Gavin, and mibbe masel respond tae the muster whae's tae luk aifter the farms?"

"Ye mean ah'll be left tae milk the coos an feed the hens?"

"Ay. An bide safe. No lik us younger eedjits."

His father sighed and let it go for the moment.

The return journey from Loudon Hill was in stark contrast to the high spirits of the morning. The new widow Rachael Weir rode in the big cart with Gavin and Janet. John, Marion and the two boys followed in the trap, their eyes forever straying to the load in the back of the cart. Behind them came Davie and Robert Steel on horseback.

It was dark by the time Waterside farm was reached and the silent convoy followed the cart as it rumbled into the cobbled yard. Gavin pulled on the reins, stopped the cart, and glanced uncertainly at his mother. Neither moved. Neither spoke. The only sound was their own breathing and the snorting of warm horses.

Rachael Weir stared at the dark outline of the farm buildings then spoke into the stillness. "Gavin. See tae yer faither. Fetch him doon and git help tae cairry him intae the guid room."

Silent helpers obeyed and minutes later Tom Weir's body was laid on the big table which was usually the centre of family celebrations.

Rachael now issued further instructions. "Ah need plenty hot water, an bring the best linen sheets frae the big kist. An ah want a wheen o they sweet smellin herbs ah hae hangin ahint the door in the wee pantry." She looked at Marion. "Ye ken whit ah need. Bring it aw here. Aifter that," she added firmly, "ye can leave me alane. Ah need tae dae this by masel." Her expression and tone brooked no argument and once everything was in place she ushered everyone from the room then closed the door against any interruption.

Rachael stood still to prepare herself. It would be far from easy to cleanse her husband's body and make it ready for burial. And so it was. The first sight of what lay within the cloak shroud was worse than she imagined. "My, my Tom, ye're an awfu sicht. Ye'll need some sortin." For a moment she wondered if she could do it. She also knew she didn't want anyone else to touch him.

Lifting her best scissors she forced herself to begin the task by slowly cutting away what was left of her husband's clothes and dropping them on a square tablecloth she'd laid in readiness on the floor. That done, she tied up the corners of the cloth and carried the bloody bundle out to the dark hall, to be dealt with later.

Returning to the bare body she stared at the mess of mud and grass mixed with congealed and dried blood. "Ye'd be horrified if ye cud see yersel," she whispered, "but ah'll dae ma best." Dipping a piece of softest muslin in a bowl of warm water she trailed it across the surface to catch up some of the crushed rosemary and golden rod leaves floating there, and with the lightest touch she began wiping and dipping, then wiping again, methodically removing every trace of the dried on mess. Gradually open cuts and long slashes and purple weals began to appear against the clean skin. Next she opened the ointment jar Marion had selected. She sniffed the mixture of lady's mantle and burnet embedded in bees wax then smeared her hands with the oily mixture. Back and forward, slowly, gently massaging the broken body and arms and legs she took care to leave extra traces of the oily mixture to fill each gaping wound. For good measure she undid a bunch of dried wintergreen leaves and placed the sprigs directly on the ointment, allowing them to stick and form an extra healing layer. Not that they'd do much this time but in her mind she was doing what she could. Tom might be dead but he deserved her love and her best care.

Now she began tearing long strips from her best linen sheet to wrap and hide her work. It was difficult to do, but she wanted no help as she lifted and rolled, lifted and rolled.

This done she turned away from the body and stepped over to the big sideboard to pull out the middle drawer then lay it on the floor. Reaching to the back of the empty space she found a tiny velvet bag. She lifted it out and undid the strings to remove two silver merks, clean, shiny, and unused. Closing the bag, and returning it to her hidey-hole, she slid the drawer back into place then took the coins over to her half shrouded husband. "Ye didna ken ah hud these," she whispered and delicately laid one coin over each shut eye. "An ah never thocht ah'd use them for this. But here ye are Tom. An may they speed ye on yer journey." With that she bound a linen strip round his head to keep the coins in place. Finally she placed sprigs of sweet smelling lavender and rosemary on another thicker sheet before rolling her husband out of sight for the last time.

Her work done she pulled a chair alongside the shrouded body and sat there staring at the shape, imagining his face as it should be, remembering what they'd shared. "Ye were some man Tom. An nae the easiest. Mony a time ah cud hae seen ye far enough." Tears welled up. "Mind hoo ah said yer impatience wud be the death o ye? Ah nivver guessed ah'd be richt. But ah loved ye onyway. Ye kent that. Ah still dae, an ah'll miss ye." Her fingers traced his name across the shroud. "Sleep weel an be at rest."

She stood up and walked towards the door, then without another glance she clicked the latch and slipped into the dark hall.

John rode on to the village to find out about funeral arrangements while his father and Davie delivered Thomas Steel to his home at Skellyhill farm. There another new widow would begin the same respectful cleansing and preparing as Rachael Weir had just done.

Well after midnight Juno's hooves rang on the close cobbles. Marion opened the door into the yard and swung the lantern against the darkness while she waited for John to bed down his beloved horse.

When he came indoors and sat down for supper he was too tired and dejected to think about food. He just stared at his plate. "If only ah'd kent an bid awa frae Loudon Hill."

"But ye didna. An supposin ye hud turned roond it wudna hae stopped onythin.It wud still hae happened," Marion cut in before he said any more. "Onyway, it wis me that wanted tae go. Ye only went tae please me an ma selfish notions." She stared into the shadows of the kitchen, dark like the depths of her growing uncertainty. How quickly everything had changed. "Ah'm scared John," she admitted, "scared for ye, the bairns, masel."

He stood up and pulled her close. "So am ah." He lifted her face, kissed her so lightly their lips barely touched.

The moment hung sweetly between them. Her eyes shone with pleasure as they shared this understanding. Their gaze held. It warmed and grew into the familiar longing. He kissed her again, hungrily this time, then pulse quickening he scooped her up and felt her snuggle against his chest. No one else had such power over him.

Exhausted as he was he managed to lift her and hold her tight while he stumbled through the hall to their room.

Dropping down on the bed together, arms already intertwined, his only thought was to lose himself completely, to disappear within this longing. Nothing else mattered. His need was in this precious moment, to be it, hold it, and somehow stay beyond the horror of today, or even the possibility of what might follow come morning.

Chapter 13

The next afternoon most of Lesmahagow crowded into the kirkyard for the burial of the four villagers whose dramatic death had elevated them to the role of heroes. A quiet crowd packed round the freshly dug trenches while people at the back stood on flat gravestones to gain a better view. The houses that bordered the yard wall on two sides had every window open with several faces cramming each space.

There had been much talk about the victory. It had grown from the skirmish at Loudon Hill to the Battle of Drumclog. The 1st of June had become a date to remember. Special pleasure had been felt at Claverhouse's disgrace, especially after the heavy fines he'd forced on so many villagers.

There was no shortage of would be recruits for the next stage. Already the list had more than fifty names, mostly horse owners. It looked as if a cavalry contingent would represent the village. Come Wednesday there would be the grand sight of men and horses trotting down the main street behind a blue banner being put together by the charge hands in Miss Ferguson's dress shop.

John had been elected captain. His head and heart had warned him to say no, but he knew he was expected to nod and accept the honour, and keep his doubts to himself. This didn't stop them growing when he thought about Loudon Hill. How quickly so many men had gone from praying to killing. He was no better himself. He'd proved it by going there against his better judgement. He also knew everything would have been different if the skirmish hadn't gone so well.

Sandy Gillon had offered to conduct the funeral service and was much put out by the curt dismissal.

"Nae need," stated the erstwhile members of the kirk session.

"Whit aboot a prayer for their salvation?"

"Their salvation is assured," had been the confident reply.

"But surely an official body wud bring mair dignity tae the occasion?"

174

"A meenister o our ain choosin will provide aw the dignity we need."

So that was that. Sandy was forced to withdraw and worry in case the sheriff got to hear about this latest event in Lesmahagow kirkyard.

Thomas Douglas appeared on the edge of the crowd. John guessed his purpose and groaned. There would be no quiet reflection on lives lost, no personal touch for a grieving family. His uncle and father-in-law, and two other villagers were about to be laid to rest, but these dead men had yet another part to play, to show all these mourners and watchers that the cause was just, to be furthered at all costs. And who better to point this out than the very man who'd triggered everything off at Loudon Hill when he called out, "Prepare tae resist." Thomas Douglas was a man to be listened to. No doubt he intended to make full use of this opportunity.

Two members of the kirk session appeared at his side and ushered him through the crowd, helping him step alongside four wooden coffins perched on the edge of the freshly dug trenches. There were gasps of surprise as the crowd realised who was here. Douglas seemed pleased by this reaction, nodding acknowledgement then holding up his hand to signify the start of the service. "Brethren. This is a sad occasion. But we can tak pride in four fine men. They gave their lives for the truth and we must never forget it. To signify this we'll begin by singing the twenty third psalm as a timely reminder of the Lord's support for us aw."

His voice rang out and everyone joined in. The high stone boundary walls caught every nuance, held every sound then allowed it to bounce free and increase in volume before soaring up in the air to carry the pent up emotion over the roof tops and along the lanes to the fields and moor beyond. The familiar words said it all. A mood of acceptance was set by the long prayer as Douglas wrung out a supplication which left few unmoved, especially when he elevated the terrible deaths to a glorious sacrifice. And then came mention of the future, emphasising its dependence on those brave men. "Aifter this we darena be found wanting in oor duty," he warned. "We canna alloo oor heroes tae die in vain."

The coffins were gently lowered, the trenches filled, and rolls of turf unrolled again. One more prayer before it was over. Respect complete. Now it was time to walk away and discover if Douglas's speech had served its purpose to secure more recruits for the cause.

"I'll cairry on whit ma faither began," Davie Steel announced in a flat voice as he shook hands with the minister at the end of the ceremony.

"Yer faither wud be proud." Thomas Douglas squeezed Davie's hand to show his approval. "Fight the guid fight lad." With that he turned to the kirk session members who were still by his side. "I'll awa tae Stonehoose for anither burial, and then doon tae Larkhall. I must seize the moment and warm up as mony brave hearts as I can."

Bursting with pride the kirk session nodded agreement and accompanied him to his waiting horse, then saw him off on his next recruiting mission.

Davie Steel stood by the newly completed graves. His face was flushed, his eyes glinting as if grief was the last thing on his mind.

John could hold back no longer. "Ah heard ye wi the meenister," he whispered. "Watch oot Davie. Ye're nae yersel."

"Whit maks ye think that?"

"My een see braw plain."

Davie rounded on him. "Tell me then. Whit dae they see?"

"Ye're cairried awa. Yer heid's fu o fancifu notions. Somethin's tellin ye ower mony wrang things, an nae jist aboot yer faither."

"Faither wis pairt o oor defiance. Ah'm prood o that. Say whit ye like it'll no pit me aff."

"Ah'm no tryin tae pit ye aff. Ah'm jist warnin ye no tae git cairried awa."

"Is that richt?" Davie almost spat out the words.

"Ay." John nodded. "Look at me. Ah wis cairried awa and led ma freends on an escapade that landed us aw in the tolbooth, wi a trial in front o Claverhoose an some fancy lord. Ah ken fine thur's a bigger picture but whit aboot us endin up wi a fine that's near crippled us? Ye need tae think aboot that. Whit aboot yer pair mither? Hoo does she feel aboot this honour that's bein shouted aboot? Hae ye even bothered tae ask her?"

Davie's strained face grew whiter. He shuffled his feet. "My heid's burstin wi aw this."

"Nae wunner," John agreed. "Whit's happened canna sit easy. Back at Loudon Hill ah saw an did things ah'd raither forget. An ah didna lose ma faither."

Davie slowly nodded as if John's words were beginning to make sense.

"Never mind whit's expected," John said gently. "Gang doon that road and ye'll end up hurtin even mair. Be true tae yersel Davie. Yer faither wudna want onythin else."

They shook hands then John said, "Ready?"

"Ay." Davie's voice sounded almost normal.

They left the kirkyard together and began walking towards the village square. The tension was gone till Davie caught sight of the new recruits waiting for John to arrive. John touched his arm. "Gang hame an see tae yer mither. She needs ye mair than this."

"Whit will the ithers think if ah walk awa?"

"Chris' sake. Ye've jist buried yer faither. Ah can add yer name tae the volunteer list, if that's whit ye want?"

Davie nodded and turned away.

John watched him walk the full length of the cobbled street and head towards the open road before turning his attention to the waiting crowd.

A few seconds later he slipped into his role as captain and the tight group of men parted to allow him access to the wide steps outside the village inn. He jumped on the top step and waited till their talking fell away. It was time to say his piece. "Guid day freends." He nodded to the rows of faces. "Thank ye for the respect ye've jist paid." He paused a moment. "An ah'm sure ye aw ken that we staund at an important moment in oor village history."

"Ay. Whit next?" an anxious voice called out.

Every back tensed and straightened.

"It seems that the next step is tae be open resistance against the government. Willin men are needed for this. If ye want tae be pairt o it assemble here in the square at eight sharp come Wednesday mornin. As mony mounted as possible, though ithers are maist welcome. We leave here tae muster wi groups in ither villages an touns. Word has gone far an wide. Thur shud be nae shortage o folk willin tae join, an the mair men we hae the mair chance we hae o success. The meenister, Thomas Douglas, tellt the Kirk session he's had word that an important lord has decided tae declare his sympathy for the cause, tak command, an lead us furrit."

"Whit aboot young Robert Hamilton?" someone shouted. "He did weel at Drumclog."

"He's happy tae serve under a new leader," John replied.

"Whit happens when we meet up wi this new leader? Whit will he want us tae dae? Will we be marchin on the capital?"

"The first intention is tae march tae Glesca an tak on the city faithers. But it'll depend on oor numbers on horse an foot, an hoo weel wur armed. If things gang richt the capital micht be next. So bring whit arms ye hae, an dinna forget food tae keep ye goin. Ah doubt if we'll be provided wi muckle tae eat." John looked round the faces, most of them eager for adventure. Fools, he wanted to say. If only he could explain how he'd swayed one way then another. Would they listen? Probably not. "Think aboot it," he warned. "Only come if ye're sure. We've jist left four guid men in oor kirkyard. Thur's a guid few ithers being buried in ither villages this day. We werena the only anes tae lose men at Loudon Hill. Awa hame. See tae yer families. If ye're still o a mind we muster on Wednesday at eight."

There was a loud clap of approval then each man turned to his neighbour and began discussing and arguing over the merits of what might or might not happen. Their new captain was forgotten. This suited him. He'd no desire to join in any of it. He wanted to find his family and go home to the sanity of his own routine.

He slipped through the chattering and was soon beyond the square and into a deserted vennel. The sudden calm and quiet was an unsettling contrast to his morning so far, and walking on past the tight row of dark, little houses he thought about Wednesday looming closer. He'd said yes to being part of all this. Now he wondered when he'd be back. Or would he be back? Did he even want to go at all?

The thought of standing against government power and the ranks of battle experienced soldiers was terrifying. This was an ordinary village, with ordinary people, leading ordinary lives just like John. His life so far had followed a predictable path, straight forward and regulated, devoted to work. He hadn't minded that. In truth he knew nothing else. But after the past few weeks how could he ever think the same way? It was little wonder that reason was struggling to make itself heard in his head.

It took some time to find Marion and the children. He couldn't remember where they'd gone after the funeral. Two wrong calls, two apologies, two conversations about Wednesday before he arrived at the right house. When he finally pushed his way into the crowded room Marion took one look at his face and mouthed, "Ah'm comin." She lifted her shawl and whispered to Johnnie and William, "C'mon, Pa's waitin. It's time we wur awa hame." She took a firm hand of both boys and hurried outside to follow John back to the main street where he'd left the horse and trap.

John busied himself adjusting the reins. As he finished his task he became aware of the quiet figure waiting beside him. She appeared calm, but the pale face spoke of her strain and grief. She and her father had been as one. Now he was gone and in the worst of circumstances. Helpless to do anything she'd been forced to watch. Ashamed of his own pre-occupation John longed to throw his arms round her, shut everything out. But not here. He turned quickly and lifted the boys into the trap. They swung through the air and both threw their arms around him. He felt their trust and doubted if any cause was precious enough to put all this at risk.

Marion touched his arm, and when he helped her into her seat she squeezed his fingers.

Before eight o'clock on Wednesday morning, the fourth of June, Lesmahagow main street was thronged four deep for its full length. The village square was packed with spectators, horses and horsemen in preparation for the off. Animals fidgeted in the tight squeeze while their riders tried not to look as uncomfortable as they felt in their best clothes. Weapons were cleaned and polished, and much in evidence, as everyone tried to play their part in the spectacle.

Marion had decided she couldn't face the crowd. Any farewells that mattered had been said during that last tearful night which had seemed all too short. Now in the village square John sat astride Juno still seeing Marion's anxious face, her brown eyes watching as he saddled his horse, her unspoken words ringing in his ears.

He'd been up and away before six that morning. The Lesmahagow contingent would leave for war when the church clock struck eight and he needed plenty of time to check that everyone and everything was in place and ready for the off.

The dew had been glistening on the grass, the stones on the farm track still wet and black, waiting for the sun's warmth to turn them grey. And the moor, his moor, had been hidden in the mist, no last view, only a hazy curtain.

His two little sons, eyes solemn and round, had stood stock still while he took the last turn in the farm track and made that last wave. Behind them the solid grey building of his home, smoke curling above the chimney as it always did, a reminder that it had been there long before John, or his father, or his grandfather, and would probably be there long after he was gone.

And then Jess, his favourite ewe, more of a pet than a farm animal, had been standing below the beech tree at the foot of the garden, watching him go, every inch of her woolly face and stocky shape showing disapproval, her cracked *baah* telling him she knew what he was about.

He'd stopped at the little bridge and looked over the narrow parapet to the trickling Logan Water with its little pools along the edge. There he'd seen patches of sky in a mirror image but had taken care to avoid catching a glimpse of himself. He didn't want that, not today.

When he'd clicked the reins and turned away the occasional chirp from the birds in the hedge had cut across his thoughts, sweet yet sharp to remind him it was still about heart over head, though he was loath to admit it. He well knew he was doing exactly what he'd warned his cousin not to do. But once again what was expected won, and like that morning on the way to Loudon Hill, he didn't turn back.

At the first stroke of eight from the church clock Captain Steel clicked the reins of his horse. Juno responded. Wull Gemmell, appointed lieutenant, signalled the others to follow. Out stepped the mounted platoon behind the bright, fluttering cloth of its newly completed blue banner, with the words Christ and Covenant sewn in large white letters across the centre. They made a bonny sight. The crowd's roar of approval had starlings rising from the eaves of the houses to cackle and stare down in disbelief at the mass of waving hands and shouts of encouragement. Everyone pushed forward to see the brave men pass, children were lifted high, sat on a shoulder, or perched on a window ledge to see the sight. Those watching knew every detail had to be noted and remembered. The place rang with the din. Some riders were hard put to hold their beasts in check let alone maintain tight formation as the contingent slowly passed between the ranks of excited faces then broke into a steady trot at the end of the street to head for the Glasgow road. Many villagers ran behind them all the way to the cross roads where the loudest cheer of all sent the new platoon off on its mission.

Those left behind wandered back along the main street talking about how fine it had been and none of the chatter mentioned the nagging doubt that maybe some of those brave men might not be clattering back up the main street. In coming days this thought would grow and the village would learn to wait, and worry, and hope.

The captain and riders settled into a steady canter and soon adapted to the discipline of riding in proper formation. It was an easy journey along the main road, and each village they passed swelled their numbers with groups of men, mounted and on foot. Spirits rose. Soon the new recruits could almost believe they were real soldiers and a force to be reckoned with.

Robert Hamilton, who'd been commander since Drumclog, rode at the head of this army. Every mile made him more aware of the responsibility. He scanned the distance for any sign of the promised leader and hoped he'd appear before they reached the city. He knew he had the men's approval. He'd handled them well at Loudon Hill but this would be different. Thousands were joining the cause, and thousands needed a leader with a breadth of knowledge and experience his youth couldn't claim.

A blue banner fluttered in the distance. He hoped this would be their promised commander and signalled halt. Everyone obeyed and waited while a group of fast riding horsemen approached.

The leading horseman juddered to a halt and looked around with a condescending air. Taken aback at the unexpected fashion plate in front of him Robert scowled at the long, pale face, ornately framed by a dark wig, powdered and prepped up as if for some extravagant pageant. The lavishly embroidered velvet surcoat was bright and expensive, but hardly suitable for a military man.

The fine gentleman eyed Robert and seemed unimpressed with such simple, rough dress. He swept a polished black felt hat with an enormous silver plume from his head and turned round to wave at the waiting troops. "I tak it this is my army?"

Robert winced at the high, sharp voice. His fears deepened. Still hoping he might be mistaken he asked, "Yer army, sir?"

"Indeed. I'm here tae commit myself tae this worthy cause and lead ye tae success against an ill government. I didna expect sae poor a welcome though." The fine gentleman bowed and fluttered his great feathery hat. "I am Sir Robert Hamilton frae Preston and Fingalton. Here for Christ and Covenant."

"Ah'm a Hamilton tae," Robert nodded. "Robert Hamilton lik yersel. My faither's a laird near Strathaven."

"Indeed." The accompanying sniff left young Robert in no doubt as to the put down.

Face red with embarrassment Robert said his piece. "Ah wis leader on Thursday at Drumclog. Ye'll likely be acquaint wi oor success against Claverhoose an appreciate we're ready tae move on an mak the government listen tae oor just demands. Ah'm still in charge. At least ah am until oor promised leader arrives."

Sir Robert waved his glove. "I am he. This is my army. I am here tae assume command. Several ither lords vouch for me on this paper." He signalled to an over-dressed young man by his side who drew out a rolled up parchment from his saddle bag and held it up for all to see.

"A meeenit sir, an nae offence." Robert Hamilton dared to stretch out his hand, "If ye please?"

The young man was so surprised he gave over the parchment.

Robert carefully unrolled the paper and read every word including the signatures. He took his time and ignored the agitated shuffling around him. At last he looked up and nodded at the outraged face. "It's aw in order. Please assume command. The men will dae their best. Ah'm sure they'll be a credit tae ye." This time Robert Hamilton doffed his own hat in a simple gesture of welcome, a welcome he did not feel.

With an ungracious nod Sir Robert positioned himself directly in front of the young man while the rest of his fine escorts lined up on either side.

"Whit noo, sir?" Robert ventured to ask the velvet covered back.

"Glasgow. I intend tae mak a direct attack on the garrison."

This alarmed Robert and he dared to speak out again. "Sir. Shud we no foregaither on the ootskirts an mak sure we're strong enough in number afore attemptin tae influence the city faithers? That way we can find oot if - "

"Of course we'll find oot," the fine gentleman cut him short. "So will the city faithers when oor action speaks louder than words."

"Surely we need artillery tae attack thick garrison walls?" Robert persisted. "As yet thur's nae cannon in oor ranks. Muskets, swords and pikes canna dent solid stane."

Sir Robert sniffed. "Resolve is enough. Stout resolve can overcome ony obstacle." He turned to his trumpeter. "Sound the off."

Robert Hamilton bit back what he wanted to say and trotted behind the expensively attired figure, the waving feather in the hat. He sniffed the heady perfume wafting towards him and muttered, "God help us when somethin lik that thinks he's a leader. Luk at him. A brainless fop in fancy claes, jist fit for prancin in some fancy lady's drawin room. He has nae idea aboot onythin military yet here he is complete wi a recommendation frae them as are supposed tae ken."

His nearest companion nodded. "It doesna bode weel. An we're no even richt sterted."

Feeling increasingly depressed Robert jogged along trying to persuade himself that first appearances could be deceptive.

By early afternoon the army was within the city gates. Glasgow's streets were deserted. Shops were shuttered, house doors and windows locked and barred. The new army seemed to have the place to themselves, with no stones being thrown at them, no shouts of abuse. They only met a few stray dogs wandering freely and picking through the middens.

There seemed to be no resistance of any kind and Sir Robert, bursting with self-importance, rode straight to the city garrison and ordered the front ranks to form up before the main entrance. He stared at the stout wooden doors and smiled as if expecting them to open. Nothing happened. His smile tightened. He turned to the nearest mounted group and waved a gloved hand. "Demand entry."

They rode forward and called out his instruction.

A terse refusal came from the tight closed garrison.

Sir Robert raged. "We need tae teach them a lesson. Advance! Storm the walls! Set fire tae the place! Smoke them oot!"

Eager for battle, the men charged forward.

The garrison commander must have been laughing as he watched the fools obey Sir Robert's command. All he had to do was wait till the right moment, signal the cannon to fire and the front line of would-be assailants took the full blast of the garrison reply. Blown apart before they even tasted battle they fell as one. The ground rocked and stones flew as the second line juddered to a halt, their hesitation perfect timing for another salvo. Some men tripped, others dropped to the ground, crawling among scattered bodies, trying to find extra shelter for now the cannon blasts were joined by musket fire. The soldiers on the garrison walls, picking off individual targets, were enjoying themselves, creating a bloody, screaming avalanche of bodies below the garrison.

It made no difference to the commander. The gloved hand rose again to signal another line forward.

Shaking with disbelief Robert Hamilton urged his horse

closer to the commander's group. He stood up in the saddle trying to attract the fine gentleman's attention.

Sir Robert ignored him.

Pushing his horse inside the protective circle he confronted Sir Robert. "Whit in God's name are ye aboot? Hae ye ony idea hoo mony men are lost for nae guid reason? Think shame man. Sound the retreat afore there's ony mair carnage."

Sir Robert flapped a gloved hand in young Robert's outraged face.

Leaning forward Robert grabbed the horse's bridle and forced the leader's two equerries aside. "If ye dinna stop this madness ah'll order a retreat mysel. We didna come here tae be yer cannon fodder."

"Ye hae nae understanding o my overall plan. I am the commander here. Hoo dare ye come furrit and try tae interfere?"

"An hoo dare ye hae nae regard for the lives o yer men?"

"These men are here tae obey, tae act as I see fit."

"An ye're here tae lead. No that ye seem tae ken whit that means."

Sir Robert chewed his lips. He seemed unsure. The darting eyes almost glazed then the face grew very red as the moment passed. No longer defensive he arched his fine eyebrows and stuck out his ornately covered chest. "I dinna require tae explain myself tae an underling. Dismiss sir. Withdraw at once." Turning to his equerry he demanded, "Get rid o him."

Robert Hamilton dared the equerry to touch his bridle. They stared at each other. It was no contest. The equerry pulled his horse back a step and Robert closed in on his commander. "If ye want me tae withdraw ah'll gladly dae so. But understaund ah'll tak every last volunteer wi me."

The two combatants stared at each other then Robert Hamilton blurted out, "For God's sake sir. Hae peety."

The commander studied the young man's set face, and saw both rage and a direct challenge to his authority.

The young man studied the aristocratic powdered face and saw open hatred. More worryingly he also saw a hint of bewilderment mixed with plain stupidity. It was obvious this man had neither plan nor strategy, for who in their right mind would ride up to a garrison expecting the doors to fly open, and everybody to come streaming out, to lay down their arms and surrender? And what leader allowed his men to be killed before his eyes for no reason at all?

Sir Robert flapped his glove again like some resentful child. "Whit a fuss." The curls of his wig trembled then shook. "If it means that much tae ye we'll sound the retreat."

With a few more salvoes from the garrison hastening the withdrawal the blue bonnets drew back to a safe distance leaving the cobbled space littered with deadly evidence while the stinking smell of death dogged every step with the stupidity of it all.

John's platoon had been positioned well to the rear. They suffered no loss, unlike the contingent from the village of Larkhall who'd been part of both advances against the garrison. Within hours of leaving home their numbers were halved.

John and his men watched rescuers run forward, attempting to lift as many wounded as possible only to be cut down by round after round of musket fire from the garrison walls while the commander's group rode back a short distance to wait in safety. No direction, no concern, no sign of leadership from the brightly attired figure who sat within his safe circle of protection and watched the tragedy unfold like some medieval play.

Beside himself with rage John roared out across the watching ranks, "Whae needs an enemy when we hae yon eedjit up front tae lead us? In God's name he's worse than a man short."

As he spoke a runner arrived with orders to retreat from the city and march back as far as Bothwell Moor, re-group and await further instructions.

"Instructions," John snarled, then waved to his tight-knit formation. "Wheel roond."

Obediently his men turned and the dispirited horde began trailing all the way back to the very spot they'd passed that afternoon.

Chapter 14

"Ah canna believe whit happened." Davie Steel buried his face in his horse's mane.

"Ay, ye're richt." John looked up from attending to his precious Juno. "It wis a sair sicht. Aw they men killed for nae reason ither than yon mad man's idea o sendin men wi muskets tae tackle rows o cannon. As for his orders tae march here then march there. Chris' sake we're back whaur we sterted this aifternoon. A few hoors ago we were ready tae face onythin. Look at us noo. At the mercy o some decked up eedjit. Ony mair o this an we'll aw be deid. He claims to be here for Christ an Covenant. No wi that attitude he's no. The real world disna even touch a man lik that. An thur's nowt we can dae aboot it." He unfastened Juno's saddle. "C'mon lass, us twa need some quiet tae oorsels. See ye later Davie." He led Juno towards the river-bank where the grass was green and untrodden.

In the commander's tent Sir Robert was unrepentant. As for listening to any criticism or advice he simply rolled his eyes, shook his expensively coiffed wig, and stared at the assembled captains. "God kens I had hope o real action back there in the city. I wis aifter something decisive tae move oor cause furrit. Sadly it didna happen." He wiped his brow and glared at the circle of angry faces. "Dinna look at me lik that gentlemen. I'll no hae it. And whit's aw this tut-tutting aboot? Back there I understood only too weel whit wis required. It's no my fault if there's a lack o resolve. Inner strength is the secret and withoot it we'll hae nae success in oor venture. It needs tae be addressed gentlemen, which means setting up camp here and taking time tae forge the richt attitude in oor men."

Experienced officers like Learmouth, Paton and Clelland had just arrived with their contingents to hear Sir Robert announce his grand plan.

Learmouth spoke first. "Whit are ye at? And whit's this

nonsense ye're spoutin aboot the lack in oor men?" He pointed a finger at Sir Robert. "No sir, quite the reverse. Ony lack rests squarely on yer ain shooders. Whit ye did shows nae respect for the lives ye command. In ma book men used as cannon fodder is unforgivable as weel as unbelievable." He turned to the other captains. "For God's sake tell this man tae use whit little brain he has afore oor cause is lost."

Clelland stepped forward to face the defiant commander. "We're here tae support, tae gie ye the benefit o mony years in the field which - "

"I accept yer experience gies ye a parteeclar view and opeenion on military matters." Sir Robert held up his hands. "On this occasion ye're wrang. Oor way furrit cries oot for a fresh approach; a new way o luking at things."

Clelland shook his head. "And while we're busy luking at things tae forge this attitude ye're aifter dae ye think oor enemy will jist hing back and alloo us that space?"

"Time is on oor side." Sir Robert sounded sure of himself. "I mean tae mak guid use o it."

Finally Captain Paton joined in. "Weel sir, I've seen service under mony a commander, and in mony a different situation, but ye're a new experience. Ane I can fine dae withoot." Before Sir Robert could respond he turned to the others. "I'm awa tae speak wi whit's left o the Larkhall contingent. They've had an ill day and nae mistake. As for whit next - " he pointed an accusing finger at Sir Robert - "I hope it's a tad better than whit went afore. This is supposed tae be a military undertaking no a kirk assembly. We shud be talking tactics no using up valuable time on hot air."

Sir Robert sniffed, "I think I've made my decision clear. Oor success rests on resolve. That's whit's missing frae oor cause. Time will nurture this, alloo it tae flourish. Noo gentlemen, if ye'll excuse me, aw this arguing is wearing me oot and it's time I had my dinner." He graciously bowed to the row of angry men and flounced out the tent.

Next morning the senior officers tried further protest.

Again Sir Robert was having none of it. He even took his idea further by insisting on sending out messengers with invites for any ministers willing to come and give divine counsel to himself, his officers, and indeed the whole army.

Many of the ousted ministers grabbed this opportunity. Here was a massive audience and they were more than happy to sermonise over the justness of the cause. Few had a tactical thought to offer.

Captain Clelland believed in the cause, the need to resist, to defend the faith,but all this philosophising and arguing chilled his heart.

Other officers seemed to agree. Not that it made any difference. Sir Robert only had ears for his own inner circle who always agreed with him.

During a particularly long sermon by a particularly long-winded minister Clelland's frustration had him interrupting the performance. "Weel sir, whit ye're saying micht be aw vera weel but no day aifter day."

The minister glared at him. "We need tae conseeder, tae explore - "

"Naw, naw." Clelland stopped him. "Ma time's ower precious tae waste on aw this. Frae noo on I'll be preparing ma recruits for whit's aheid." He turned to the watchers. "Bide if ye want. I'm awa."

The minister watched him go then picked up where he'd left off.

Nothing changed after Clelland's outburst. Ministers came and went. A week passed, and there was still no sign or even mention of action. News of the vast assembly spread throughout the country; along with it went a growing whisper that the government itself was under threat, maybe about to fall. Now more than eight thousand strong, this rebel army could have used its advantage and marched on the capital. But no move was made.

"There's still much tae learn," Sir Robert insisted and everyone stayed on Bothwell Moor while every aspect of every policy was dissected and wrangled over. The more they talked the more they became divided. Sir Robert seemed to approve, always in the thick of any heated argument, encouraging more discussion till the air above and around the camp was hot with reasoned and unreasoned debate while nothing was resolved.

John complained each morning when he and Wull reviewed their platoon. Apart from insisting on proper maintenance of their allocated space, and making sure the horses were well tended, there was little else to do. Eventually Wull said what they were both thinking. "Is it worth oor while bidin?"

"We'll gie it a few mair days," John said. "If there's nae plan for ony action we're awa. The men are fair scunnered wi aw this palaver. In fact ah'm surprised thure still here. Whae in their richt mind jist sits an waits for trouble tae arrive?"

Sermons and endless debate had replaced plans and tactics. Decision and action were forgotten. This left the army vulnerable. The men became restless. Mischief raised her unpredictable head. At first it was good-natured but gradually opportunities to settle old scores grew. Then there was stealing. John became involved in one such incident when a sergeant shouted, "Come quick. We've jist caught a man riflin thru the meenisters' baggage."

John hurried over to find the culprit flat on his back with both arms pinned down by heavy boots. Beside him lay a bulging bag.

"Let him stand," John commanded.

The man struggled up.

"Whit's yer name?"

"They caw me Gumsy."

"Richt then Gumsy, whit's this aboot? Explain yersel."

"Ah'm a pair man."

"So are we. Some pairer than ithers," John replied. "But ye must be sorely bereft when ye resort tae stealin frae yer ain comrades, especially meenisters."

"It's aw this hingin aboot," Gumsy spat. "Ah cudna help it. Onyway, the meenisters hae mair than they need."

"That's nae excuse."

"Ah'm fed up daein withoot."

"That's as maybe but stealin is stealin. Ye need tae return the goods an show some regret for whit ye did."

"Whae's gonna mak me?" Gumsy spat again.

John turned to the sergeant. "Maybe a sharp lesson will bring him tae his senses. March him ower tae the leader's tent an request permission tae use the whip on him."

At this Gumsy struggled violently then threw himself on the ground again and refused to move.

"If he's no for walkin git a squad tae cairry him," John ordered.

And so the prisoner arrived feet first among the commander's select group just as Sir Robert was lecturing his ministers on an appropriate theme for their next sermon. They looked as if they welcomed the interruption.

"A thief," the sergeant announced. "He wis caught stealin frae the meenisters' baggage. Captain John Steel sent me tae request permission for a floggin."

"Just so." Sir Robert, more annoyed by the break in his discourse than the supposed crime against the ministers, advanced on the prisoner. "Whit hae ye tae say for yersel, felon?"

Silence.

"Dae ye hear me?"

Gumsy sat up. "Ay. Loud and clear. But ah'd raither no." He covered his ears.

Sir Robert glared at the man. "Hoo dare ye speak lik that tae yer commander?"

"Commander." Gumsy spat on the ground then slowly looked the fine gentleman up and down. "Jist luk at ye."

Sir Robert flinched. His face reddened. He raised a hand as if to strike Gumsy then seemed to change his mind and stepped closer to the defiant face. "Go on. I dare ye. Speak yer mind."

"Whit for? Ye're no worth speakin tae let alane listenin tae."

Head on one side like a blackbird studying a worm Sir Robert scanned the filthy face and stared into a pair of hard, little eyes.

Gumsy met his gaze then showed his gums and three uneven, blackened teeth. He winked and grinned in further insult.

Sir Robert pulled back.

Gumsy's grin widened till he was almost laughing.

Sir Robert stroked his chin and seemed to be thinking. He nodded to himself and straightened his shoulders then turned to an officer by his side. "This prisoner disna want tae listen. So, we'll help him. Cut aff his ears. Baith o them."

No one moved.

Sir Robert clapped his hands and glared at the officer.

The officer hesitated.

Sir Robert clapped his hands again. "Whit are ye waiting for?"

The officer nodded and signalled two of his men to bring the prisoner closer.

Gumsy writhed and kicked as he was dragged in front of the officer.

The officer's face was fixed but chalk white. "Lay him doon on his back."

The two soldiers tried to obey but Gumsy almost managed to fight them off, all the while threatening Sir Robert. "Ah'll hae ye so ah will. Torturin a pair man fur yer ain amusement. Ah hope ye roast in Hell." He spat out the words till one soldier sat on his chest and winded him. He choked and stopped struggling. The other soldier seized his chance and pinned down Gumsy's arms.

Now helpless, Gumsy seemed to realise that the threat was about to become reality. Face wet with tears, he drummed his feet on the grass and began to scream for mercy.

The officer drew his sword.

"Get on wi it," Sir Robert snapped

The officer took a deep breath. "Keep the prisoner still." He raised his sword, swiped on either side of Gumsy's head and two ears lay neatly on the grass along with a few strands of matted hair.

For a long moment there was silence. Everyone stared at the ears and the prisoner who seemed to have passed out with shock. Sir Robert smiled at the evidence. "Noo get that trash oot o here."

The officer sheathed his sword and nodded to the two soldiers who seemed unable to move.

Sir Robert clapped his hands yet again. The officer stepped forward to help the two soldiers lift the unconscious prisoner. This seemed to revive Gumsy. His eyes opened and he tried to lift his head. "Ah'll hae ye - " No more words came as he fell back again in a faint, his blood soaking into the grass beside a pair of pink ears.

Sir Robert turned to his stunned audience. "I trust that meets wi yer reverends' approval? Noo as I wis saying - "

The unconscious man was dragged away to have his head bound while the sergeant hurried back to tell John what had happened. "An the meenisters jist sat watchin an did naethin. They didna even try and stop Sir Robert. Ah ken yon thief deserved a whippin. But baith ears cut aff."

"Ah need tae see this for masel." John headed in the direction of the screams.

Gumsy had recovered consciousness and was sharing his pain with everyone. He'd almost worked himself into a fit with his tongue rolling, and high-pitched screams coming one after another till he choked and vomited. As soon as he had enough breath the whole performance would start again.

John pushed his way into the struggling group and stared down at Gumsy rolling and kicking on the grass.

"He's in a bad way," one of the men said. "We can hardly keep him still enough tae tie up his heid. He's clean oot his mind wi fricht an pain, an threatenin tae kill the commander."

"Kill Sir Robert?"

The soldier nodded. "Ye can see yersel he's nae richt."

"Far frae it," John said grimly. "It's the maist sensible thing ah've heard in days."

The man looked shocked but John was already turning to face the onlookers. He said no more. He didn't need to. A path opened before him as he walked away. Anger drove him; all he wanted was to distance himself. To stay and try to explain or argue his point would only make matters worse.

Within minutes he was beyond the edge of the camp. Ahead lay the fine beech wood, part of the Duke of Hamilton's vast estate. Here were tall trees, mature and strong yet softly graceful with the pale green, lacy canopy that beech drapes over itself before the heat of summer roughens the leaves and darkens them to a duller shade. One behind another they stood steady and re-assuring. Here he could enjoy the whiff of woodland with no hint of the pervading stink from unwashed bodies too close together, where the smell of stale and badly cooked food hung in the air, along with boredom and growing resentment in a grand mix with horse and human shit.

He sat down below one of the tallest trees and leant against its solid trunk. In front of him line after line of tree trunks and branches almost blocked out the sprawling encampment by the riverbank. *If only*, he wished. The thought of what he might do to Sir Robert took him to places he'd never imagined before. He went willingly. And then the doubts came back. He needed his special comfort. Now he sought the picture of a vast stretch of undulating grass and heather above his farm, wide and open and empty below an ever-changing sky. Like Lucas Brotherstone, not many weeks before, he realised there are no questions out there, no answers. This brought relief and, eyes closed, he sat on. Gradually his anger slid away and his mind stilled. He became aware of the wood sounds, the gentle scuffles of tiny creatures in the undergrowth, and bird songs close by and further within the wood. A bee buzzed past the end of his nose. The sound made him smile and imagine the hurtling black and yellow striped ball, all wings and legs and pollen. His fingers traced the grass fronds and felt the various shapes of leaves, different sizes, some smooth some rough. "This is a daisy," he whispered. "This feels like a wee dandelion. Ay, it's got a mop for a heid. And here's clover beside it." He leant closer. "Ah can smell its sweetness." He opened his eyes to check if he was correct. There by his thumb a tiny ladybird, her bright red back covered by five round black spots, was steadily marching across a broad dandelion leaf. He watched her progress from one edge to the other before she slid to the underside then re-appeared on the stalk before climbing all the way down to the ground, never hesitating, never missing a beat until she vanished among the lower leaves. He sighed. "At least she seems tae ken whit she's aboot."

Way above his head came a light pitter pat. Looking up through the network of branches, finer and finer as they touched the sky, he saw glistening raindrops beginning to bounce from leaf to leaf, dropping through the tiny spaces and dancing towards him.

Pure water splashed on his upturned face and he began to feel clean again.

A flustered looking Gavin appeared. "So there ye are," he accused. "Ah've been lukin awhaur. Ye're the talk o the place aifter agreein wi yon thief."

"Ah cudna help it," John shrugged. "Thief or no, ah agree wi him. Mibbe no for the same reason, but he's richt - we'd be a lot better aff withoot Sir Robert."

"But daein awa wi yer leader? Ye canna say that, John. Wur aw scunnered. But we need tae try an mak the best o it."

"Ay weel. Ah'm jist aboot done tryin. This isnae workin oot, is it?"

"Naw," Gavin agreed.

After this they sat together staring into space.

Eventually Gavin said, "Yer ain worst enemy, that's whit ye are."

John smiled. "Me and eight thoosand ithers."

They both smiled then Gavin stood up again. "Ah'd best gang back. But ye'd best bide on a wee while till the steer settles."

John watched the young man walk back to the camp. Far from feeling ashamed he wondered if it really was down to him and his tantrum or had this incident opened up doors that Gavin might have preferred to keep shut.

The rain grew heavier. The earlier raindrops multiplied into a curtain of fine drizzle. Now it was difficult to make out the haphazard lines of dark tents, the belching smoke from the many fires, the variety of figures scurrying back and forward. From where he sat it all seemed unreal. *If only,* he wished again, and looking down at the grassy fronds by his feet he tried to catch another glimpse of the ladybird. She was not to be seen.

"Weel did ye find him?" Wull Gemmell pounced on Gavin on his return.

"Ay. Jist leave it at that."

Knowing John as they did the Lesmahagow platoon had a good idea what he meant.

"Whaur is he onyway?" Wull asked.

Gavin pointed towards the trees.

"Time ah hud a word." Wull turned and walked towards the wood.

"That should be interestin," someone said. "Ane's as bad as the ither."

The others laughed. John and Wull were made for one another.

When Wull found John he began with, "Eedjit. A prize eedjit

195

so ye are. Drawin attention tae yersel lik that. Hae ye ony idea whit that mad commander micht dae tae ye?"

"He's mad aw richt. If folk canna see it wi thur ain een they need tae be tellt. Ah dinna care whae hears or kens or - "

Wull almost smiled. "Ay. Lik ah said, ye're a prize eedjit. God sakes John, will ye nivver learn that it's no wise tae mooth aff withoot thinkin?"

"Ay, weel." John looked down at the grass and kicked at a tree root. "It jist happens."

"So it seems." Wull did smile and sat down beside him. "That's why we git on sae weel."

John sighed but said nothing.

They stayed where they were for a long time in companionable silence. Wull's solid figure had its usual calming effect, his very presence somehow allowing John to wrestle with his demons and finally swallow them without a word being spoken. It was dark before they returned to the camp. No one saw them arrive and in the morning no one said anything about the day before.

The camp continued to wait with no decision from Sir Robert and no indication as to what might happen next.

Each day John worried about Marion, the boys, his farm, all the work his father had to cope with. Despite all this he didn't leave. And while he stayed so did the Lesmahagow platoon.

The camp was restless but Sir Robert remained content as a cockerel in the midden. Rumour after rumour began to circulate about the king sending some great duke from England with ten thousand regulars to wipe out the rebels and put an end to their defiance. This threat made no difference. The religious debating and wrangling continued. Men came and went at will. Numbers rose and fell daily. The camp began to assume a semi permanent identity as some of the volunteers from the nearby town of Hamilton returned home for a few days and then wandered back again.

At the end of the third week an army of regulars lined up on the opposite bank of the river Clyde. Reality had finally arrived with disciplined campaign veterans in formation. These battle-scarred men must have wondered at the strange sight on the other side where mass disorder was apparent. What confronted them certainly didn't look like determined rebellion.

A stone toll bridge with a fortified guardhouse stood at the point where the river Clyde curved out of the wide valley. To defend this important causeway the rebels had one small brass cannon brought from Douglas castle, the only cannon in the whole army. When the Duke of Monmouth, leading the king's troops, heard this report he laughed, "The narrowness of the bridge micht aid the fools for an hoor or twa but withoot proper artillery we'll soon sweep them awa. Once across it's simply a matter o rounding them up. As for that crack-brain in charge, he's as guid as on oor side. Cudna be better. He micht even be open to some kind o offer and gie us a surrender withoot the need for a pitched battle."

Three officers were despatched to the end of the bridge. They waved the white flag of truce then called out, "We bring a message from the Duke of Monmouth. Disarm and no undue harshness will be used against ye."

They were met with stony silence.

The officers waited a moment then shouted, "How say ye?"

This time the answer from the bridge came from Sir Robert himself. He leant over the stone parapet. "Wi a guarantee like that we'll see oorsels hanged next."

His inner circle laughed and clapped their hands in approval. The men standing behind glared at the well-decorated figure and said nothing.

Monmouth's officers went back with this reply.

He blinked. "Go back and gie the fool a chance tae reconsider. I'd raither hae live prisoners as deid bodies littering this bonny spot."

"No surrender," was the next reply.

When Monmouth heard this he accepted the inevitable. But before briefing his colonels he took the precaution of announcing, "Tak note I made a generous offer o clemency. I did it more than once. The rebel leader chose tae refuse and is noo responsible for the spilling o his men's blood. They may be traitors and a mere rabble but I'll tak nae pleasure in killing so many, so easily."

Monmouth had done himself proud with eight experienced commanders who were well aware of what was expected. The Duke of Montrose led the cavalry, the Earl of Linlithgow the infantry; Claverhouse, more than eager to make amends for his recent disgrace at Drumclog, was at the head of his dragoons. The Earls of Home and Airlie were in charge of their own troops, and Lord Mar commanded a huge infantry on foot. Their discipline and singularity of purpose was in stark contrast to the Covenanting army, still without strategy, let alone orders, or any sign of leadership.

Among the rebels each contingent was trying to prepare for its own independent action with no senior officer passing through the ranks to set up proper distribution of powder and shot. Few muskets had a second round. They were far from able to match the equipment of the government troops let alone the organisation and yet the battle they'd longed for was about to commence.

Chapter 15

Just before dawn on Sunday June 22nd, the Duke of Monmouth signalled advance in the name of the king. The rebels guarding the bridge over the River Clyde caught sight of the royalist musketeers blowing their matches as they walked forward in the half-light.

The attack had begun.

One of the guards raced to tell Sir Robert and was astounded at his leader's lack of reaction. He simply ordered everyone to remain as they'd been since the night before when they'd been split into two divisions without anyone named in control of either division. This had been his token preparation for battle. Unit captains had no idea how much musket shot would be available or how it might be distributed. They'd have to decide everything from deployment of men to use of weapons. As for liaising further up the line of command there was no mention of how and when or even if it should take place.

A smaller battalion was posted on the bridge as a first line of defence. The main body of men was positioned along the slope from the river to the wooded area, and well away from the bridge approach, but no formal orders had been given whether they were intended as back up. Well clear, on higher ground, and almost on the edge of the trees, Sir Robert sat astride his charger. From here he had a good view of the disciplined ranks facing the almost casual line of his own men. The disparity was obvious yet he seemed content to make no alteration, issue no instructions, no stirring address for his troops, no encouragement of any kind. He simply sat, waiting for the performance to begin.

On this occasion the devil was not in the detail. There was no detail. More worrying was the lack of an overall plan.

John Steel sat aside his precious Juno and stared round at the sea of blue and white banners fluttering bravely and defiantly against a line up of a huge, well-armed enemy on the opposite bank.

He studied their disciplined ranks and wondered how things might be in a few hours time.

The Lesmahagow contingent was part of the battalion positioned by the old stone bridge over the River Clyde. This made him feel safer. The narrow causeway, no more than twelve feet wide, was a real asset, easy to defend if the enemy ever made it over the rocky barricade his men had built at the other end.

So long as the bridge held the enemy would be forced to march several miles upstream where the river was shallow enough to cross. He hoped Sir Robert knew this, had made plans to meet the advancing line when it emerged from Hamilton Palace Wood with little chance of a full bloodied charge. Definitely an advantage. "Ay," he said aloud. "Jist so lang as we haud the bridge."

Gavin sat alongside him and nodded. "Thank God they Douglas men brocht thur wee cannon frae Douglas Castle."

John frowned. "It's oor only cannon. Hae ye seen the heavy pieces the government troops are linin up against us?"

As he spoke the royalist artillery sent the opening salvo. The Douglas men responded and the little cannon held its own. Maybe it was the higher position, maybe the enemy hadn't expected a cannon, even a little one, to fire so directly at them. Whatever the reason it was enough to have the royalists abandon their big guns and retreat up the broad bank.

The men on the bridge cheered and watched them go. Confidence increased as they enemy stayed well back for more than half an hour before cautiously advancing again. This time their approach was different; guns trained on the wall of the bridge itself, they let fly. Each blast shook the solid stonework. Gaps began to appear when great slabs fell into the water below. Clouds of dust flew out, swirling towards the attackers and settling on their metal helmets as they drew closer to the damaged wall.

On the causeway several men were blown apart where they stood on the castellated rampart. They were the lucky ones. Those who lost their footing or were blasted off the parapet had a long fall before hitting the river. Once in the water they were carried away by the surging current or dragged under to eventually surface among the tangled weeds further along the river-bank. Any who survived this ordeal were fished out the water and systematically hacked to pieces by the front line of Lord Mar's infantry.

Those on the bridge could hear the shouts of terror mixed with vain screams pleading for mercy. They could also see the flashing of sword blades rising and falling, slashing and cutting, turning the water ever more red.

Earlier hope vanished but there was no option but to keep going, to try and counter each volley till the muzzle of the little cannon almost glowed. Against the odds they did hold their own and prevented the enemy from advancing any further.

And then they ran out of ammunition for their cannon. Desperate shouts for more made no difference. There didn't seem to be any more, other than some musket shot.

John saw this and knew mere muskets were of little use against the heavy armoury. The well-equipped royalists had the best of it. They'd soon be across the rocky barrier. Soon be on the bridge itself.

Just then David Hackston, one of the killers of Archbishop Sharpe, ran back through the swirling smoke on the bridge. John recognised him. So, he thought, noo ye're showin whit ye're aboot fleein lik a coward. And then he heard the man's roars for help, the desperate shouts for men, any men, to come and resist, to stop the onslaught, to hold the bridge before it was too late.

John turned to see what was happening behind. There like a beautiful peacock sat Sir Robert, the spectator on a fine charger, safe on the edge of the first line of trees. "Damn ye," he roared. "Damn ye tae hell an back." Jumping off his horse he shouted above the din to Gavin, "Bide here. Keep haud o the horses. Wull, Davie, an masel will tak the platoon an see whit can be done on the bridge."

"But - " Gavin started to argue.

"Dae as ye're tellt," John punched his chest. "Bide put. An keep haud o they beasts. Ah'm relyin on ye. We'll need them afore lang."

The three men disappeared into the mêlée and Gavin was left grappling with four agitated horses who were fast becoming desperate to take off and escape the bangs and flashes around them. Strong as he was he had to dig his heels in hard and lean back. His hands were damp. They began to slide down the leather straps so he twisted the thongs round his wrists and hoped this would be enough to hold on. And all the time he kept repeating, "Easy noo. Easy." Gradually his strength and persistence paid off, and he managed to quieten Juno, the lead horse. Once she settled the others sensed her acceptance. They lessened their straining though their eyes and ears still flicked back and forward at the gusts of smoke and clashing steel which seemed to grow more frantic by the minute.

By now Gavin had guessed why he'd been ordered to do this. Determined not to let John down he hung on to the leather straps and tried to ignore the surge of bodies around him. It was difficult to simply concentrate on the anxious animals but he did his best.

Three hundred and more had thundered to join Hackston and meet the disciplined mass of the battle hardened king's troops who were already a quarter of the way along the causeway. The fresh wall of swords, pikes and halberds worked, stalling the advance. After a few hectic minutes of hand-to-hand fighting the rebel front line began to push the enemy back.

The sun began to rise. The air grew hot. Men were fighting in a blinding sweat in the relentless push from Monmouth's men who were constantly reinforced by fresh hands. There was no respite, no relief for the blue bonnets. Over and over again the desperate men on the bridge called back for support, but no more volunteers ran forward. Like their commander, those on the grassy slope stood and watched the relentless push as if it had nothing to do with them.

A sensible commander might have sent forward a keg of powder to blow the bridge and put a stop to the advance before it was too late. Since there was none to send Sir Robert did nothing. He continued to sit in the safe shelter of the wood. His face grew tighter and whiter as time passed. His attendants glanced at him, whispering to each other while the battle unravelled in the way that one or two had secretly expected.

John was facing his demons. On the bridge his sword hacked and thrust with the best of them, his rage giving him added strength as he damned and swore against the man responsible for this fiasco. The others fighting alongside seemed driven by the same force as they doggedly tried to resist the government's fierce attack.

Eventually a runner appeared from Sir Robert and gasped, "Retire," before vanishing into the mêlée.

Beyond exhaustion the rebel defenders needed no telling. They already knew they'd no chance of holding the bridge any longer. In a tight formation, each supporting and protecting the other, they managed to achieve an orderly retreat along the full length of the causeway. The way was now clear for an enemy advance, and moments later the king's army began swarming across the bridge with heavy artillery spitting death to all in its path.

Stumbling off the bridge the exhausted defenders could hardly have received a worse reward for all their efforts. Expecting to find themselves part of a stout defence from the thousands crowding the moor they were confronted with men pushing each other aside in their desperation to be gone. Worst of all they saw their commander in full flight, his horse racing up the long slope and away into the wood beyond. Leaving the volunteers to their fate Sir Robert took off to save his own skin. It was a grim sight for those who'd fought so hard and long. Now their effort meant nothing, but few were surprised.

That night the grand gentleman would lie between clean sheets in a comfortable bed in Loudon Castle, with little care for the fate of his once fine army. Within days he'd be further south, aboard a ship, heading for the safety of Holland where he'd boast of his exploits and berate those left behind.

In no time seven hundred were dead. Some of the would be fighters who saw this had enough sense to flee, racing through Hamilton Palace Woods, hoping to reach the town and disappear. More than twelve hundred others did nothing, simply dropping what weapons they had to become abject prisoners, forced to strip off and lie face down on the ground. Wrists bound, noses sunk in stinking, churned up mud, their bare rumps fully exposed it must have felt like the ultimate humiliation.

How wrong they were.

That would begin with a forced march in bare feet all the way to Edinburgh. Once there they'd be penned up in a walled section of Greyfriars church with no shelter, hardly any food, and tainted water to drink. Weeks spent in the Scottish summer rain would give way to an autumn of desperation. When winter frost and snow set in their suffering would be complete. Many would die from their wounds, or hunger, or freeze to death. Some would go mad. Come spring the survivors would be marched to the port of Leith, dropped into the airless holds of elegant tall ships, and transported to the West Indies. Those alive at the end of this journey would be sold as slaves, and it would be many years, if ever, before they'd see their homeland again.

One of those elegant ships, the *Crown of London*, its hold crammed with rebels, would founder on rocks at Mull Head off Deerness. Savage winds and waves along the Pentland Firth would put an end to her journey before it was properly begun. Worse, the soldiers on board would refuse to open the hatches and two hundred and seventy-nine captives would drown where they stood in the dark, cramped space. Another forty eight would somehow manage to escape and make it into the raging sea, but few of those would reach the shore, only to be recaptured and shipped on to slavery. Whatever their reason for joining the cause against king and government, the cry for Christ and Covenant would seem hollow indeed.

By ten o'clock that morning the battle was all but over. Already a courier was galloping towards the capital with news of the royalist victory.

Monmouth now decided it was time to cement his success and unleashed the cavalry. Among them John saw Claverhouse, the huge white plume on his hat waving like a banner, as he charged forward on his black horse, relishing his promise to make the so called rebels pay for his recent disgrace.

Linlithgow's dragoons came behind, killing methodically while they progressed along the river bank, then fanning out, still capturing and cutting down.

The sight of so much slaughter turned John's stomach but didn't surprise him.

Drumclog had shown him what hate could do. This time it was all about revenge.

Forty miles away Sandy Peden stood in a peaceful valley, about to begin an open-air service. It was a beautiful summer day, no word of troopers in the district, nothing to alarm the villagers who'd arrived for his sermon. Everything seemed calm. But today Sandy had nothing to say that those around would want to hear.

His tiny congregation sat on the grass and waited in silence while the gaunt figure in the patched cloak and leather mask made no move to speak.

Behind the mask Sandy closed his eyes and opened his mind to the great darkness that had been hammering against his brow for hours and now filled his inner eye. Here he saw a great swirl of blue bonnets, torn and tattered and covered in blood. He knew what this was, knew what it meant, and bowed his head in despair.

"Sir?" someone asked gently. "Whit ails ye?"

Only after a second asking did Sandy respond. "Ah see an end tae oor cause for richt noo death an revenge is claimin mony a life in a terrible battle. Extremists amang us hae scorned ma council for peaceful prayer as the best way furrit. That pains me for noo they're payin a heavy price an takin ower mony innocent men wi them. There will be nae sermon this day. Ah need tae be on ma ain, tae pray for their souls. An ma freends, I entreat ye tae dae likewise. Pray for them aw, an pray for a future. Pray that we'll hae yin, an let it be free frae sic terrible hate."

He held up his hand in blessing then turned and quickly walked away leaving a startled group staring after him. Days later news of the battle would come, and they'd understand his strange words, and there would be much talk and fear of the great man's power of second sight.

By then Sandy would be on the outskirts of Hamilton, seeing for himself, and accepting that it was too late to change anything after what happened at Bothwell Bridge.

A sudden trumpet call gave warning as the king's cavalry signalled the start of a two-pronged advance. Caught between dragoons and cavalry the men remaining on the wide river-bank were being swept relentlessly into the centre and corralled like helpless sheep.

John realised this was the moment he'd been dreading. He saw how close it was and roared, "Back tae the horses afore it's too late."

Davie and Will needed no second telling and quickly found Gavin where they'd left him.

Astride their horses they were about to wheel round when the Earl of Airlie's cavalry unit caught sight of the little group and bore down on them. Aware of the lead horse approaching John tightened his sword grip yet again. He'd no intention of becoming a prisoner or dying if he could help it.

Airlie drew level and shouted, "Surrender!" Over-confident and expecting little resistance he didn't see the flat edge of John's sword swing in a great circle. He felt it when the broad band of steel met him full in the face with a loud smack. He rocked backwards and scrabbled to recover. John was ready for him, stabbing downwards with his sword to slice through the thick leather of the great earl's saddle strap. The loosened saddle slipped sidewards; the earl went with it, losing control. His legs shot forward then flailed in the air. Dropping his sword, he hung onto the reins, trying to pull himself back up. It was too late. His weight, and that of his heavy armour, tipped the balance. He fell from his great charger and crashed to the ground with a roar. His head rocked back. His neck jerked. The underside of his metal helmet dug into his skin, the thick chin-strap pushing upwards, momentarily choking him. He lost focus but not before his well honed survival instinct clicked in. Even in his daze he knew to roll sidewards, and pushing hard against his unwieldy metal breast-plate he forced his body over again and again. His metal coat gave some protection from prancing hooves while he kept rolling, seeking safety. Finally he curled into a tight ball until a clear space began to grow around him. Aware of this he stared up and saw his circle of men who'd pulled their horses back to create an area of safety. He saw their faces and read their amused expressions.

Instead of relief, rage took over

Those few vital seconds were enough. John, Davie, Gavin and Wull seized their chance and galloped through the panicking crowd of rebels. In no time they reached the slope beyond and headed for the wooded area around Hamilton Palace.

Before the battle Duchess Anne had sent Monmouth a written request that the ground around Hamilton Palace should be respected. With gentlemanly politeness the commander had agreed and forbidden any chase into the fine woodland.

To the earl's men this didn't matter. Their only concern was their fallen master, and they made no move to stop the four escaping horsemen. Several leading rebels also saw their chance and took it. Once through that woodland and beyond they'd quickly disappear into the wilder lands of the south to become a recurring thorn in Clavers' flesh. From here they'd harry his troopers and try to thwart his every move to enforce the law. He'd be after them for months with little success until frustration would force him to complain to the king himself that Monmouth's gesture to the duchess was not only ill considered but the main reason why the so-called rebellion was not completely crushed in the south of Scotland.

The earl's young lieutenant jumped down to aid his master. Unfortunately he couldn't resist smiling as he held out a hand to the old man still spread eagled on the ground.

"Whit are ye grinning at?" Airlie glared at him.

"Naething, sir," the young man lied.

Naething," the earl growled. "Ye saw whit happened. That peasant tried tae mak a fool o me. Fetch the scoundrel here till I show him whae's the fool."

"I canna sir. He's awa." The lieutenant helped the earl to his feet. "It aw happened sae quick. In the heat o the moment things can - " He got no further.

"A name. I want a name!" the earl roared. "Get me a name!"

The lieutenant flushed.

"Did ye hear me?" Airlie pushed his lieutenant backwards. "I need a name."

"Sir." The young man hurried over to the nearest line of prisoners, demanding if anyone had seen his master fall from his horse. Within minutes he had found a witness and called to Airlie, "Sir. This man kens something aboot yer attacker."

The earl strode over to the group of prisoners, hurled them aside and grabbed hold of a small man cowering behind the lieutenant. He shook him several times then held the quivering figure clear of the ground. "Ye ken something. Whit is it?"

The man struggled but said nothing

The earl's great hands tightened their grip.

The man squealed.

The earl allowed the man's feet to touch the grass. He steadied him then switched his grip to the scrawny throat. "Whae wis it cut my horse traces?"

"Captain John Steel whacked ye aff yer horse." It all came out in a stammer then unwisely the man added, "Ye didna staund a chance."

"Is that so?" The old earl lifted the prisoner again, swinging him several times before punching him to the ground. He then rounded on his gaping lieutenant.

Guessing what was coming the young man stepped back. He was too late. The earl's fingers reached his collar and held on. The lieutenant found himself pulled towards the angry face.

"Find this Steel," the earl hissed.

"He's awa, sir," the lieutenant repeated. "He could be onywhaur by noo."

"I want him." Another pull at the young man's collar.

"Sir. The man isna worth the effort."

"It is tae me." Airlie let go of the lieutenant's collar and turned back to the prisoner still lying where he'd left him. The toe of his riding boot prodded the man's side. "Whaur dae I find this Captain Steel?"

No answer.

Kneeling down to grab the long, lank hair the earl yanked the terrified face up towards his own red one. "I asked ye a question." Drawing his dagger he held the flat of the cold steel blade against the sweating skin and pressed his victim's throat till the man's eyes bulged.

"Lesmahagow yer honour," the prisoner gasped. "Ten miles distant." He pointed in the general direction. "But ye're wastin yer time."

"Hoo come?" The blade pressed again.

"Ye'll nivver catch him."

Airlie struck the prisoner senseless then jumped to his feet shouting, "I hae a man tae catch. Find me a fresh horse and a man as kens the road tae this village whaur I'll find John Steel."

"Sir." The lieutenant raced off to obey.

Claverhouse appeared with a line of captive ministers stumbling in front of his horse.

When he saw Airlie's expression he asked, "Whit's wrang?"

"Naething I canna deal wi mysel," the old earl snapped and made to turn his horse.

"Leaving the field aready?" Clavers expressed surprise. "There's still a lot tae dae."

"Nae doubt. But I hae a rogue tae find. He cut my saddle traces."

"And ye landed on yer arse wi a thump." Clavers could barely hide his smile.

"And when I get haud o him he'll pay for it."

"Nae doubt. But whaur is this rogue?"

"Gone. But I hae a name and ken whaur tae find him. It's Lesmahagow if ye must ken."

Clavers' eyebrows rose. "The name wudna happen tae be John Steel?"

The earl gaped. "Hoo did ye ken?"

"Jist a guess," Clavers replied. "Be careful my friend. Ye've maybe met yer match wi that yin. He made a fool o my platoon a few weeks back, and when brocht tae book and fined he still managed tae trick me ower a horse I'd demanded."

"And ye let him aff wi it?"

"At the time I wis mair amused than affronted. There wis nae real harm done."

"Sir." Lieutenant Crichton, who was riding alongside Clavers, saluted Airlie and spoke up. "If ye're aifter John Steel, ah'm yer man. Ah ken exactly whaur tae find him."

"Dae ye indeed?" Airlie smiled and looked hopefully at Clavers. "Hae ah yer permission sir?"

Clavers shook his head and frowned at Airlie. "My lieutenant has plenty tae dae here that's mair important than chasing the country side tae satisfy an auld man's daft pride. It's no worth the bother."

"It will be when I get a haud o Steel."

"Sir - " Crichton dared to interrupt.

Clavers ignored his lieutenant and scowled at Airlie. "So ye think yer spite against ane man is mair important than aw this? Chris' sake Airlie, get yer priorities richt." He turned his horse. "Richt then Crichton, we hae work tae dae."

"Ay sir." Crichton turned his horse and followed his master.

Airlie stared after them. For a moment the grand, old earl was speechless at Clavers' put down then turning towards his lieutenant he snapped, "Report tae Montrose. Inform him I've a business needing urgent attention awa frae the field. Aifter that follow on yersel."

"Whaur tae sir?"

"Ye heard yon prisoner, Lesmahagow. Get directions and dinna be lang aboot it."

Airlie galloped off with with his troopers struggling to keep up.

The young man stared after the fast disappearing group of riders. He shook his head and wondered how he'd explain this piece of nonsense to Montrose.

He needn't have worried. Airlie's reputation went before him. Montrose laughed at the story. "Nae fool lik an auld fool. Especially ane wi sic a fine opinion o himsel."

The young lieutenant flushed. "Sir. May I hae yer permission?"

"Ay." Montrose waved him away. "On ye go and chase aifter yer daft, auld maister. And much guid may it dae."

Lucas Brotherstone sat at the window of his tiny attic room, high above the uneven cobbles of Patrimonium Stratt. He'd lodged in this strange, squinty looking house since arriving in Utrecht only weeks ago to become a tutor at the Scots College.

Five minutes walk from his work, centrally situated but quiet, this spot allowed him to step into the bustling street life or step back as he felt the need.

Below him stretched rows of steep, pantile roofs, while beyond soared the graceful spire of the Domtoren with its carillon of fifty bells ringing out their noontide message across the city.

Unaware of all this his mind was picturing a faraway village where not so long ago he'd been a happy man.

That part of this life was supposed to be behind him but today's news about the battle at Bothwell had changed all that, shaming his selfish interest, and triggering the urge to think again.

Patrimonium Straat was known as the street of lost souls. At first this had seemed amusing but now he felt like one, and longed to be in his real home again.

With a sigh he gathered up his books and clattered down the steep, rickety wooden stairs. In another ten minutes he'd be in front of his students, giving his lecture on Matthew 5 Verse 5, *'Blessed are the meek: for they will inherit the earth.'* He'd chosen this text yesterday, before hearing the news from Scotland. Now it was all wrong.

Chapter 16

After picking their way through the dense wood John's group of riders came out on the edge of the open parkland by Hamilton Palace. Now they could break into a gallop again.

Four horses cut across this grassy space making the duke's famous white cattle bellow and scatter when the trespassers thundered past to jump the broad boundary hedge and land on the road beyond. The beasts gaped at all this noise and speed then shook their long, graceful horns and turned away to resume their orderly grazing.

John led the group past the bottom edge of the town. They had it to themselves. There was no sign of life. News of the royalist army on Bothwell Moor had scared the Hamilton residents and every door was shut with everyone intent on staying out of sight. The main road too was strangely empty. There was nothing to hold the riders back in their headlong dash away from the disaster behind them.

They were just in time. Government platoons were already pounding off the battlefield, chasing after defeated rebels who were streaming along that same road.

It had been three weeks since the platoon had left the village and news gradually drifted back about the encampment at Bothwell. Robert Steel could barely believe an army would simply stay put while the leaders and ministers argued among themselves. He spent hours worrying about this and in the evening he'd pace the cobbled yard at Logan Waterhead trying to make some sense of a situation that seemed nothing short of madness. Most of all he thought about John, the one who usually acted first then thought about it.

Marion watched him torture himself and her own worry increased as her vivid imagination wrestled with all manner of guesses. Often her two boys bore the brunt of her tongue and then she'd feel guilty, or she'd go for hours without uttering a word which upset them even more. By the end of the third week her nerves were almost at breaking point and one evening she joined her father-in-law in his pacing. They went up and down the yard a few times before she said, "Faither. We need tae ken."

He nodded. "Ah'd like that."

"Somebody shud go an find oot. Mibbe as far as Hamilton. Folk ther must ken whit's happenin." She hesitated then took his hand. "Will ye dae it?"

"Whit aboot the farms? It's no easy keepin it aw goin wi ane auld man an three women."

Marion smiled. "We'd manage the extra work for a day or twa. It wudna be that bad, an the bairns wud help. Wur aw desperate tae hear some richt news."

They left it at that and walked on in silence.

Two days passed. On the third morning Robert Steel packed his big canvas satchel and put on his best leather jacket. In a mixture of childish excitement and nagging worry he led his horse out from the stable. The three women warned him several times about taking care then watched the old man plod down the long track to the beech avenue and begin the twelve mile journey to Hamilton. He didn't hurry for he was still of half a mind to stay and wait. But neither did he turn back.

Once Robert Steel's gaunt figure had disappeared among the beech trees the women returned to the kitchen deciding how to tackle the extra work. Robert Steel had been doing the milking. A rota must be agreed. As for the other tasks only the most urgent would take priority; anything that could wait, would wait. After all, the men had been away three weeks, surely they must be home soon.

Robert Steel had an easy journey with few travellers on the main road to the city. He arrived mid morning on the 22nd of June to find the town of Hamilton deserted. There was no one to ask. Having come this far he pressed on towards Bothwell.

At the moment John's group was racing away from the town his father had reached the road leading to the moor. He gaped at the surge of fugitives running towards him, their terrified faces telling their own story, warning him to turn. And he did try - but even then it was too late. The government dragoons were close behind and they had their orders. Muskets fired then reloaded. Several running figures fell, some stumbling but forcing themselves on through the smoke now belching out around them.

Arms and legs scrambled past Robert Steel's farm horse, and unused to crowds, let alone all the screaming and banging of gunfire, the beast froze. In a panic Robert struggled with the animal, trying to turn him and escape the horror, but within seconds a musket ball hit the old man in the centre of his chest, bursting his leather jacket apart and ripping a gaping hole in his rib cage. He rocked back and fell out of the saddle as the dragoon who'd fired the shot, drew alongside to deliver a final sword thrust.

Robert Steel's horse would be taken as booty, and like many others killed on that road outside Hamilton, his body would be swept up and buried in a mass grave. His family would never know his fate.

Unaware of what was happening to his father, indeed unaware his father was anywhere but back home on the farm, John and the others galloped on.

Lesmahagow was only twelve miles away, and easily covered if they stuck to the main road. Keen to avoid being seen they were careful to leave the wide road outside the village of Larkhall and skirt round by little used lanes and farm tracks where they met no one. Once in open country they were less anxious and felt confident enough to ease their pace. For the next two miles the horses were allowed to trot or walk although they didn't dare stop. They needed distance, a reaching towards their own patch where they could lie low for a while.

The horses were fit, well cared for, and moved along with ease although their ears were still flat against their heads, their eyes still flashing with fear from the memory of men and metal clashing and surging together for hours.

Further on they passed a few people working in their fields but no heads looked up or paid any attention to the travellers. Here was normality, a proper routine with no hint of terror or any battle sounds, and yet the riders sensed all that would soon change.

Before the next two villages again they left the road and took the long way round. They were pleased to find everything quiet, no sense of alarm.

And so it continued till the smoking chimneys of Lesmahagow beckoned. Even then they followed their new routine and veered off the road to make a wide arc through the fields and old birch wood and come in behind the kirk yard. They did this quietly, trotting in single file and hoping no one was about. Their return was as secret as their departure had been public.

Turning down towards the river Nethan they were well shielded by overhanging trees. Here Wull left the group and headed up the steep bank towards the hamlet of Brocketsbrae. John called out, "Go weel," as his friend disappeared among a thick clump of broom.

The others trotted along the river to the bend beyond the village. There they splashed through the shallows and began the long climb up towards the edge of the moor. It was all so familiar yet somehow eerily strange.

Once past the tree line they stopped. Here Davie would veer off towards his farm at Skellyhill. John leant over to grasp his cousin's arm. Davie turned and squeezed the outstretched hand. There was nothing worth saying.

John and Gavin watched while Davie's horse picked its way along the long slope towards the farm track. The beast moved slowly and carefully but the ears were up as if sensing home territory. At the end of the slope the horse broke into a trot. Davie gave a quick wave, and was gone.

John turned Juno's black head and set off in the opposite direction. Five minutes later he and Gavin could see the long beech avenue which lined the highest stretch of the road. Together they picked their way through scraggy heather towards it. When they reached the first green field instead of jumping the drystane dyke John worked his way along to the wooden gate, dismounted, opened the gate and led Juno through. He looked up at Gavin. "She's ower tired for jumpin. It's the least I can dae."

Gavin nodded and walked his own horse through the opening then waited while John shut the gate and remounted.

Once across the field he headed for the second gate and did the same before they stepped onto the shingly road. Neither hurried but trotted along pleased with the welcome sight of familiar fields, some fresh and green, some yellowy where the hay had been cut and stalked. Here and there cows and sheep wandered and grazed. All so natural and peaceful compared to the unnatural sights and sounds they'd left behind.

John stopped at the top of his own farm track "This is me then. Anither mile and ye'll be hame tae."

Gavin nodded and tried to smile but weariness had caught up with him and he remained set-faced as he trotted away.

John stayed where he was till the young man was out of sight before he swung Juno down the long curved track towards the little hump-backed bridge across the Logan burn. He'd ridden along this track every day for years and never thought about it. This time the stones, the bushes, the overhanging trees, the waving grass, the wild flowers, even the nettles stood out as if he was seeing them for the first time. The sweet smell of buttercups and the last of the hawthorn blossom filled his nostrils. He knew he'd remember this moment.

He crossed the bridge and caught a glimpse of soft grey smoke lazily curling up from the high chimney of Logan Waterhead, almost exactly as it had been that morning he'd left to join the new formed village platoon. He stopped Juno and patted her neck. Her ears went up when he whispered, "Hame lass."

Tired as she was the horse almost galloped up the last incline and in through the close to the cobbled yard.

Marion was in the little garden behind the farm-house. There she'd established two small beehives. She enjoyed tending to their simple needs, and it paid off for each year the bees produced more honey that she put to good use during the winter months. The boys loved its sweetness spread on her new baked bread and it worked wonders for coughs and colds.

She usually enjoyed watching the busy, organised life of these tiny creatures as they flew back and forwards gathering pollen from the garden and moor beyond. But over the last few weeks their dedication and selflessness to each other had made her think of her own wilfulness. John indulged her. She knew that, and she often played on it. But what if she hadn't been so determined to attend those secret meetings, and then Loudon Hill?

She had laid down her basket to open the latch gate when she heard the familiar clip clop on the cobbles. Basket forgotten she rushed through the gate, into the yard, and there he was, filthy, exhausted, but alive.

As soon as Marion appeared John forgot his disappointment, anger, and fear. Even his disillusion vanished. He jumped down from his horse, wrapped his arms round her, and nothing else mattered but each other.

Sandy Gillon enjoyed driving his horse and trap around his parish. He was out and about so often he'd become a well-known figure. It was one of the few things about his charge that brought any pleasure. Most days he persuaded Meg to come with him, and they'd rattle along and chat about what they saw, and make no mention of Kirk, or sheriff, or rebellion. Even an hour in the fresh air allowed them to return in a better mood. It didn't last though and every few days it seemed necessary to hitch up the horse and trap, to escape into the open, away from kirk and manse, and the constant reminder of being trapped in a situation of their own making. These little outings helped keep some of their arguments at bay. At least it had until that day the village platoon marched away. After that Meg's mood had darkened. She grew more unsettled with their false existence. And of course she would always add, "Whit aboot they decent folk in the pews each Sunday? It's the law maks them come. An we're pairt o it. Can ye no see, it'll aye be them an us. We dinna belang here. Never huv."

There was no answer to that.

Was there a way out? Sandy asked himself this question every day but never heard an answer. And so he limped on in a spiral of doubt and self-recrimination. However, today was sunny. The church service was past. The strain of confronting a reluctant congregation was over for another week. This cheered him up. He felt it was time to try and regain Meg's support. If she'd ride out in the trap with him he'd try and explain yet again how he'd come to make such a terrible mistake. If only he could talk about his stupid dreams in a way she could understand. If only he could make her listen.

He hurried round to the stable to hitch up the horse and trap for an outing. It was no longer a task. He'd had weeks of practice and confidently walked the horse to the front of the house then tethered him to the railings.

He knew Meg was in the kitchen so he stopped in the hall and practised a smile before walking in to find her bent over a small wooden butter churn, steadily turning the handle. She looked up at this interruption.

"Ah wis wonderin." He stopped then gaped at her. "Meg. Whit are ye daein? This is the Sabbath. A day o rest. We're supposed tae set an example."

"Is that so?" She sounded defiant.

"Ay weel," he said more gently. "If ye must. Onyway, whaur did that wee churn come frae?"

"The back scullery. It's been weel used. And noo it's ma turn." The little churn rotated smoothly under her guidance.

"Hoo come?"

"We hae a Glebe field," Meg said.

"Whit's that got tae dae wi it?"

"Mary Forrest came tae the door yesterday when ye wur shut in the front room writin yer sermon. Ye ken whae she is. She sits in the third pew frae the front. Sma, fat, roond face, black curly hair, smiley een. Her man's related tae the man frae the bakehoose. She tellt me she used tae keep her coo in the Glebe field. But she hudna liked tae let it bide on aifter the meenister went awa. She wondered if we'd alloo her tae pit the beast in ther again. She said she gied the meenister's wife a wee churn an showed her hoo tae use it. Aifter that she delivered a jug o milk every day, an cream aince a week for makin the butter. She thocht the churn micht still be ther. We taen a luk, an so it wis. That's when ah said ah didna ken hoo tae work it. She offered tae show me, an wis that keen she went straicht hame for some cream so we cud git stairted. We had a practice an aifter that ah helped her pit the beast in the field."

"Shud ye no hae asked me first?"

218

"Whit for?" Meg snapped. "Ye nivver consult me aboot onythin. Ye dae whit ye want. Ah'm jist daein the same. At least we'll git some benefit frae this."

He tried to ignore her sarcasm. Neither spoke while Meg continued to turn the handle of the little churn. She was clearly in a bad mood but he tried anyway. "Ah wis goin tae suggest a run wi the horse an trap. It's a fine day an ye ken hoo wee Isabel enjoys bein oot an aboot."

"Richt noo she's happy enough playin in the garden," Meg replied. "Onyway ah canna stop or it'll aw go tae waste. An aince the butter's made ah need tae rinse it, pat it, put it in covered dishes, an then lay them in the cauld cupboard."

"Ye'll be ready for a sit doon aifter that," he persisted. "Ready for a wee jaunt in the trap. The fresh air wud dae ye guid, an we'd hae a chance tae talk."

"For God's sake Sandy." The churn handle turned even faster. "Aw ye ivver dae is talk. But ye nivver listen."

"Ah will this time. Ah promise."

"Promise. As if. Awa an talk tae yersel an gie me peace." The churn rumbled on and Meg stared at the rotating drum as if it was the only thing in the room worth her attention.

Finally she said, "It's no easy pittin up wi aw this an whiles ah jist need space tae masel."

"Ah ken. Ah'm sorry."

"If ye say that word ane mair time." Her voice sharpened. "Jist tak a luk at yersel. A guid, hard luk an see whit ye're at."

Today he'd no strength to resist her attack. Today any persuasion was out of the question. All he could do was stand there listening to the little churn creak and rumble as it turned. Meg was surprising. He had to admit that. This was the first time she'd organised anything on her own without a word to him.

He gave up and left her to it, and wandered down the long hall to the front door. He opened the door then stopped to call back, "Ah'd like ye tae come."

His only reply was the churn's regular beat. He sighed. "Wrang again. An ah dare say she's got it richt." Closing the door he ran down the front steps, undid the horse's reins from the railings with every intention of going back to the stable, except it was easy to jump into the driving seat of his little trap, and even easier to click the reins. After that the horse made the decision for him and simply trotted away down the lane as it often did of an afternoon.

It was a lovely day with a warm breeze. The world seemed full of summer promise. The horse sensed this and trotted along with its head held high while the narrow wheels of the trap rattled from one stone to another in a rhythm of their own. He listened and liked what he heard. His mood lifted. He began to whistle and allow the picture of Meg's angry face to soften. Out here her resentment seemed less of a worry. Now he could think of the kind Meg, the thoughtful, caring Meg, the Meg he loved. And one of those days she'd smile again when he put this mistake behind them and made things right again. "Ay," he promised the beautiful day. "So ah will."

At the cross roads he stopped and wondered which way to go. Not that it made much difference. It was the joy of the journey and what he'd see as he travelled along. He sat in the sunshine and listened to the hum of insect wings. He sniffed the blossom. It was all very pleasant.

He was jerked out of his reverie by a crowd of mounted men who thundered out of nowhere and surrounded him. Startled by their aggression he hung onto the horse's reins and tried not to look as scared as he felt when the leading rider, a grisled, elderly man in battle armour, leant forward and barked, "John Steel. Dae ye ken him?"

"Steel's a common name aboot here." Sandy flinched and drew back.

"Youngish man, big made, behaves as if he's somebody important."

"There's a few lik that."

"This ane's a rebel against the crown. He's a captain in the renegade army that's jist been routed back there at Bothwell. He escaped aff the field. I'm aifter him. We hae a score tae settle. Dae ye ken the man?"

"A John Steel did become captain o the village platoon. He's a local farmer."

"Near here?" A heavy leather glove thumped against the side of the trap.

Sandy was so scared he almost gave the answer the old man

was looking for. His curate's voice at the back of his head was encouraging him, reminding him the law's the law and must be upheld. A rebel's a rebel, and deserves no protection.

Even as he thought this his sense of fairness warned him to look at this man and see the danger in his power. This man would settle any score with no thought for anything or anyone but himself. John Steel would have no chance. He'd be as good as dead, with a rope round his neck, or a sharp sword plunged deep in his chest.

"Hae ye lost yer senses?" the angry earl demanded. "I havena aw day."

Sandy could see the revenge in the old man's eyes. He was tempted to say what was wanted and be done, left to continue his ride through the countryside.

The awful glint in the great man's eye seemed to cut through his confusion and left a strange sympathy for the odd farmer he hardly knew. This shocked him. He tried to swallow this feeling but it refused to go.

Raising a finger to point in the opposite direction he managed to stammer, "Ah'm no sure, but ah think the Steel ye're aifter has a farm on the far side o the village. At the next crossroads ye'll see a sign sayin Brocketsbrae. Go straight on, up the hill then turn richt an follow a narrow track for aboot a mile an a half."

Without so much as a nod the earl turned his great horse and the troopers were gone.

Sandy stared at the swirling dust cloud and could hardly believe what he'd just done. He felt sick. His fingers shook. His head pounded. He could hear his curate's voice raging against such stupidity. He took another deep breath and tried to steady himself. It was followed by a surge of terror at what might happen once his lie was discovered.

He jumped down from his seat to loosen the shafts of the trap. Within seconds he was astride the horse for the first time, digging his heels into its rounded flank. The beast responded and he hung on as best he could while hedgerows flashed past on either side reminding him what he was doing and where he was going. All he could think about was reaching John, to warn him before someone put that grisly old earl right and told him where the Steel farm really was. And then that band of troopers would come thundering back. He dug in his heels again.

Minutes later the horse burst through the close mouth of Logan Waterhead and Sandy roared out John's name.

John ran out the stable to stare at the last person he expected to see.

"Get awa John!" Sandy waved his hands like a mad man. "A government platoon's aifter ye. They've ridden hard an long an look terrible determined. Their leader's a big, grisled man, an it's ye he's aifter."

"Hoo dae ye ken?"

"He named ye. Says he has a score tae settle. Somethin tae dae wi a battle at Bothwell. If ye value yer skin git movin afore it's ower late."

John gaped at him then looked towards the house.

"Nae time."

"Ye'll wait and tell her?"

"Ay. For God's sake man, jist go."

Running across the yard John leapt the dry stane dyke of the vegetable patch and headed for the top field, scattering baaing sheep on either side. At the edge of the field he was over the last fence and could begin the long climb up and away to the moor.

Sandy watched the big man pound over the rising ground and admired how he ran, how easily his strong legs skimmed through the rough heather. *If only,* he thought, and wished he was up there, running away. But having promised to stay he was left struggling against every nerve in his body which was shrieking for him to get as far away as possible before it was too late.

The thought of the troopers decided him and he was turning his horse when Marion opened the door of the house. She blinked at the sight of the curate sitting on a sweating horse in the middle of her yard.

"Troopers," was all Sandy said.

No explanation was necessary. They could both hear the flurry at the end of the farm track.

"Are they aifter John?" She hurried down the steps towards her unlikely visitor

"Ay."

"Whaur is he?"

Sandy pointed beyond the field to the stretch of moor above the farm.

They could both see a dark figure running fast, already past the clump of pine trees, almost on the sky line.

Marion turned towards Sandy. "He's safer oot ther than onywhaur. John has the advantage on the moor, no them."

"Ah hope so," Sandy whispered.

Neither spoke then Marion reached up to touch his arm. "That wis kindly meant Maister Gillon. Thank ye."

Jumping down from his horse he grasped her outstretched hand. His own stupid ambition and pretence meant nothing now. John Steel was real, and the danger he was in was very real. The white face staring at him mirrored his own thoughts, and he nodded in recognition. Marion Steel hooked her arm through his and allowed Sandy's free hand to cover her trembling fingers, then slowly she returned his nod.

With perfect understanding the rebel farmer's wife and the would-be curate turned as one to face the close entrance. They stood straight and still; an unlikely pair, awaiting the soldiers' arrival.

END

Historical Figures in Changed Times

John Graham of Claverhouse, Viscount Dundee: Stout supporter of Stewart kings who relied heavily on his ability to keep order in South West Scotland. One of the most successful Scottish soldiers of his time. Considered a ruthless opponent by Covenanters, earned title Bluidy Clavers. Administered justice throughout Southern Scotland, captain of King's royal regiment, member of the Privy Council, created Viscount in 1688. Killed at Battle of Killiecrankie 17th June 1689 where his men were successful.

Archbishop Sharp of Saint Andrews: Originally a Presbyterian minister. Changed sides and became a significant figure in Episcopal Church. His attitude and treatment of Covenanters ended in his murder on Magus Muir near Saint Andrews on 3rd May 1679 where he was dragged from his coach and stabbed seven times. A severe backlash followed this event.

David Hackston of Rathillet: Present at Sharp's murder. Fought at Drumclog, Bothwell Bridge, Airds Moss where he was captured, tortured then hanged and quartered in Edinburgh's Grassmarket on 30th July 1680.

William Cleland: Fought at Drumclog, Bothwell Bridge. Escaped to Holland. Later returned and remained as a fugitive in Ayrshire and Lanarkshire. Leader at siege of Dunkeld 21st August 1689 where Covenanters held out. He was killed during this siege. Claimed to have shot John Graham at Battle of Killiecrankie.

William Dingwall: One of the murderers of Archbishop Sharp. Killed at Drumclog.

Reverend Alexander Peden: One of the most significant Covenanter ministers. Inspirational preacher. Outed from his parish at New Luce in Wigtonshire he spent most of his life living rough and taking secret religious meetings. Famous for wearing a leather mask. Credited with second sight and described as Peden the prophet.

Ambushed in June 1672, sent to the Bass Rock for four years then ordered aboard the St Michael for transportation to America. The ship put in at Gravesend in England where the captain set all the prisoners free. Returned home then wandered between Scotland and Northern Ireland. Died at his brother's house 26th January 1686 aged sixty. After burial troops dug up the corpse with intention of staging a hanging. Local laird intervened and corpse was buried at foot of the gallows.

James Ogilvie Earl of Airlie and Strathmore: Stout royalist supporter. Cavalry leader at Bothwell Bridge. During final stage of battle he tried to capture John Steel. John Steel fought back, knocked Airlie off his horse then escaped. Airlie then tried to hunt down Steel. Unsuccessful. In revenge he claimed the Steel farm and land.

Sir Robert Hamilton of Preston and Fingalton: A poor leader of the Covenanters at Bothwell Bridge. Almost first to leave the field and flee to the safety of Holland. Returned to Scotland after 1688.

Thomas Weir: Tenant farmer at Waterside near Lesmahagow. Fought at Drumclog where he was mortally wounded. Considered a hero of the battle.

John Steel: Bonnet laird with three farms. Lived at Logan Waterhead near Lesmahagow. Fought at Drumclog and Bothwell Bridge. As a consequence was declared a rebel with 1000 merks reward for his capture. Lost his property and spent ten years on the run. Was never caught. Captain in Cameronian Regiment in 1689 to oversee ousting of English curates without bloodshed. Buried in Lesmahagow Old Parish Kirkyard under a plain thruchstane. Date unknown but after 1707.

Marion Steel: John Steel's wife. As a rebel's wife she was forced to live rough on the moor with her family after Bothwell Bridge. Endured ill treatment from government.

Robert Steel: John Steel's father. Disappeared near Bothwell on day of battle. Fate unknown but assumed to have been killed by government troopers.

David Steel: Cousin of John Steel. Lived at Skellyhill farm near Lesmahagow. Fought at Drumclog and Bothwell Bridge. Fugitive till 1686 when he was caught and shot.

Thomas Steeel: Father of David Steel. Killed at Drumclog. Named as a hero of the battle.

About Ethyl Smith

Ethyl Smith is a graduate of Glasgow School of Art and a Fellow of Manchester School of Advanced Studies. She is also a graduate of the University of Strathclyde Novel Writing course and the Stirling University M.Litt. Creative Writing course.

Ethyl followed a career in illustrating and design lecturing, before following an interest in holistic therapy & hypnotherapy, which she now teaches.

Her short stories have appeared in a range of magazines including Scottish Field, Gutter, Scottish Memories, Mistaken Identities (edited by Jame Robertson), Mixing the Colours Anthology, and Scottish Book Trust Anthology.

Her interest in Scottish language and history, particularly 17th century, led to a trilogy based on covenanting times, where greed, power, and religion created a dangerous mix. Changed Times is the first in that series.

More Books From ThunderPoint Publishing Ltd.

Mule Train
by Huw Francis
ISBN: 978-0-9575689-0-7 (eBook)
ISBN: 978-0-9575689-1-4 (Paperback)

Four lives come together in the remote and spectacular mountains bordering Afghanistan and explode in a deadly cocktail of treachery, betrayal and violence.

Written with a deep love of Pakistan and the Pakistani people, Mule Train will sweep you from Karachi in the south to the Shandur Pass in the north, through the dangerous borderland alongside Afghanistan, in an adventure that will keep you gripped throughout.

'Stunningly captures the feel of Pakistan, from Karachi to the hills' – tripfiction.com

A Good Death

by Helen Davis
ISBN: 978-0-9575689-7-6 (eBook)
ISBN: 978-0-9575689-6-9 (Paperback)

'A good death is better than a bad conscience,' said Sophie.

1983 – Georgie, Theo, Sophie and Helena, four disparate young Cambridge undergraduates, set out to scale Ausangate, one of the highest and most sacred peaks in the Andes.

Seduced into employing the handsome and enigmatic Wamani as a guide, the four women are initiated into the mystically dangerous side of Peru, Wamani and themselves as they travel from Cuzco to the mountain, a journey that will shape their lives forever.

2013 – though the women are still close, the secrets and betrayals of Ausangate chafe at the friendship.

A girls' weekend at a lonely Fenland farmhouse descends into conflict with the insensitive inclusion of an overbearing young academic toyboy brought along by Theo. Sparked by his unexpected presence, pent up petty jealousies, recriminations and bitterness finally explode the truth of Ausangate, setting the women on a new and dangerous path.

Sharply observant and darkly comic, Helen Davis's début novel is an elegant tale of murder, seduction, vengeance, and the value of a good friendship.

'The prose is crisp, adept, and emotionally evocative' – Lesbrary.com

The Birds That Never Flew

by Margot McCuaig

Shortlisted for the Dundee International Book Prize 2012
Longlisted for the Polari First Book Prize 2014
ISBN: 978-0-9929768-5-9 (eBook)
ISBN: 978-0-9929768-4-2 (Paperback)

'Have you got a light hen? I'm totally gaspin.'

Battered and bruised, Elizabeth has taken her daughter and left her abusive husband Patrick. Again. In the bleak and impersonal Glasgow housing office Elizabeth meets the provocatively intriguing drug addict Sadie, who is desperate to get her own life back on track.

The two women forge a fierce and interdependent relationship as they try to rebuild their shattered lives, but despite their bold, and sometimes illegal attempts it seems impossible to escape from the abuse they have always known, and tragedy strikes.

More than a decade later Elizabeth has started to implement her perfect revenge – until a surreal Glaswegian Virgin Mary steps in with imperfect timing and a less than divine attitude to stick a spoke in the wheel of retribution.

Tragic, darkly funny and irreverent, *The Birds That Never Flew* ushers in a new and vibrant voice in Scottish literature.

'…dark, beautiful and moving, I wholeheartedly recommend' scanoir.co.uk

Toxic

by Jackie McLean

Shortlisted for the Yeovil Book Prize 2011

ISBN: 978-0-9575689-8-3 (eBook)

ISBN: 978-0-9575689-9-0 (Paperback)

The recklessly brilliant DI Donna Davenport, struggling to hide a secret from police colleagues and get over the break-up with her partner, has been suspended from duty for a fiery and inappropriate outburst to the press.

DI Evanton, an old-fashioned, hard-living misogynistic copper has been newly demoted for thumping a suspect, and transferred to Dundee with a final warning ringing in his ears and a reputation that precedes him.

And in the peaceful, rolling Tayside farmland a deadly store of MIC, the toxin that devastated Bhopal, is being illegally stored by a criminal gang smuggling the valuable substance necessary for making cheap pesticides.

An anonymous tip-off starts a desperate search for the MIC that is complicated by the uneasy partnership between Davenport and Evanton and their growing mistrust of each others actions.

Compelling and authentic, Toxic is a tense and fast paced crime thriller.

'...a humdinger of a plot that is as realistic as it is frightening' – crimefictionlover.com

In The Shadow Of The Hill
by Helen Forbes
ISBN: 978-0-9929768-1-1 (eBook)
ISBN: 978-0-9929768-0-4 (Paperback)

An elderly woman is found battered to death in the common stairwell of an Inverness block of flats.

Detective Sergeant Joe Galbraith starts what seems like one more depressing investigation of the untimely death of a poor unfortunate who was in the wrong place, at the wrong time.

As the investigation spreads across Scotland it reaches into a past that Joe has tried to forget, and takes him back to the Hebridean island of Harris, where he spent his childhood.

Among the mountains and the stunning landscape of religiously conservative Harris, in the shadow of Ceapabhal, long buried events and a tragic story are slowly uncovered, and the investigation takes on an altogether more sinister aspect.

In The Shadow Of The Hill skilfully captures the intricacies and malevolence of the underbelly of Highland and Island life, bringing tragedy and vengeance to the magical beauty of the Outer Hebrides.

'...our first real home-grown sample of modern Highland noir' – Roger Hutchison; West Highland Free Press

Over Here
by Jane Taylor
ISBN: 978-0-9929768-3-5 (eBook)
ISBN: 978-0-9929768-2-8 (Paperback)

It's coming up to twenty-four hours since the boy stepped down from the big passenger liner – it must be, he reckons foggily – because morning has come around once more with the awful irrevocability of time destined to lead nowhere in this worrying new situation. His temporary minder on board – last spotted heading for the bar some while before the lumbering process of docking got underway – seems to have vanished for good. Where does that leave him now? All on his own in a new country: that's where it leaves him. He is just nine years old.

An eloquently written novel tracing the social transformations of a century where possibilities were opened up by two world wars that saw millions of men move around the world to fight, and mass migration to the new worlds of Canada and Australia by tens of thousands of people looking for a better life.

Through the eyes of three generations of women, the tragic story of the nine year old boy on Liverpool docks is brought to life in saddeningly evocative prose.

'…a sweeping haunting first novel that spans four generations and two continents…' Cristina Odone/Catholic Herald

The Bonnie Road

by Suzanne d'Corsey
ISBN: 978-1-910946-01-5 (eBook)
ISBN: 978-0-9929768-6-6 (Paperback)

My grandmother passed me in transit. She was leaving, I was coming into this world, our spirits meeting at the door to my mother's womb, as she bent over the bed to close the thin crinkled lids of her own mother's eyes.

The women of Morag's family have been the keepers of tradition for generations, their skills and knowledge passed down from woman to woman, kept close and hidden from public view, official condemnation and religious suppression.

In late 1970s St. Andrews, demand for Morag's services are still there, but requested as stealthily as ever, for even in 20th century Scotland witchcraft is a dangerous Art to practise.

When newly widowed Rosalind arrives from California to tend her ailing uncle, she is drawn unsuspecting into a new world she never knew existed, one in which everyone seems to have a secret, but that offers greater opportunities than she dreamt of – if she only has the courage to open her heart to it.

Richly detailed, dark and compelling, d'Corsey magically transposes the old ways of Scotland into the 20th Century and brings to life the ancient traditions and beliefs that still dance just below the surface of the modern world.

'...successfully portrays rich characters in compelling plots, interwoven with atmospheric Scottish settings & history and coloured with witchcraft & romance' – poppypeacockpens.com

The House with the Lilac Shutters: and other stories

by Gabrielle Barnby

ISBN: 978-1-910946-02-2 (eBook)

ISBN: 978-0-9929768-8-0 (Paperback)

Irma Lagrasse has taught piano to three generations of villagers, whilst slowly twisting the knife of vengeance; Nico knows a secret; and M. Lenoir has discovered a suppressed and dangerous passion.

Revolving around the Café Rose, opposite The House with the Lilac Shutters, this collection of contemporary short stories links a small town in France with a small town in England, traces the unexpected connections between the people of both places and explores the unpredictable influences that the past can have on the present.

Characters weave in and out of each other's stories, secrets are concealed and new connections are made.

With a keenly observant eye, Barnby illustrates the everyday tragedies, sorrows, hopes and joys of ordinary people in this vividly understated and unsentimental collection.

'The more I read, and the more descriptions I encountered, the more I was put in mind of one of my all time favourite texts – Dylan Thomas' *Under Milk Wood*' **– lindasbookbag.com**

Talk of the Toun

by Helen MacKinven

ISBN: 978-1-910946-00-8 (eBook)

ISBN: 978-0-9929768-7-3 (Paperback)

She was greetin' again. But there's no need for Lorraine to be feart, since the first day of primary school, Angela has always been there to mop up her tears and snotters.

An uplifting black comedy of love, family life and friendship, Talk of the Toun is a bittersweet coming-of-age tale set in the summer of 1985, in working class, central belt Scotland.

Lifelong friends Angela and Lorraine are two very different girls, with a growing divide in their aspirations and ambitions putting their friendship under increasing strain.

Artistically gifted Angela has her sights set on art school, but lassies like Angela, from a small town council scheme, are expected to settle for a nice wee secretarial job at the local factory. Her only ally is her gallus gran, Senga, the pet psychic, who firmly believes that her granddaughter can be whatever she wants.

Though Lorraine's ambitions are focused closer to home Angela has plans for her too, and a caravan holiday to Filey with Angela's family tests the dynamics of their relationship and has lifelong consequences for them both.

Effortlessly capturing the religious and social intricacies of 1980s Scotland, Talk of the Toun is the perfect mix of pathos and humour as the two girls wrestle with the complications of growing up and exploring who they really are.

'Fresh, fierce and funny...a sharp and poignant study of growing up in 1980s Scotland. You'll laugh, you'll cry...you'll cringe' – KAREN CAMPBELL

QueerBashing

By Tim Morriosn

ISBN: 978-1-910946-06-0 (eBook)
ISBN: 978-0-9929768-9-7 (Paperback)

The first queerbasher McGillivray ever met was in the mirror.

From the revivalist churches of Orkney in the 1970s, to the gay bars of London and Northern England in the 90s, via the divinity school at Aberdeen, this is the story of McGillivray, a self-centred, promiscuous hypocrite, failed Church of Scotland minister, and his own worst enemy.

Determined to live life on his own terms, McGillivray's grasp on reality slides into psychosis and a sense of his own invulnerability, resulting in a brutal attack ending life as he knows it.

Raw and uncompromising, this is a viciously funny but ultimately moving account of one man's desire to come to terms with himself and live his life as he sees fit.

'...an arresting novel of pain and self-discovery' – Alastair Mabbott (The Herald)

Lightning Source UK Ltd.
Milton Keynes UK
UKOW05f0617130417
299009UK00006B/84/P